LAYCE GARDNER

A Perfect Romance

Bella
BOOKS

2013

Bella Books, Inc.
P.O. Box 10543
Tallahassee, FL 32302

Printed in the United States of America on acid-free paper.

First Bella Books Edition 2013

Editor: Medora MacDougall
Cover designer: Kiaro Creative

ISBN: 978-1-59493-343-1

About the Author

Layce is a novelist, screenwriter, playwright and sassypants. Her novels include *Tats* (2012 Goldie winner), *Tats Too: The Case of the Devil's Diamond*, *Wild at Heart*, and the short stories "The Day I Tried Out for Cheerleader and Other Stupid Stuff" and "Save the Last Dance for Me". You can read more about her at *Laycegardner.com*.

Other Bella Books by Layce Gardner

Tats
Tats Too: The Case of the Devil's Diamond
Wild at Heart

For Saxon.
I wish I'd met you sooner so I could love you longer.

CHAPTER ONE

"My girlfriend is a slut," Dana Dooley said, gripping the steering wheel with two hands. It was the first time she'd put that thought into words and it felt good and weird at the same time—like she'd let the air out of a balloon and the balloon was her stomach and her stomach was whipping around the car as it deflated. "The thing is," she continued, "even though Kimmy's the one screwing around on me, I still feel guilty. Like I should apologize to her for making her have to cheat on me. Does that make any sense?"

"That's your low self-esteem talking, Double D," Trudy said from the passenger seat. Trudy had a way of putting things into perspective in the simplest way possible. "People, women especially, will take advantage of the fact that you want to please other people. I don't see why you think your girlfriend would be any different. Some people—you, for instance—have a tendency to attract other people—Kimmy, for instance—who will take advantage of the fact that you'll do anything to avoid confrontation."

"Have you been watching Dr. Phil again?"

Trudy rolled her eyes, but since it was dark inside the car the gesture was wasted on Dana. "Who is it who keeps picking up strays and bringing them home? Then expecting them to love you back?"

"Me," Dana sighed.

Trudy nodded. "And who is it who drops everything they're doing to go rescue their Neanderthal brother out of his messes all the time?"

"That would be me."

"And who is it that still lives with her grandmother because she can't tell her she wants to move out?"

"That's not true," Dana objected. "Maw Maw needs me to help out. Plus, the rent is free. And someday that house will be all mine. I'm insuring my inheritance."

"Mmhmm," Trudy said like she didn't believe her. "Maybe you should consider telling people 'no' once in a while."

Dana shook her head. "I can't, Trudy, you know that. It's scary."

"It's easy," Trudy said. "I'll show you. Ask me some questions."

"C'mon…"

"I'm serious. Ask."

"Okay." Dana caved in. "Will you help me move this…"

Dana didn't even get to finish the question, before Trudy blurted, "No."

She asked another. "Can you loan me…"

"No."

"Can I have…"

"No."

Dana laughed. "Okay, okay, I get the point."

"Good girl. Now try repeating after me: No, Kimmy, it is not all right to cheat on me with everything in town that has a pulse."

"No, Kimmy, it's not all right to cheat on me with everything that has a pulse."

"Now pack your bags and don't let the door hit you in the ass."

"I can't say that," Dana said.

"Why not?"

"What if she's not sleeping with somebody else?"

"You just said you knew she was."

"I *think* she is. I'm pretty sure she is. But I don't have concrete proof," Dana said. "All I have is a gut feeling and I don't want to convict somebody of adultery on a gut feeling."

"You're nuts, you know that?"

"I come by it naturally," Dana said. Truer words were never spoken. All the Dooleys in Dana's family tree were a little nutty. In fact, one could say her tree was chock full of nuts and squirrels. Dana Dooley and five generations of her ancestors had lived in the little town of Dooley Springs, Oklahoma. The town was named after her five-times great grandfather, Donald Dooley. Donald was already middle-aged when he took off from Tennessee to cash in on the California gold rush. He only made it as far as Oklahoma (then it was called Indian Territory) before he decided that going clear to California to get rich quick was a fool's errand. He found a natural hot springs nestled in the Cookson Hills of northeastern Oklahoma and put the word out that he'd found the real fountain of youth with super-dooper healing powers. People came from all over to bathe their crippled and aging bodies in the springs and give Donald Dooley all their money for letting them sit in a muddy creek. It took about a year before they realized he was a charlatan. Once their pockets were empty, they filled up with self-righteous loathing and lynched him from the highest tree. He left behind his wife and two sons. All the cripples and looneys who came to bathe and got suckered didn't have the money or the wherewithal to leave Dooley Springs and that's how the town got started. The entire town descended from a lineage of fools and crazies and charlatans. That made for some very interesting Saturday nights and full moons.

Trudy continued. "People commonly mistake niceness for a weakness."

"Mmhmm, so true," Dana said. And what she thought but didn't say was, "That's why I am driving you to an AA meeting on a Thursday night when all I really want to do is sit on my couch with a pint of Bluebell Birthday Cake ice cream, nursing my toothache and watching a woman-in-jeopardy TV movie on Lifetime. Then maybe I could lie in bed with a Karin Kallmaker lesbian romance novel and pretend my girlfriend isn't out screwing somebody else behind my back."

Dana wadded up her fist and pounded the steering wheel (but not hard enough to hurt). "I'm tired of being the nice person. I'm tired of always being the one who gets run over, pushed down and screwed around on. For once I'd like to do the running, pushing and screwing."

"Puddle!" Trudy yelled.

Dana saw the puddle from last night's storm glistening in the middle of her lane and reflexively swerved into the left lane in order to avoid it. Dana's car was an old VW Bug. She named her Betty Boop because she squeaked a lot. Betty also used to be bright cherry red before the rust took over and became the predominant color. Dana didn't want to complain too much because she was pretty sure it was the rust that held Betty together. Betty had a big hole in the middle of her passenger-side floorboard. Whoever was riding shotgun had to sit with their legs spread and could watch the highway pass only six inches beneath their feet. The hole came in handy on long road trips because you didn't even have to pull over to go to the bathroom. That was the good part. The bad part was that hitting a puddle in the middle of the road going fifty miles an hour wasn't as fun as you'd think it would be.

Hoooooonnnnkkkk blared an approaching semi-truck. Headlights momentarily blinded Dana and she swerved back to the right, barely making it back into her own lane in time to miss the oncoming truck.

"Whew…That was a close call," Dana said, stretching a smile over her fear.

To look at Trudy you wouldn't know she'd had a near-death experience that lasted exactly 3.7 pants-peeing seconds. The only hint she gave that she was even remotely scared was that she took an extra hard puff off her unlit Marlboro.

Carrying on as if she didn't almost get smashed by six tons of metal rolling ninety miles an hour on eighteen wheels, Dana said, "I wish I could be as self-assured as you. I've always thought if they wrote a book or a movie about my life, I wouldn't even be the main character. At best, I would be the overweight best friend or the whacko neighbor who makes everyone else seem normal by comparison."

"Well, I know I'm not a lesbo," Trudy said, "but I still think if I found my girlfriend cheating on me, I would toss her out on her ass." She pretended to take another long drag off the cigarette. Both of them quit smoking together almost three months ago, but Trudy liked to pretend puff. She could give up the nicotine, but she couldn't quite kick the image of smoking. She liked the way she looked holding a cigarette, like all those women in the Virginia Slims ads she had admired growing up. Those women were in control of their lives and happy. As long as they had a cigarette in their mouths, they didn't need a man.

"That's the problem," Dana said snatching the cig from Trudy's lips and taking her own pretend puff. "I can't prove she's cheating on me. I know she is," she blew the fake smoke out the closed window, "but until I catch her actually doing it, I don't know she is for sure." Trudy took her cigarette back and ashed on the floor. "You need to hire yourself one of those private investigators to tail her and get some pictures in the act. You could get that Kinsey Milhone woman to do it."

"Kinsey Milhone is a fictional character," Dana said.

"I bet Stephanie Plum would do it."

"Another fictional character."

"I know that. I meant somebody like them." Trudy took another drag.

"Or I could save the money and do it myself. I could tail her until I catch her red-handed."

Trudy exhaled out the side of her mouth, making a noise that sounded like a dog farting. She said, "Good luck with that. I've seen your stealth mode. And it isn't, what's the right word? 'Stealthy.'"

Dana shot her a withering look and made the dog-farting noise back at her.

"Oh, don't get all up on your hind legs, Double D. You know you're the biggest klutz in the tri-county area."

In the interest of preserving their twenty-some-odd-year friendship, Dana chose to ignore that last remark. "If she's cheating on me, I'll find her out. She'll wish she'd never done me wrong," she said. "Hey, that sounded like the lyrics to a country song."

"Beats the stuffin' outta me what you ever saw in her in the first place," Trudy said.

"Two things." Dana waggled her eyebrows up and down like a demented Groucho Marx.

"Well, anybody with four grand in their pocket can buy big boobs. Maybe next time you shop for a girlfriend, you'll look deeper."

"Maybe," Dana said. But even to herself she didn't sound too sure.

"Puddle!" Trudy yelled.

Dana swerved, this time checking the left lane first, but instead of missing the puddle, she plowed straight through it.

Dana guided Betty back into the right lane and looked over at Trudy who had her feet planted on the dashboard like she was in a gyno's stirrups. She held her skirt out like a sail over the current of air flowing up from the floorboard hole. She wore a silly grin on her face.

"You got a floorboard douche and you're smiling?" Dana asked.

"It tickled my woo-hoo," Trudy said, all giggly.

Dana laughed despite her foul mood.

Trudy pulled a bottle of peppermint schnapps out of her purse, pooched her lips out real big and used the inside of them to suck from the bottle so she wouldn't smear her lipstick. She looked like a fish drinking from a bottle. Trudy didn't like the taste of peppermint schnapps but she figured if she was going to drink she may as well have minty fresh breath.

"Do you really think you should be drinking right before we go into an AA meeting?" Dana asked.

"When should I do it? During the meeting?"

"No. The other alcoholics might think it's rude." Dana mocked a grade school teacher's voice, "If you didn't bring enough to share with everyone, then you can't have any."

Trudy laughed even though it wasn't all that funny. That was the good thing about Trudy—she laughed easily and never ceased to find Dana entertaining. Dana and Trudy had been best friends since second grade when Dana tried to kiss Trudy in the girl's restroom and Trudy socked her in the mouth.

"Are you sure you want to go to this meeting?" Dana asked.

"I fished the pond dry in all the bars," Trudy replied. She took another drink, swished the schnapps around in her mouth and swallowed. "I need to cast my net further. There's gotta be some decent men out there. I've married enough drunks. I want a sober man, so where better to find a sober man than an AA meeting?"

Trudy had been married three times. Twice to the same man. Dana didn't know if that counted as once or twice, but she had been maid of honor for all three weddings and that was what she was counting.

Truth be told, Dana hoped Trudy did find a sober man. Maybe the sobriety thing would rub off on her a little. She was starting to worry about the shape of Trudy's liver. She was looking a little yellowish around the gills. Or maybe she had put on too much foundation. Trudy had a notorious heavy hand with the Merle Norman. You could see where the makeup ended and her real color began halfway down her neck. It made her look like she was wearing a turtleneck. It was probably one of the side effects of her job as the hair and makeup lady over at the funeral home. It was Trudy's dream job. She got to make over people and they never complained. Plus, her parents owned the funeral home so she couldn't get fired if she drank on the job.

"How do I look?" Trudy asked, turning sideways in the car seat and striking a ridiculous pose that involved elbows sticking out and showing lots of thigh.

"That wig's my favorite," said Dana.

"You told me the one I was wearing yesterday was your favorite."

Dana sidestepped, "That was yesterday. Today, this one's my new favorite. What color is that anyhow?"

"Champagne. It's real hair too. Ordered it special from China. You know how many Asian women had to die to make this wig?" Trudy machine-gun laughed for the next quarter of a mile.

When she was laughed out, Trudy flipped down the visor and looked at herself in the mirror she'd duct-taped there. She scooched the wig forward on her head and made kissy noises at herself. Dana didn't understand how she did it, but Trudy was a regular man magnet. It might've been Trudy's boobs, but Dana's boobs were much larger and the only thing she ever attracted were chiggers.

Dana turned on the left blinker when she spotted the neon VFW sign blipping on and off alongside the dark highway. She counted the blinks and the intermittent dark pulses: long blink, pulse, pulse, blink, pulse, long blink, long pulse. She wished she knew Morse code so she could figure out the secret message the sign was sending her.

"Let's discuss signals," Dana said. "You want to use the ones we always use?"

"Sure," Trudy said. "If I find a guy I want to go home with, I'll pull on my right earlobe. If I want you to come rescue me from a creepy guy, I'll scratch my ass."

"Okay, but what if you want to go home with a creepy guy? Are you going to pull on your ear and scratch your ass at the same time?"

Trudy laughed. "You're the one that hooks up with creeps, not me."

"Right. You just marry them," Dana said, adding under her breath, "three times."

"You better not be picking up anybody," Trudy said. "I'm counting on you to be my designated driver."

"But what if I get an itch for some strange?" Dana asked.

Trudy socked Dana in the arm hard enough to make her swerve into the other lane. "You already have a girlfriend."

"Yeah," Dana admitted, aiming the car back into the right lane. "Only problem is she's off scratching somebody else's strange."

"Ewww," Trudy said. "That's not a good visual."

Dana pulled into the VFW parking lot, downshifting into first. The gears ground together louder than her teeth at night. She said a quick silent prayer that Betty didn't drop her transmission at this godforsaken place.

The Veteran of Foreign Wars building was made out of native stone and was long and narrow. They called it a shotgun building—because you could stand at the front door, fire a shotgun and shoot a coon standing in your backyard. Neon beer signs lit up the blacked-out windows. A handwritten sign in black magic marker was taped to the door: "AA Meeting in Back. 7:30." Only in Oklahoma would they think holding an AA meeting in the back of a bar was normal. Of course, this was the same state that thought it was fine to name the Will Rogers International Airport after a man who died in a plane crash.

There was another homemade sign on the door that proclaimed: "No Firearms." Dana wondered if the pistol range next door had a sign on its door that read: "No Drunks."

Trudy finished off the schnapps, swishing it around in her mouth, tilting her head back, gargling for exactly nine seconds (Dana counted) and finally swallowing. She tossed the empty bottle into the back seat floorboard and was out of the car and strutting for the front door before Dana even had the key out of the ignition.

Trudy was anxious to get inside and have first dibs on all the available men before some other hussy showed up and gave her competition. Dana got out of the car a lot slower because she wasn't looking forward to spending prime time Thursday watching Trudy weave the web to catch her next male victim.

Dana slouched through the front door and followed in Trudy's wake. She tried to hold her breath all the way through the bar and into the back room. She could easily hold her breath for over a minute and closer to a minute and a half (now that she didn't smoke), but she neglected to take a deep breath first and only made it halfway through the room before she had to let go and suck in some air. As soon as she inhaled, she knew it was a mistake. Smells of the stinky variety accosted her—cigarette smoke, cheap perfume, whiskey, body odor and more cigarette smoke. The fumes burned her nose and the back of her throat. She wished for the umpteenth time that day that she still smoked. Her sense of smell was duller when she smoked and, as it turned out, that was usually a good thing.

Dana walked by two old men sitting at the end of the bar like antique bookends. They wore faded overalls and straw cowboy hats, and had wrinkled walnut-colored skin and gray stubble on their chins. One of the men had a cigarette perched on his bottom lip and, miraculously, it didn't move when he talked. Dana overheard part of his conversation as she walked by. "I'm just saying that coloreds don't know their rightful place nowadays. Don't get me wrong, I'm not a racist or nothing. I fought in Nam elbow-to-elbow with a colored boy from Alabama that we called High Pockets on account of him being so tall. He carried me over his shoulder and toted me all the way back to our platoon the day I took that shrapnel in my right buttock and as much as I 'preciated that, I still wouldn't have voted on him to be president." He stopped and sucked hard on his cigarette for a second, then almost as an afterthought, he said with smoke streaming out of his nostrils, "They call it the White House, you know, not the Black House."

Dana opened the door to the back room and the toe of her flip-flop hung up on the metal thing that hides the carpet seam and she accidentally flipped her shoe backward and flopped her body forward. She ended up with her end up. The tossed shoe landed only God knows where. She knew she shouldn't have worn flip-flops. Every time she did, she threw shoes faster than a Kentucky race horse.

Dana tripping over her own feet was second nature. She'd been a klutz ever since she could crawl. In fact, she was the only baby she ever heard of who used to fall on her butt while crawling. That was before she got wise and took up rolling. If she saw something she wanted across the room, she would lie on her back and roll until she reached her destination.

Dana would still prefer to roll places if it weren't for the social stigma of it. It sure would've saved her a lot of bruises. By the time she was in third grade her name had become a verb. Kids used to call falling down and skinning their knees "pulling a Dooley." In her career as a bumbler, she had Dooleyed off bicycles, porches, roofs, boats and once she even Dooleyed out of a car going down the highway at sixty miles per hour. She wasn't driving, thank God.

So, after Dana Dooleyed through the door, she got up, brushed off and walked around the room looking for her shoe while pretending not to be looking for her shoe. She finally gave up after she'd walked the perimeter of the room twice.

What the heck, it was a rubber flip-flop that cost a buck ninety-eight. Actually, it came as a pair so the single flip-flop cost ninety-nine cents. And if you divided that by three it comes out to thirty-three, so that's a good omen according to my personal numerology.

Dana gave up on the shoe manhunt and concentrated on the Trudy womanhunt instead. As she looked around, she surmised that the room hadn't been redecorated since the last foreign war. (She made a D in high school history so she wasn't entirely sure what the last foreign war was and besides weren't all wars foreign except for that one civil war?) Gray metal folding chairs sat in crooked lines facing a podium and a weathered American flag. The cracked linoleum was guacamole-colored with yellowed rips here and there. The walls were the color of corn that'd been boiling on the stove top all day and the ceiling was littered with water stains, giving it a tortilla-that's-burnt-around-the-edges look. Dana thought the room was unappetizing, even if Texican was her favorite ethnic food.

She scoured the crowd and located Trudy holding court by the coffee urn and donuts that were set out alongside the wall on the ping-pong table. Actually, Dana couldn't help but find her because she was the shiniest thing in the whole room. Trudy was lethal with a Bedazzler gun. They should make her have a permit to carry one. One evening Dana had fallen asleep on her couch and when she woke up she found that Trudy had bedazzled "Tuck Fexas" across the chest of her Longhorns' sweatshirt. She'd been wearing it at the time.

They'd been at the meeting only ten minutes and Trudy already had men swarming all over her like flies on a pile of honey. Trudy thought it was because of her brilliant conversational skills, acerbic wit and her talent for making a delicious casserole out of a can of cream of mushroom soup and a bag of Lay's potato chips. Dana thought the men buzzed around Trudy because she was black and therefore exotic and taboo by Oklahoma standards. Dana knew better than to remind her that she was black, though. Trudy was indifferent to her race and hated it if you referred to her as African American. She maintained that she wasn't from Africa and she was pure American. If you mentioned her roots, she thought you were talking about her hair. She was the only black person in all of Dooley Springs. Her white parents, Jerry and Ellie Engleman, had adopted her when she was a baby. They raised her up white and she didn't even know she was different until kindergarten when the school nurse put a flesh-colored Band-Aid on her skinned knee and the color was off by ten shades.

Dana hobbled over to the snack table, poured lukewarm coffee into a Styrofoam cup, dumped in three packages of dry creamer and two artificial sweeteners and used one of those red and white swizzle sticks to beat the hell out of the concoction. She hated it when she sucked up one of those creamer globs and got a mouthful of chalky stuff.

She eavesdropped on Queen Bee Trudy telling a story to her swarm of worker bees. "And that's when I said, 'Honey, I'm more man than you'll ever be and more woman than you'll ever get.'"

Dana mentally rolled her eyes. Trudy's stories about marrying Bruce the Fag were her favorites, but she didn't like to show her amusement because as the only openly lesbian representative in Dooley Springs, she felt compelled to exhibit a sense of solidarity with the gay population.

Bruce the Fag was really flamey, and she never understood how Trudy could not have known he was gay. There were so many red flags on that relationship it bordered on the ridiculous. Bruce the Fag didn't watch football. Didn't own one single camouflaged item of clothing. Had no inkling when deer season started. And he could recite all the lines to the movie *Funny Girl.* On Halloween he dressed up as Carol Channing and sang "Hello, Dolly!" to every trick-or-treater who rang the doorbell. Trudy married him anyway, then proceeded to get upset when she came home from work and caught him playing catch with the Unitarian minister. He wasn't even the pitcher.

Dana felt sorry for Bruce the Fag. He married the only woman in town who actually wanted to get nailed by her husband.

"Hi, are you missing something?" asked a voice. Startled, Dana turned and found herself face-to-face with her missing flip-flop. Peeking out from behind the rubber shoe was a woman who had short brown hair that stuck straight up on her head like she'd licked her finger and stuck it in a light socket. She was about Dana's height, but her hair made her seem a couple of inches taller. She had brown-almost-black eyes like melted dark chocolate and a smile that reminded Dana of strawberry cheesecake. Her smile itself didn't exactly remind Dana of cheesecake; it's that the smile gave her the same feeling as looking at a slice of strawberry cheesecake.

"You found it!" Dana said a little too energetically. She immediately toned her reaction down by a few notches. "Where was it?" she asked, accepting the shoe. That was what Dana said out loud, but inside her head were whirling dozens of questions like: *What's your name? Are you a lesbian? Do you believe in love at first sight? Did you sue Supercuts when they did that to your hair?*

The woman smiled—Dana's stomach gurgled—and answered, "It was playing hide-and-seek in the rubber tree plant over by the door. I think it thought it was its mother."

Dana laughed too loud. Several alcoholics turned and looked at her like she was disturbing their quest for sobriety.

Dana downshifted to a more reserved chuckle and said, "You're funny."

Ellen (Dana finally noticed the woman's name tag) said, "It wasn't that funny."

Dana quickly covered her embarrassment by shaking her finger at the flip-flop and scolding, "Bad shoe, bad, bad shoe. What've I told you about hiding from me?"

Ellen laughed.

"That wasn't all that funny either," Dana said. She knew right then and without a doubt that Ellen was A.) stupid, B.) trying to impress her, or 3.) being nice.

"Then we're even."

"How'd you know it was mine?" Dana asked.

Ellen looked down at Dana's one bare foot and the other foot wearing the twin flip-flop and said with a shrug, "Lucky guess."

Dana looked at her naked foot and wished she had painted her toenails and she also wished she weren't so stupid when it came to flirting with attractive women.

Dana dropped the flip-flop to the floor and tried to stick her foot into it, but she got her big toe caught on the wrong side of the thingie that went between the toes and when she tried to extricate her foot for a do-over it got twisted up more. She stood there with a forced smile on her face and shook her foot like she was trying to fling dog doody off her shoe, and the harder she shook, the worse it got stuck. She shook her foot while holding her cup of coffee away from her body with her right hand.

You do the Hokey Pokey and you turn yourself around. That's what it's all about.

Then Ellen did the darnedest thing. She knelt and gently slipped the offending shoe off Dana's foot. She wrapped a hand around Dana's bare ankle and slid her naked foot back into the flip-flop the correct way.

Dana had never felt anything more intimate, and judging by the reaction of her nipples, they thought the same thing. Obviously, her nipples were hardwired directly to her toes. Either that or it had been way too long since she had been touched by anybody.

Still kneeling, Ellen looked up at Dana and smiled like she was Prince Charming and Dana was Cinderella and the flip-flop was the glass slipper. "Thanks," Dana said. "I really need to go before I turn into a pumpkin."

"But the meeting hasn't even started yet."

Ellen rose to her feet and smiled at Dana with those lips and that mouth and that nose and those eyes and Dana knew she needed to get out of there fast before she humped Ellen's leg like a toy poodle in heat.

"You're new here, right?" Ellen said. "We could sit together if you want company."

"I'm here with somebody."

"Oh?" Ellen said like it was a question and she wanted more of an explanation.

Dana halfway gestured somewhere in the general vicinity of where she last saw Trudy. Ellen didn't even bother to look. She took the smallest step into Dana's space. Not so close that Dana could easily kiss her—

God, I want to kiss those lips.

—but close enough that she got a big whiff of pink Jolly Rancher when Ellen exhaled. Anybody who had ever known Dana knew one thing for sure: She loved watermelon-flavored Jolly Ranchers. They were her kryptonite.

"I've never seen you here before," Ellen said.

"That's weird," Dana said. "I've never seen you here before either."

Ellen turned that over in her mind. "So then you've been here before?"

"Nope."

Ellen wrinkled her nose.

Dang, she's cute when she does that.

Dana smiled to let her know she was kidding and Ellen grinned. "I'm sorry," Dana said, even though she wasn't really sorry at all. "Social situations make me nervous and I sometimes act inappropriately and say weird things."

"Maybe you have Asperger's Syndrome," Ellen joked.

"No," Dana deadpanned, "I'm just real bad at reading people's faces."

"That's what Asperger's is."

"I know." Dana smiled.

Ellen laughed and grabbed a Styrofoam cup off the upside down stack and held it under the coffee spigot.

"Alcoholics sure drink a lot of coffee," Dana remarked.

Ellen looked at her a little surprised, then laughed.

"I'm sorry," Dana said, "I shouldn't have said that. It was a needless observation that I was using as a space filler or as a transition into another topic of conversation, but it came out sounding rude and I didn't mean it that way. See, when there's a hole in the conversation I feel this urge to stick something in the hole. In fact, there's very few people in this world I'm comfortable being around and not sticking something in their hole."

Ellen raised her eyebrows.

Dana blathered, "Not their hole-hole, you understand. The hole of the conversation."

Ellen nodded and smiled.

"You think I'm bizarre. I don't blame you. Most people do."

"I think you're interesting," Ellen said. "And you're right. We do drink a lot of coffee."

There was a long silence. Dana was determined not to stick anything in the hole. She bit the inside of her cheek to keep herself from talking. Ellen filled the hole, "You can always tell how long somebody's gone without a drink by how much they've gnawed on their cup."

Dana glanced around the room and saw that what she said was true. Everybody's cup was decorated with teeth marks and had tiny shark bites around the rims.

"I like to chew on Styrofoam too," Dana said.

"I have a thing about popping bubble wrap."

"Me too!" Dana said.

Dang it, she thought, *I shouldn't have said that with an exclamation mark. Now Ellen's going to think I am overly excitable.*

She continued in a calm library voice, "Though I don't think those two things are indicative of anything. Most people can't resist bubble wrap popping or Styrofoam nibbling. It can be construed as a nervous tic, but really I do it because it's fun."

"When I was a little kid I used to suck on my hair," Ellen said. She blew on her coffee, then added, "I sucked on it so much that my mom finally cut it short."

Dana glanced up at the top of Ellen's head where her hair was sticking straight up like it was scared. She wanted to touch it really bad, but resisted because she didn't know Ellen well enough and touching another person's head wasn't a socially acceptable thing to do when you first met them. She offered up her own confession. "I used to suck on my arm in first grade. Had hickeys all up and down my arm."

Ellen laughed for real this time. Dana liked the sound of her laugh, the way it ran up and down the musical scales and had a sense of freedom to it. Most people's laughs sounded like they were penned in behind barbed wire, but Ellen's laugh was like jazz music, irregular and frenetic, yet oddly exciting. Dana closed her eyes and let Ellen's laugh wash over her.

This was the kind of real conversation Dana had always fantasized about having with a girlfriend. On the surface they were talking about bubble wrap and arm hickeys, but underneath where the subtext resided, they were really talking about deep issues like love and death and relationships and serial monogamy and lactose intolerance and IBS and …

Dana opened her eyes and was shocked to see Ellen's green eyes peering at her over the rim of her Styrofoam cup. Dana stumbled backwards a step. She used her tried and true technique for calming her nerves—reciting the multiplication tables. She closed her eyes and got clear up to three times seven before her breath evened out enough to talk.

"Are you okay?" Ellen asked.

"What color are your eyes?" Dana asked. "One minute they're brown and the next they're green."

"Hazel. They turn green when I'm experiencing intense emotion. Or when I have the flu."

Dana hoped Ellen wasn't sick. Especially since she had handled her shoe and her bare foot and she could have nasty flu germs all over her hands.

Dana blinked. She had to force herself to stop looking into those hypnotic eyes. Ellen was sucking all the information out of her brain through those kaleidoscope eyes. She closed her eyes and silently recited the Pledge of Allegiance.

"What's so funny?" Ellen asked.

Dana realized she must have been staring into space and grinning. That was when she knew that she was doing exactly what she accused her girlfriend, Kimmy, of doing. Well, she wasn't actually *doing it* doing it, she was only thinking about doing it. Dana was well aware that her moral compass was a bit askew—she once saw a man drop a five dollar bill on the ground and she stuck it in her pocket without telling him—but she was not a cheater whoredog slut of a girlfriend. That was where she drew the line.

"It was nice meeting you," Dana blurted, "but I really have to go."

"Was it something I said?"

"No, I need to go." Dana hurried over to where Trudy was madly scratching her butt. Trudy was cornered by a man who was gnawing on a Styrofoam cup like it was an ear of corn. Her eyes had that telltale glazed-over look that said he was talking about hunting or fishing or football.

Dana tapped Trudy on the shoulder. "Excuse me for interrupting," she said, "but aren't you the woman who was just released from prison for chopping off her husband's penis?"

Trudy replied, "He dropped those charges when I returned the organ in question." She looked back at corncob man and smiled with all her teeth showing. Trudy elbowed the man like she was sharing an inside joke and said, "I put his severed penis on ice first, I'm not all bad."

And, presto, the man disappeared.

"Where the hell were you?" Trudy said under her breath. "I've been over here scratching my butt for ten minutes. People are going to think I have fleas."

"I need to get out of here. I'm a little overstimulated." She grabbed Trudy's hand and pulled her toward the door.

A man's voice called out, "Okay, people, have a seat. Let's get this meeting started."

Trudy yanked her hand out of Dana's grip. "I haven't made the rounds yet. Men outnumber women here ten to one. I need to play those odds." She stuck her bottom lip out like an overgrown baby and pleaded, "Pleeeezzzeeee."

"Okay," Dana relented. "I'm going to go wait in the bar. I'll give you thirty minutes to find your next husband before I leave without you."

Trudy turned her charm wattage up to high and sashayed off to a cluster of men in the far corner, leaving Dana to marvel how she could look so sexy while wearing red plastic cowboy boots.

Dana gave a last look around the room and spotted Ellen. She was already talking to some other woman. Dana's tits were bigger, but the other woman definitely had her beat in the big-hair department.

She sighed.

CHAPTER TWO

Dana listened to the song for the dozenth time while she slurped at her drink. She had never realized how much she and Carrie Underwood had in common. They were born and raised about fifty miles from each other, each had cheating lovers and each owned Louisville Sluggers.

The jukebox sucked up her last five-dollar bill and she punched in A9 twenty more times.

"Hey, lady, give that song a rest, will ya?" an old man with suspenders called out from his perch on a barstool.

Of course it would be a man who said that. She sat back down at corner table and waved at the bartender to make her another drink. She had asked for a drink that had ice cream in it because if she was going to drink her calories then she wanted to thoroughly enjoy it. But since they didn't have ice cream at a bar (explained the bartender with a haughty tone) she opted for a White Russian instead.

She slurped down the dregs of her second drink. These things tasted better than hard rock candy. She wouldn't mind pouring this stuff over her Cheerios.

Dana didn't drink all that much. She never had. She already felt like her life was out of control and drinking seemed to exacerbate that feeling. But between Kimmy's philandering and her own incessant toothache, Dana figured self-medication was warranted. The alcohol helped with her toothache, especially when she swished it around in her mouth before she swallowed. She could still feel the pain, but now she didn't care. The throbbing was persistent, but it was more like a distant third cousin on Thanksgiving who was relegated to sitting at the kid's table.

Dana moved her jaw from side to side and listened to it pop. *Bubble wrap.*

She wondered what scared-hair woman was doing. Was she sitting next to big-hair woman? Were they exchanging pheromones and phone numbers? Was she in there talking about how she bottomed out, woke up homeless on the street, sold handjobs in dark alleyways and then vowed to get sober and straighten her life out? Did she start drinking because some woman broke her heart?

Dana could kick herself. She finally met a woman she could relate to, maybe even enjoy talking to and what did she do? She ran away. And got drunk. And the woman was a recovering alcoholic.

She slurped some of the ice cubes into her mouth and crunched. She shouldn't be thinking about this woman. She should be concentrating on how to get her relationship with Kimmy back on track. Or rather, how to catch her cheating butt so she could break up with her and be free to pursue women with pokey hair.

Ouch! Note to self: don't crunch ice on a broken molar.

She stuck her finger in her mouth and gingerly touched the sore tooth.

Dana woke up every morning with an aching jaw from clenching her teeth while she slept. She didn't grind, she clenched. In fact, she clenched so hard and so often that she finally snapped off her second molar. Last week, she had given in to the pain, opened her hemophiliac wallet (it bled money nonstop) and went to see her dentist, Dr. Asshole (not his real name.)

"Open wide," Dr. Asshole said, aiming a lethal-looking hypodermic needle toward Dana's face. "You're going to feel a little prick."

"That's a joke, right?"

"What?"

"Open your mouth? Feel a little prick?"

His smile turned upside down. The rest of the exam got worse from there.

"You're clenching your teeth in your sleep," A-hole explained. "You have too much stress. I can make you a night guard to wear."

"How about you write me a script for valium instead?" she asked.

This time he laughed. And Dana wasn't trying to be funny; she was dead serious. He fitted her with a temporary crown to wear until her new gold crown was made. She chose gold because she liked the bling factor. She imagined herself sipping a dry martini at a cocktail party, pinky finger extended, laughing at her own joke. She tilted her head back and laughed and— *bling bling bling!*—people were awestruck by the flash of gold and the twinkle in her smile like in the toothpaste commercials.

She would be the only white person in Oklahoma with a gold tooth. It would be her distinguishing characteristic if they ever had to identify her body.

Dr. Ass of Hole burst her bubble when he said, "The crown's too far back in your mouth to be seen."

The temporary crown that he stuck over her ground-down-to-a-nub molar had fallen out twice. The first time it fell into the toilet bowl while she was brushing her teeth and peeing at the same time. (She liked to multitask boring activities.) She had to boil it before she stuck it back in her mouth. The second time it fell out when she was painting her privacy fence like Tom Sawyer (except she couldn't con her friends into painting it for her.) The crown plunked into the open can of paint. She had to boil it that time too. She finally got smart and stuck it back on with some crusty Polident that she found in Maw Maw's bathroom.

Since then Dana had had trouble sleeping at night not only because of the teeth-clenching, but because she was scared that she was going to suck the temporary crown down her windpipe and suffocate like Tennessee Williams did with that cap to the nasal spray.

The bartender brought another drink to her table. "Hey," Dana slurred. "This one's not white."

"You drank all the milk. What do you think this is, the Dairy Barn?"

She handed him a ten-spot. "Keep the change."

Why'd I do that? He's mean to me and I give him a tip. Trudy's right, I let people walk all over me.

"Thanks for the tip," he said, walking away.

Dana grabbed his arm and spun him around. "You want a real tip?"

Resigned to listening to drunks, he shrugged. Dana raised her voice so she could be heard over Carrie's singing and said, "Don't ever fall in love!"

Everybody in the bar turned to look at her. Dana hopped up onto her chair and pointed her drink accusingly at all five patrons. "There's no such thing as true love!" She gestured at each person, "There's no such thing as romance! It's all a sham to sell Valentines cards and chocolate. There's only lust and pheromones and loneliness and the need to procreate." When she said "procreate," she demonstrated with a few pelvic thrusts so her audience wouldn't miss the point. "Women are bitches! Every last one of 'em, stone cold bitches! They'll rip your heart out and feed it to the pigs! Whoops." That last "whoops" part was because she slung half her drink in a wild arc across the floor when she gestured a little too emphatically.

The bartender frowned. "You're cut off."

"Eff you," Dana mumbled. She swung a loose fist at the bartender. Unfortunately, she had forgot she was standing on a chair so when she swung she ended up crashing to the floor. She raised what was left of her drink above her head and clunked it on the table. Then she grabbed the chair and pulled herself up and into it.

Dana grabbed her drink, toasted the patrons and downed it. The bartender shook his head and walked away. Then she slumped over the table with her head in her arms.

She was down to her last effing drink. Her last effing dollar. Her last effing chance at effing love. Effing Carrie Undereffingwood should sing a song about that. Or maybe she'd write a book about it. That was the ticket. She'd write a book about Kimmy and all this crapola.

* * *

Dana had been writing The Great American Novel for the past fifteen years. She had written 2,471 single-spaced pages and, not surprisingly, most of those pages centered on her various travails with women. Her book was titled *Bad Romance*, and she thought of it as an anti-romance/revenge fantasy loosely disguised as a romantic comedy. It was a semi-quasi memoir/fiction. A cross between fact and fiction. A faction, if you will. If the Lifetime Channel for Women ever made it into a TV movie, the crawl under the title would read:

"Inspired by a true story. The following events may or may not have happened. And if they did happen and you think this is about you, then go ahead and try to prove it, bitch."

* * *

I've had more than my fair share of Lisas. Five of them in fact. Once I tried to work out the statistical odds having five girlfriends in a row named Lisa and the best I could come up with was that I have a better chance of getting eaten by a shark. Which explains why I won't set foot in an ocean. Well, that and the fact that there are no oceans in Oklahoma.

My first Lisa was an accident. I was fresh out of college and working on my novel and I was full of dreams, hopes and aspirations for my newly-framed

English lit degree. I was typing on my Maw Maw's Smith-Corona typewriter in front of the picture window and saw an old Chevy van roll to a stop right in front of my house.

Lisa Number One jumped out of the van and threw open its hood. Black smoke roiled out and little flames jumped out of the engine.

Lisa Number One was tall, trim, athletic and I liked the way her butt looked in those cut-offs. She had cornrowed hair and I thought that was a real interesting choice for a white girl. I ran outside and turned my water hose on the engine. The flames sizzled out and the hot metal hissed as we stared at each other.

She more or less invited herself into my house. I fed her some cold, leftover pizza, and then she invited herself into my shower and into my bed.

The next morning, we rolled the van into my driveway and she unloaded some of her clothes and we went back to bed. We got out of bed about a week later and that's when I realized she was living with me and I didn't really know much about her.

According to the little she'd told me in between bouts of lovemaking, she was from New Jersey and was a wannabe stuntwoman. She was following her dharma to Hollywood when her van broke down.

I had made the classic young lesbian mistake and confused sex with love. Turned out I was horny. As soon as the horny wore off things started going downhill fast.

Five months went by and Lisa Number One refused to go get a normal job. She said she had to practice her stunts for when Hollywood came calling. I didn't point out that they couldn't call because she didn't own a phone.

So I spent my days typing my magnum opus and she spent her days lighting herself on fire and hurling her body over parked cars.

One day when I was sitting at my typewriter, I looked through the picture window and saw a big crowd of people standing around in my front yard. They were all craning their necks, looking up at the roof of my house and pointing. I ran outside to see what all the commotion was and found Lisa Number One standing on my third story roof. She had dragged the neighbor kids' trampoline over to my yard and it was set up directly underneath her.

"Jump!" somebody yelled.

My front yard was full of looky-loos and cars were stopping on the street. A few people had set out lawn chairs and somebody even had an ice cooler and was selling Coors Lite at three bucks a bottle.

Lisa Number One responded with some exaggerated deep-knee bends and shoulder rolls, though it was beyond me why you had to warm up to fall off a roof.

I had my mouth open to yell at her not to jump, but then I clamped my mouth shut. Would it really be so bad if she jumped? What if she broke her neck and died? I'd have to spring for the funeral, that's what. Plus, I'd have to wear black for a week and walk around looking all bereaved and accepting casseroles from the neighbors. That would suck. But even worse—what if she severed her spinal cord and didn't die? She just got paralyzed? Then I'd be stuck with her for life, wiping her ass and spoon- feeding her green Jello. That would suck even worse.

I cupped my hands around my mouth like a megaphone and yelled, "Don't jump!" But my words were drowned out by a group of little kids chanting, "Jump! Jump! Jump!"

Lisa Number One had the crowd eating of her hand and she was playing this like a pro. She cracked her knuckles and popped her neck from side to side. She licked her index finger and held it up to test the direction and velocity of the breeze.

A purple Gremlin screeched to a stop in the street and farted a cloud of black smoke out its tailpipe. CeCe White climbed out of the car. She was the star reporter for the *Dooley Springs Dispatch*. CeCe wore a mumu-type dress that had big Hawaiian flowers on it and a pair of Birkenstocks that were older than me. Around her neck hung a big camera with a zoom lens. Her permed hair was all mooshed down on one side like she'd just rolled out of bed.

The entire crowd was yelling "Jump-Jump-Jump." All the beer was gone and the natives were getting restless. It looked like Lisa Number One needed to hurry up and dive or somebody was going to push her off the roof.

CeCe didn't waste any time. She raised her camera and clicked so fast it sounded like a tiny machine gun.

Lisa Number One threw the crowd a big thumbs-up signal, shouted, "Geromino!" and executed the best swan dive I'd ever seen outside of the Olympics on TV.

All the people's heads followed her arcing descent off the roof; their heads bounced when she hit the bull's eye of the trampoline; and their heads followed her skyrocketing bounce back up in the air. She cannonballed up higher than the third story she'd jumped from.

As soon as she hit the apex of her ascent, she hung in limbo for a moment with a surprised look on her face. I heard CeCe's camera machine gun again and knew that was the shot we'd see in tomorrow's paper.

Lisa Number One screamed and flailed her arms and legs, looking like a deranged marionette dancing a jig. Then her strings were cut and she started falling again. All that flailing around had her off balance and this time when she hit the trampoline she shot sideways instead of up. If it hadn't been for the walnut tree she would've ended up over in the neighbor's yard.

A teenage boy scampered up the tree and scooched on his butt out to the limb where Lisa Number One was draped like a wet towel hung over a clothesline. He put a finger on her neck and shouted back down, "She's alive!"

The whole crowd went wild, clapping and yelling, like OU had won the Orange Bowl.

I went inside and called the fire department to come rescue her out of the tree, but I was told that the trucks were out fighting a blaze in some farmer's barn. So, I did the next best thing and shot her out of the tree with my garden hose. (Actually, I aimed the stream of water at her face, it woke her up and she fell out of the tree.)

The next day I had her van towed in and fixed. A week later I had Trudy call her on my home line and pretend to be a big Hollywood producer looking for a stuntwoman for Sandra Bullock's newest film.

Lisa Number One was packed up and long gone by the time I got home.

* * *

Dana was slumped over in a chair by the jukebox, her forehead pressed against the edge of a wooden table, arms hanging limply at her sides, fingertips dangling only inches from the floor, muttering "Lisa" and "jump" over and over when someone lightly touched her arm.

Dana turned her head and, keeping her cheek pressed against the table, looked up at Ellen. "*There* you are," she said like she'd been waiting on her the whole time.

"Here I am."

"Prince Charming," Dana slurred.

Ellen laid her cheek on the table next to Dana's. Their noses were only three inches apart. Dana giggled.

"What's so funny?" Ellen asked.

"You have three eyes." Dana giggled again.

"Do you need a ride home?"

Dana didn't hear the question. Her clouded mind was still focused on threesomes. "I have a thing for threes. They're a good omen. I once knew a woman who had three nipples."

"Awesome," Ellen replied.

"You know where her third nipple was?"

"On her third boob?"

Dana laughed. Then she hiccupped. "No, she only had two boobs. The third nipple was under her arm."

"Oh, right."

"Next to her belly button. Her belly button wasn't on her belly. It was in her armpit. Right under the third nipple."

"Please don't tell me anything else was under her arm too."

Dana said, "When she was naked, she looked like a Picasso painting." She laughed and hiccupped at the same time. At last she focused her eyes on the top of Ellen's head.

"Can I touch it?" she asked.

"My armpit?"

"Your hair. How do you get it to stick straight up like that?"

"Gel."

"It makes you look like a hedgehog."

Ellen smiled uneasily.

"Or a shoe brush."

Ellen's smile faded.

"Or maybe a porky-pine."

"Are you insulting me?" Ellen asked. "Should I be offended?"

"Nope. No offense intended. Your hair is exciting and different. I like it ever so much. I'm an authority on being different, you see, and I deem your hair most different and exciting."

"You deem it so, thusly, it must be so." Ellen laughed. "And might I ask, on whose authority you are basing this knowledge?"

"Huh?"

"Your name, m'lady?"

Dana sat up and straightened her shoulders. She hiccupped twice, then said, "I am none other than Dame Dana Dooley"— *hic*—"of Oklahomadom in the village of Dooleyshire."

Ellen sat up and faced Dana. "Oklahomadom? And what kingdom is that realm located in?"

Dana furrowed her brows a moment, then smiled and said, "Kingdom Come."

"Well, Dame Dana Dooley of Kingdom Come," Ellen held her arm across her waist and bent forward as she continued, "I bow before your supreme weirdness."

Dana drew an imaginary sword from the imaginary sheath on her hip and tapped it on Ellen's real left shoulder, saying, "I, Dame Dana Dooley, knight you Sir...loin of beef." She tapped Ellen's real right shoulder, "Sir...rhosis of liver. Sir... han Sirhan."

They laughed. Dana reached out with her palm and lightly patted the top of Ellen's head. "Ouch," she said. "Your hair is prickly."

"That's what you get for being so handsy. I usually have a 'no touching above the neck rule' on first dates."

Dana closed one eye and looked at Ellen with the other. It was a double-dog-dare-you type of squint. "Are we on a date?" she asked.

"Would you like to be on a date?"

"I would if I could," Dana said, "but I can't, so I won't."

"Are you straight? I had the feeling that you…you know, were a lesbian."

"I am, but I'm kind of involved with somebody right now."

"So am I," Ellen said with a groan. "So I can't go out on a date with you either."

"Maybe we could *not* go out with each other together," Dana said. This train of thought appealed to her. "We could *not* go on a date, and *not* kiss, and I would definitely *not* pat you above the neck and we would *not* fall in love and you would *not* cheat on me and *not* break my heart."

"Is that what's happened to you? Somebody cheated on you?"

Dana looked away and frowned. The moment passed and when she looked back at Ellen she was smiling again. "Would you *not* go out with me if neither one of us were attached?"

"No," Ellen said, "I would definitely *not* want to *not* go out with you."

"In that case, can I *not* buy you a drink?"

"I don't drink, remember?"

"I'm confused," Dana said. "You don't drink or you don't *not* drink?"

"Can I *not* have what you're *not* drinking?"

"Yes," Dana said, shaking her head no. That was hard to do—say yes and shake your head no. It would have been hard sober, let alone drunk. Dana laughed. "You probably think I'm an alcoholic."

"Are you?"

Dana shook her head. "Most certainly I am *not*."

"Okay," Ellen said, crossing her arms over her chest.

"You don't believe me."

"No, it's not that. I'm a little confused by what you're *not* and what we're *not* doing and what we're *not* talking about."

Dana laughed and stood. She wobbled. Ellen reached up and put a hand on Dana's hip, helping to steady her. The hand on the hip thing made Dana's mind race. Well, her mind was too drunk to exactly race, but it did perk up and do a sexy dance. "I wanna dance. Will you dance with me?"

"Here?"

Dana grabbed Ellen's hand and pulled her to the middle of the room. She pressed her body into Ellen's and snuggled her face into the crook of her neck. She breathed in deep. Ellen smelled like cookie dough. She let out the breath and took another deeper whiff of the vanilla scent. Yummy. First watermelon and then vanilla. Dana melted quicker than a double dip cone from Braums in the middle of July.

She closed her eyes, leaned into Ellen's arms and swayed to the music. When she opened her eyes, she realized that she wasn't really swaying. It was the room that was swaying. Her knees crumpled and she would've Dooleyed to the floor big time, but Ellen caught her under the arms and held her up. Dana giggled. It was a good thing there was nothing under her arms but armpits.

Ellen held Dana tight against her and Dana felt like she was on that ride at the carnival that goes round and round so fast that when the floor drops out from under your feet, you're still plastered against the wall.

"Centipede force," Dana mumbled into Ellen's neck.

"What?"

Dana giggled. "I mean centrifugal force. I don't usually drink this much. I've had a bad day. A bad week. A bad life, really. A bad romance, for sure." She giggled again. "That's the name of the book I'm writing, *A Bad Romance.*"

"You're a writer?"

Dana closed her eyes and rested her head on Ellen's shoulder. Ellen tilted her head and pressed her cheek to Dana's. Dana was starting to think the floor dropping out from under her feet had nothing to do with the White Russians. She whispered into Ellen's ear, "I'm working on a book. But I can't think of a plot. I suck at plots."

Ellen whispered back into Dana's ear, "I like spooning with you."

Dana replied, "I prefer forking myself."

Ellen looked at her wide-eyed and Dana laughed. "Sorry. Sometimes I say socially unacceptable things. It has nothing to do with being drunk. I do it when I'm sober too."

Ellen chuckled. "You should know that I'm *not* enjoying this and I'm definitely *not* thinking about kissing you."

"I think you're a terrible dancer and I hate your exciting hair and beautiful brown and green eyes and the last thing on my mind is kissing you back."

"I'm in love with my girlfriend," Ellen said.

"I love my girlfriend too," Dana said back.

They were both lying. And each knew the other was lying too. They looked into each other's eyes for a full thirty seconds (Dana counted and was pleased that it was a multiple of three.) This was a moment fraught with unsaid what-ifs and impossibilities that could become possibilities if either one knew the right thing to say or do.

Each waited for the other to initiate the first kiss. Neither one wanted to be the one who first cheated on her girlfriend. If Ellen ignited the kiss, then Dana was largely blameless because who could turn down an incoming kiss when they were drunk? If Dana ignited the kiss then Ellen's reputation remained untarnished because wasn't she helping a fellow AA member and how was she to know a drunk woman was going to kiss her? Of course they knew deep down in their heart of hearts that it wasn't the initiating or the igniting of the kiss that would be hard—it was ending the kiss that would be next to impossible.

So, by mutual, unspoken agreement arranged solely by eye contact, Dana and Ellen closed their eyes, tilted their heads a tiny bit to the right and slowly leaned in, aiming their lips in the general vicinity of the other's.

But as fate would have it, their lips were only a fraction of a centimeter, half a heartbeat, a tiny breath apart, when a hand grabbed Dana's shoulder and spun her around.

"I turn my back for five minutes and you go and get all cozy with this piece of white trash?" Trudy bellowed.

Dana blinked rapidly, six, nine, twelve times. "Huh?" is all she managed to sputter.

"I'm sorry," Ellen stammered. "We weren't…It wasn't what you think…"

Trudy interrupted, "Yeah, I can see you weren't doing what I wasn't thinking."

"Trudy, c'mon…" Dana sputtered.

But Trudy pushed Dana behind her and continued, "Now why don't you get your scrawny ass on outta here before I throw it out." She pointed at the door in case Ellen didn't know where it was.

Ellen said, "I really wasn't trying to…"

Trudy interrupted her again. "I said, 'Git!'" She backed Ellen up five paces, saying, "Girl, don't make me take off my wig and beat you with it."

Ellen back pedaled her way to the door. She turned to open it and Dana called out, "Don't go!"

The door swung closed behind Ellen. Dana looked around the bar. Everyone was turned on their bar stool watching the real-live reality TV unfold before them. "What're you all looking at?" Dana hollered. Everyone spun back around on their stools and Dana flopped into the nearest chair. She put her elbows on her knees and her face in her hands. "She's gone," she sobbed, "I'll never see her again."

Between the slobbering and the sobbing, Trudy couldn't understand a word Dana said. She plopped into the chair next to Dana. "I scared the cuss outta her and I didn't even try all that hard."

"She's gone…"

"Is that's what's wrong with me?" Trudy asked.

"She could've been the love of my life," Dana said, "and she's gone."

"Do I scare men off?"

"And I effed it up."

"Are men afraid of me?"

"I let her get away."

"Am I too masculine?"

Dana and Trudy asked simultaneously, "What's wrong with me?"

Dana peered at Trudy through her tears. "Why'd you do that?"

"Do what?"

Dana took a closer look at Trudy. Her wig was a little askew and her lipstick was smeared in the corner of her mouth. "Why'd you run her off like that?"

"You were scratching your butt."

"No, I wasn't."

"Yes, you were," Trudy said. "I came out here after the meeting was over, which by the way was a big, fat bust—sober men are boring—and she had you in a bear hug and you were scratching your butt like some ol' mangy dog. So I rescued you."

"My butt was itchy! Dangit, Trudy, you scared off the only woman I've been interested in —in my whole life maybe—and you ran her off!" Dana turned on the faucet full force. Her shoulders shook, her nose ran, the works.

"Well, it's not my fault," Trudy huffed. She dug Dana's keys out of her front pocket, slung her purse over her shoulder and high-stepped for the door, saying, "Maybe you should put some lotion on your dry ass."

Trudy walked out and tried to slam the door behind her, but it had one of those hydraulic arms that only let it ease shut. She dug her heels in and pushed on the door until she was out of breath, so she stopped pushing, stepped back and gave it a good kick instead.

The door slammed shut.

Silence fell on the room like a guillotine. Dana looked over at the jukebox and saw the old man with suspenders holding the pulled power cord in his hand. "Enough of that damned song," he muttered. He tossed the cord to the floor and moseyed back over toward his barstool.

Dana looked at the drunks watching her. If this were one of her beloved TV movies, this would be the close-up of the star right before the commercial break.

"What the eff are you all looking at?" Dana yelled. The drunks grumbled and turned back around on their stools.

Dana took a long shaky breath, cowgirled up and wiped her nose on the tail of her T-shirt. She stumbled out the door. "Trudy, hold up!"

Trudy was backing Betty out of the parking space when Dana tripped and fell forward, sprawling over the hood of the car. Trudy slammed on the brakes and Dana's forward momentum smashed her up against the front windshield. Lying across the hood on her belly with her face mashed against the front windshield, Dana said out the side of her mouth, "Sometimes you're the bug, sometimes you're the windshield."

Five minutes later, Dana was squeezed into the passenger seat of her own car with her feet braced on the dashboard, watching the highway blur by in the hole between her legs. She felt like that jukebox with its power cord pulled.

"So, let me get this straight," Trudy said as she steered Betty between the yellow stripes. "Kimmy is cheating on you, so you wanted to get even by cheating on her with a woman you just met."

"No, that's not what I was doing," Dana said in a "methinks the lady doth protest too much" type of voice. She didn't know whether she was trying to convince herself or Trudy when she added, "I wasn't trying to get even. I'm drunk and depressed and hormonal and she was cute and sweet and I like her and she has the most amazing eyes and when she touches me it feels like her fingertips are scorching my skin and, oh crap, is that what I was doing?"

"Seemed that way to me," Trudy said.

"You're right. I don't even know this Ellen person. I was subconsciously trying to exact revenge on Kimmy. In fact, the more I think about it, the more I realize I hate her. I hate Ellen for taking advantage of me while I was in a vulnerable spot. I loathe her. I loathe her hair. I loathe her sense of humor. I loathe her eyes. I loathe the way she smells so delicious. I loathe her cute ass. I loathe everything about her."

"Good Lord," Trudy said, "you're in love."

"Yeah, I think I am," Dana said right before she passed out.

CHAPTER THREE

Dana unglued her eyes and silently screamed when the bucket of bright sunshine splashed in her face. She shivered, groaned and shrank back under the bed covers. Only then did she realize she was naked from the waist down and she had a mighty toothache. She sincerely hoped those two things were unrelated.

Once again, she was waking up alone in bed with no idea if Kimmy had come home, slept and left for work already or if she had never come home at all. Most likely the latter.

Asscat crawled onto Dana's ample chest and flexed his claws on her boobs, working his paws up and down like little pistons. He loved to knead kitty bread on her chest every morning. Dana grabbed him by his scruff and tossed him to the floor, growling, "Go catch another squirrel."

Asscat's real name was Riff Raff, but Dana called him Asscat because he murdered squirrels. He didn't kill them and leave them for dead either. He ate them. He devoured them—all of them. *Almost.* He ate everything except their tails and buttholes.

These choice remains he deposited on the welcome mat at the front door.

Dana was always and forever digging miniature graves in her backyard and burying the asses of squirrels. That was how Asscat earned his name.

Asscat squalled his displeasure at being heaved out of the warm bed. He padded out the door with his tail quivering high in the air and as straight as an arrow.

Dana moaned and rubbed her eyes. Last night was such a wasted drunk. She had been hoping that she would come home late and plastered and it would make Kimmy jealous. Maybe Kimmy would think Dana had been out with another woman. Then she'd be so jealous that she would straighten up her ways and they would live happily ever after. Instead, Kimmy was none the wiser and Dana had a hangover of the third degree.

Dana heard something strange. She sat up. It sounded like a vibrator. A muffled vibrator. A vibrator that was inside something. No, wait, it was her cell phone that was vibrating. She stuck her hand up her shirt and down her bra and under her boob and extricated the cell phone. She kept her phone there because she'd lose it otherwise. Chances were she'd always know where her left boob was and, by default, she'd know where her cell phone was. The only problem with that reasoning was that she kept forgetting that it was wedged under her boob and getting in the shower with it. She'd ruined many a phone that way.

She squinted at the phone and saw there was a text. She didn't recognize the number.

The message read, "How r u feeling?"

She slid out the qwerty keyboard and typed back with her thumbs, "Who is this?"

Several seconds passed then a new message lit up the screen. "You tried to rub my head last nite n ur gf threw me out of vfw."

It was Ellen! Dana jumped for joy. Which was weird because she was still lying in bed, so it ended up looking more like she was bouncing up and down on her butt. She typed back, "Howd u get my #?" She hit send, then realized that her message may have sounded like she didn't want Ellen to text her. So she typed another, "But Im glad you did." She quickly sent that text.

She only had to wait a few seconds before her screen lit up again. "Ur # was on ur shirt."

Dana looked down at the front of her shirt. She was still wearing her orange Slave Labor shirt and, sure enough, her phone number was printed right under the logo.

"Lol," Dana typed, "silly me."

"Lol," Ellen typed back, "meet for lunch 2day? not a date."

Dana mused on those last three words. She was no expert on women or dating or dating women, but Dana was enough of a woman to know that when you out-and-out say something like "It's not a date" or "I just want to be your friend" the opposite is really true. In fact, the last time Dana had told someone "I'm not trying to get in your pants," she was in said pants within the hour.

"Sounds good," Dana texted. "Picnic? City park? Noon?"

"K," Ellen wrote back, "Ill bring fud."

Dana threw back the covers and jumped out of bed. This time instead of wincing at the bright sunshine, she marveled at how the morning was perfectly reflecting her mood.

* * *

I started my own business about eight or nine years ago. After taking out a huge student loan and spending five years in college to get my English lit degree, I began writing the Great American Lesbian Romance Novel. Unfortunately, collection agencies kept calling and waking me up in the middle of the afternoon. I turned my creativity to the task of earning money. I printed up a stack of flyers and stuck them under every windshield within a fifty-mile radius of my house. The flyers were neon orange with giant black letters proclaiming the name of my new business, Slave Labor. Under the company name was my logo, a cartoonish version of a man's leg from the knee down with a ball and chain attached to the ankle. The slogan read: "We'll do almost anything for next to nothing."

Within two hours of passing out the flyers, a chicken farmer called. "I need you to sex my chickens," he said.

I almost hung up on him before he explained, "All's you got to do is separate the boy chicks from the girl chicks. I'll pay you a hundred bucks for the day's work."

I showed up at his farm in my bright orange T-shirt that Trudy had silk-screened with the words "Slave Labor." (The irony did not escape me that a black person was helping a white person become slave labor.)

It may have taken me five years to get my college degree, but it only took me three minutes to find out that baby chicks are cute in a cage at the Tractor Supply store, but they weren't so cute when there were two thousand of the little suckers pooping on you.

I sexed those chicks for thirteen grueling hours. The work consisted of picking up a chick, squeezing its pooper and checking its anus for a bump. Bumps are boys, no bumps are girls. At the end of the day, I collected my hundred dollars and felt like a useful member of society.

I had to throw away my brand new Slave Labor T-shirt, though. Chicken shit is a stain that doesn't wash out.

Work got better after that but not by much. I did odd jobs like walk dogs and buy belated birthday presents for wives and clean out garages and attics. I had a few regular clients, like the agoraphobe whom I'd never actually seen. I just delivered the weekly groceries to her front porch. A woman's hand—it looked more like a claw with little blue worms squiggling under the pale skin—thrust money at me through the mail slot. Once every three months or so the country club paid me to wade in its pond and pick out the golf balls. If I weren't deathly afraid of the killer swans, this would have been a great job. Then there was Wanda who hired me to come in every Friday and clean her beauty shop, The Best Little Hairhouse.

The building used to be home to a Kentucky Fried Chicken franchise. When KFC moved uptown where all the lunch hour traffic flowed, Wanda moved her beauty shop from her garage to the old KFC building. Wanda joked about her choice of buildings a lot. Like when a customer would ask her for a perm she would say, "Regular or extra-crispy?" Or when they got a manicure, she would say it was "finger-lickin' good."

She kept the front part of her shop like the old KFC with the big picture windows overlooking Main Street and using the tables as waiting areas and a manicurist station. Wanda turned the kitchen area into shampoo sinks and hair dryers and she had two hair-cutting stations—one for her and one for whoever she had hired to help out.

The building still smelled like fried chicken and brown gravy from the twenty years of grease embedded under the baseboards. The secret recipe had steeped into the paint. Every time I left the shop after work a pack of stray dogs would follow me home.

One Friday I showed up to do my weekly cleaning and when I walked in Bella and Donna, two seventy-year-old sisters, were sitting under hairdryers with the hoods pulled down over their curlers. The sisters were fond enough of food that their wrinkles were plumped out and they didn't look a day over sixty. I read somewhere once that fat made you look younger. Of course, it also made you look fat.

Bella and Donna were shouting at each other with their outside voices so they could be heard over the noise of their hair dryers.

"It's one of those half-and-half jobbies," Bella said.

"Bullroar. There's no such thing. It's got to be one or the other," Donna said.

"That's why it called 'piecake.' Because it's half pie and half cake," Bella insisted.

I tickled the air at Wanda who was busy ratting and bumping up the back of Jenny McCoy's hairdo. Jenny was a mousy little thing with a flat chest who put all her self-worth into the care and maintenance of her hair. She felt about her hair the way a teenage boy feels about his penis. She couldn't keep her hands off it. She was constantly touching, patting and twirling it.

Jenny was the hoity-toity type who held her nose so high up in the air it looked like she couldn't bear the stench of her own upper lip. She was married to Bob McCoy, who was the preacher over at the Last Chance Baptist Church. I always felt sorry for her because Baptists think female orgasms are demon possessions.

I went all through school with Jenny. We became enemies when we both got invited to Marlene Williams's slumber party in the eighth grade. Jenny was on her period and she wore those thick sanitary napkins when all the other girls wore tampons. (Only Satan's harlots wore tampons.) She woke up sometime in the middle of the night and went to the bathroom. When she came out she was shaking and out of breath. She flipped on the overhead light and waved something around, babbling about stigmatas and Jesus. I finally got her to sit down and breathe and that was when she showed it to me. She held out her used sanitary napkin and said, "Look! I bled a perfect likeness of Jesus in my Kotex!"

When we went back to school the next day, Marlene Williams told everyone that the movie *Carrie* was based on Jenny's life. Jenny never got invited to another slumber party and she blamed me for it.

Well, to be truthful, I think she blamed me for stealing her bloody Shroud-of-Turin and listing it on eBay. I got over forty bucks for it. I tried to split it with her, but she got all huffy puffy about it.

Twenty years later, Jenny was sitting in The Best Little Hairhouse getting a fifty-dollar color and curl and I was cleaning the toilets. Go figure.

"Dana, you judged the last pie contest at the county fair. Will you please tell my sister that she can't enter her piecake in both categories? She needs to pick a dang category and stick to it," said Donna.

"I judged the pie-*eating* contest. I'm not qualified to answer your question."

"Shoot fire and save matches," Donna grumbled.

Bella smirked and wagged a finger at her sister. "You wait and watch. I'm gonna win both categories. Mark my word."

Wanda gave me a smile as I opened the closet and extracted the little carry-all of cleansers. Wanda had brand-new dentures which were pretty to look at, but according to her they didn't fit right. She couldn't keep them glued down. She made awful clicking noises when she talked and every time she bent over they popped out and hit the floor. She claimed the three-second rule and popped them right back in without rinsing them first.

Wanda said, "Dana, you want your hair cut, *click*, the new girl, *click*, I hired isn't busy."

Wanda paid me in cash and haircuts. I usually got my hair cut every four months, so she was getting off cheap. "New girl?" I asked, nervously tucking a stray strand of hair behind my ear.

She whispered behind her hand (in a voice loud enough for everyone to hear), "I hired her, *click*, three days ago and nobody's wanted to be the first, *click*, one to test her out."

"I don't want to be anybody's guinea pig," I whispered back.

"Ssshhhh," she said, darting her eyes to the closed restroom door. "I thought that since you don't put as much stock, *click click*, in your looks as other women, that you wouldn't mind, *click*, giving Kimmy a test drive."

Jenny giggled.

There were so many insults in Wanda's statement I didn't even know where to begin. So, I did the next best thing and ignored it. I pulled out a roll of paper towels and squirted one of the mirrors with glass cleaner. It was no accident that I squirted Jenny's reflection right between the eyes. I could feel Jenny's eyeballs burning a hole in my back.

I squirted the reflection of Jenny's boobs, first one, then the other. I wiped on the mirror, making swirly-cues around her titties. She glared hate rays at me. I squirted her mirror image directly in the crotch. I scrubbed at it vigorously, pretending there was something on the mirror that I couldn't get off. I made sure to smile lasciviously while I did it.

The toilet flushed and the rest room door opened. I looked into the other side of the mirror to see the new hairstylist walk out. My hand froze in mid-swipe.

No wonder every woman in town was suspicious of her. She was drop dead gorgeous. She could give Miss America a run for her money.

Kimmy walked to her empty station chair and sat down. She picked up a file and commenced to work on a nail. I studied her reflection. Her hair was the color of a Hershey's milk chocolate candy bar. Her eyes were blue like my favorite M&M's. Her lips were as pink as fresh-spun cotton candy. Her dress was the color of pistachio pudding, and her breasts were like twin mounds of whipped cream with a cherry on top.

My stomach growled.

I resumed cleaning the mirror, stealing sidelong glances at her.

Miss High-and-Mighty, Jenny McCoy, must have thought this was a prime opportunity to out me. Or embarrass me. Or both. "Dana, my friend Claire's nephew is coming to town. I could invite you over for Sunday dinner. He's from California, you know, a liberal type who might find you…interesting."

Kimmy flicked her eyes up at me and back down to her filing.

"No, thanks," I said.

"Are you still in your lesbian phase?" Jenny said the word "lesbian" like it burned her lips.

Kimmy's file stopped.

"Yes, Jenny, I am. And I can prove it too."

Kimmy resumed her filing and a small smile played across her lips.

"Seems to me you might want to switch to something more lucrative," Jenny snorted.

I wiped at the mirror harder.

Jenny continued, "You're not going to have much luck finding a man as long as you keep saying you're a lesbian."

"You never know. Lesbians turn men on. That's a proven fact."

I distinctly heard Kimmy giggle. Wanda and the sisters were quiet. I think they were silently placing bets on how long it would take me to explode.

"Men like real women, Dana. Not women who are pretending to be men," Jenny said.

I scrubbed so hard the mirror squeaked.

Wanda took that opportunity to jump in and change the subject. "Did you all hear Davy Arbuckle, *click click*, is getting divorced?"

"Where'd you hear that?" Bella asked.

I glanced over at Kimmy and found her looking at me. She smiled and went back to filing her nails.

Wanda said, "Mona told me. Said she was going to divorce him this summer right after they take the kids to Disney, *click*, World."

Jenny was like a dog with a bone. "I bet you could catch him, Dana. He's never been particular."

"I don't think I could ever go out with a man who did that to a dog," I said.

"Did what?" Bella asked.

"You mean you all haven't heard about Winston, his prize bulldog?"

"What about him?" Wanda asked.

"Davy gets a stud fee off that ugly dog, you know."

"Yes, but what of it?" Donna inquired.

"Well, Winston is too short to mate. His hind legs are too short to allow him access to the female, you know," I explained. Everyone was staring at me, including Kimmy. "So when it came time to breed Winston, Davy had to do the honors."

"Do the, *click*, honors?"

"You know..." I said. I moved my fist back and forth in front of my crotch. "Do the honors. He jacked off his dog, collected the bulldog stuff, and carted it back to the vet, and Dr. Amos injected it into the female."

Bella gasped. "Davy Arbuckle did that to his dog?"

I nodded. "Now that dog follows him everywhere. He can't get rid of it to save his soul."

They all laughed. Well, except for Jenny, of course, but she never laughed. She probably thought mirth was the eighth deadly sin.

"No wonder Mona's divorcing him," Donna said.

"Maybe I'll ask Mona out," I said.

Bella interjected her opinion, "I wouldn't mind being a lesbian. Except for the sex part."

"Couldn't be any worse than having sex with my husband," Donna said.

Jenny said, "Being a lesbian is an excuse a woman comes up with when she can't get a man. I don't believe in lesbians. They don't exist."

"Well, I don't believe in you. Therefore, you don't exist," I said.

Bella chimed in, "I saw a lesbian on TV the other night." She smiled at everyone and said proudly, "I have cable now."

Jenny stood up and brushed the wrinkles out of her skirt. "Lesbians are like unicorns. Everybody's heard of them, but nobody's ever seen one."

"Why, Jenny, didn't you used to have a poster of a unicorn in your bedroom?" I sniped.

"I most certainly did not," she said.

"Oh, that's right," I said. "My bad. I was thinking of that poster of Darlene from *Roseanne* you had hanging up on your wall."

"She was an exceptional actress," Jenny said, turning three shades of red.

"Yes, she was," I said, grabbing an imaginary pair of boobs and squeezing. Everybody laughed.

Jenny harrumphed, threw some folded money on the counter and pranced out the door like a circus pony.

After Jenny's grand exit, Kimmy stood up and swiveled her chair around toward me. "Let me cut your hair. Give you a new style," she said. "You can be my first."

Wanda and the sisters stared at me expectantly. "I don't know," I said. "I've had this same hairdo forever. I don't adjust well to change."

"Jennifer Anniston would be proud." Kimmy patted the back of her chair. "But, honey, it's time to let go."

I tried to think of reasons why I shouldn't let her cut my hair. 1) I could end up looking like a fool, and 2) I would have to wear a hat the rest of the summer.

I tried to think up reasons to let her cut my hair. 1) If I sat in that chair, I'd be eye level with her boobs.

"Why not?" I said. "Let's cut my hair."

I eased into the chair while she gathered all her instruments and laid them out like a surgeon. She selected a pair of pointy scissors and snipped the air, testing them out.

"Who do you want to be?" she asked.

"You mean I get to be somebody else?"

"Sure," she said with a knowing smile. "That's what the beauty biz is all about. You come in here to be somebody else, look like somebody else." She snipped the air around her like David Carradine catching flies with chopsticks. "I am the magic-maker who transforms you into who you want to be," she said with an ultra-straight face.

"Isn't that line from *Willie Wonka*?"

She laughed. "Isn't there anybody you'd like to be?"

My mind raced with all the endless possibilities. "How about Wonder Woman?"

"Lynda Carter?"

"No, Wonder Woman. I'd kill for a magic lasso and those golden arm bands."

She laughed. "When I was a kid I had a Wonder Woman nightlight. She was sitting inside her invisible airplane."

"How could you see it?"

"Huh?"

"If she was inside her invisible airplane, how could you see the nightlight?"

"I don't know. I never thought of that."

"Maybe your mom lied to you. Maybe she told you there was a nightlight but it wasn't really there."

She laughed again. I liked it when she laughed. It made her boobs jiggle. I made a pact with myself right then and there to make her laugh as much as possible.

"How about short hair? Short hair will make you look younger," she said.

"I'm okay with looking my age. How about you make my butt smaller instead?"

"No problem."

She lifted a hunk of hair off the back of my neck and chopped. Her scissors blurred as she hacked, sawed and axed. After fifteen minutes her scissors slowed and she swiveled me around in the chair a couple of times, pumped a glob of gel into her palm, rubbed her hands together like she was trying to start a fire with twigs and then applied it all vigorously to my head.

She held a hand mirror up in front of my face so I could see the back of my hair in the mirror and said, "What do you think?"

I'd never paid much attention to the back of my head before. I'd always thought of it like the play sets that I helped build in high school: only the front mattered. The back was masking tape and boards. I realized I'd been selfish my whole life by not paying any attention at all to the people behind me.

Kimmy turned my chair until I was facing myself in the mirror.

"What do you think?" she asked again.

I looked like me except with less hair and more face.

I raised my eyes and saw Bella, Donna and Wanda standing behind my chair, scrutinizing Kimmy's job.

"I never knew you were so pretty, Dana Dooley," Donna said.

"That style brings out your eyes," Bella said.

"And your cheekbones," Donna added.

I blushed more shades of red than Crayola has in their 124-pack while the sisters chatted all the way back over to their hairdryers. "You see, she's like me. An artist. We don't follow recipes," Bella said.

"You know who needs to make an appointment with her?" Donna asked.

"Gertie?"

"Mmmhmmm, she's always wanting to try new things. I'll call her up tonight."

Wanda winked her approval at Kimmy and went back to sweeping up hair.

"Thanks," I murmured.

"Thank you for being my guinea pig," she said. "I owe you one."

* * *

Dana spent the better part of the morning plucking her eyebrows and waxing her mustache. She even tweezed her nipples. Not because she thought Ellen would actually see her nipples at the city park picnic, but because it made Dana feel in control. There were so many things about her body that she couldn't control—like hunger, where fat stored itself and pimples—that she liked to control everything she could.

She stopped short of shaving her legs even though she definitely had a five o'clock shadow. Shaving her legs was as good as admitting that she wanted to have sex with Ellen. And she didn't. Well, she did want to have sex with her, she just didn't want to have sex with her over lunch on a first date. Having unshaved legs would act as a chastity belt. Or at least a speed bump.

CHAPTER FOUR

Dana was twenty-one minutes early (a multiple of three) even though she drove around the park three times (another multiple of three) before parking. She sat on top of the monkey bars so she could see the whole park at once. She swung her feet back and forth and thought about the date that wasn't a date. What if Ellen got a good look at her in broad daylight and decided she didn't like what she saw? What if Ellen really did mean that this wasn't a date and she had tweezed her nipples for nothing?

"Hey!"

Startled, Dana flinched and almost fell off the monkey bars.

"Sorry," Ellen said. "I didn't mean to scare you."

"That's okay, I'm used to falling," Dana said, then immediately felt stupid.

She scooted back further on the monkey bars and surreptitiously looked Ellen over. She was wearing baggy jeans hanging low on her hips with her boxers peeking over the waistband, brown Converse tennis shoes and a T-shirt that read "I like cats. I just can't eat a whole one by myself."

"Sorry, if I'm late," Ellen said. "There was a long line."

"You're late?" Dana said. "I thought I was early." She grimaced at how easily she lied. She didn't want to start off lying to Ellen. She wanted this whatever-it-was to be different. "I'm sorry," she said. "I lied to you. I was completely aware that you were late. Seven minutes late to be exact."

"Sorry," Ellen said.

"It's okay," Dana explained, "I felt bad about lying to you. I don't even know why I did it."

Ellen nodded like she understood. "You going to come down?" she asked.

"Why don't you come up? It's cool, you can see the whole park from here. I like to sit up here and pretend to be God. God of the park."

Ellen laughed. "Okay, God, here goes." She clenched the bag between her teeth, scrambled up the bars and scooched on her butt until she was sitting in the middle of the monkey bars next to Dana. She took a deep breath and looked down on the park. There were a few wooden tables scattered around the perimeter, the creek tumbled over a small waterfall and the swings moved back and forth in the light breeze. It was picture perfect and peaceful.

"Look," Ellen said, "all the little people down there on Earth look like ants."

"Those are ants."

"Oh, sorry, God. You're right."

They laughed.

Dana said, "This is my happy place."

"I can see why."

Dana's stomach growled loudly. Ellen laughed. "Somebody's hungry." She opened the bag and handed over a six-inch sub and a bag of chips. "I forgot the drinks," she said apologetically.

"That's okay," Dana said. She unwrapped her sandwich and was happy to see that it was loaded with three types of meat and a good three inches of everything else.

"I told them to put everything on it. I figured you could take off what you don't like."

Dana smiled. "I like my sandwiches Dagwood style," she said. And to prove it, she took a humongous bite. While she chewed, she wracked her brain trying to think of a good conversation starter and all she could come up with was, "I got my very first kiss up here."

"Oh, yeah? How old were you?"

"Twenty-seven."

Ellen looked at her wide-eyed.

"Just kidding," Dana said. "I was seven."

"Who was it with?" Ellen bit into her sandwich.

"Jenny McCoy. I planted a big kiss right on her lips, she screamed and fell off. Sprained her wrist."

Ellen laughed.

"She's hated me ever since. I seem to have that effect on women."

"I seriously doubt that," Ellen said. "So, that was your girlfriend last night?"

"You saw my girlfriend?"

"Yeah, she threatened to beat me with her wig, remember?"

"No, that's Trudy, she's my best friend. She thought she was supposed to rescue me from you, but our signals were crossed and...Sorry about that."

"She must be a really good friend."

"She owed me. I had just rescued her from a guy who smelled like fertilizer."

They chuckled and popped chips in their mouths. They swung their legs and chewed until Ellen asked, "So how'd you get to be here?"

"I climbed like you."

Ellen laughed. "I meant this town. Have you lived here your whole life?"

"Not yet. I'm kidding. Seriously, I've never lived anywhere else. My family's been here for five generations. The town was named after my grandpa."

"Really?"

"Mmhmm. He was a real scoundrel, though. That's why there's no statues of him or anything."

Ellen laughed.

"What's so funny?"

"I've never heard anybody call somebody a scoundrel before."

Dana shrugged. "He was a rascal too."

Ellen laughed, then said, "So that means your last name is…?"

"Dooley. Dana Dooley, that's me. Some people call me Double D 'cause of my initials."

Ellen smirked. "I don't want to make you mad, but there might be another reason they call you Double D."

Dana laughed. "How kind of you to notice."

"Are you blushing?"

"Am I?"

"I think so."

Dana popped another chip in her mouth, then finally asked, "So what's your last name?"

"Fisher. Not nearly as interesting as yours. And, before you ask, they don't call me double B."

They laughed and bit into their sandwiches.

* * *

I decided to celebrate my new haircut (which I had come to think of as a metaphor for the new life I was embarking on) by going out on the town. It was Friday night, I was single, I was sober, and I was on my way to DeWayne's Bar, hoping to go home later that night neither single nor sober. Or, at the very least, not sober. I was dressed to the nines in my green gypsy skirt with the embroidered flowers and the little bells dangling from the hem. I had chosen my white peasant blouse to go with it because it de-accentuated my ample boobage. I thought I looked Italian and earthy—like I should be stomping grapes in a vat.

DeWayne's was strategically located on the outside of the county limits. Dooley County was a dry county and this way hard liquor could be served and the sheriff didn't have any say in the matter.

I was pushing Betty's pedal to the metal and chugging along at fifty miles an hour when I saw a pair of weak headlights in the road up in front of me.

I had a moment of thinking it was an alien's (the outer space kind of alien) UFO that had crash-landed out in the country. But when I got closer I saw that it was Hank riding his lawnmower down the right-of-way. I downshifted to first and set myself at his pace while I rolled down the passenger window. Hank looked over at me and his face broke into a big grin. I like to see Hank grin. His smile takes up most of his face and divides it into different planes like one of those cubist paintings. He tipped his John Deere ball cap at me and winked. Hank's one of those throwback old-timers who still tips his hat and opens doors for women.

"Hey, Hank," I yelled.

"Howdy, Dana Dooley," he yelled back. "You get a new haircut?"

"No, my butt's smaller. I didn't see you in church this past Sunday."

"I was there," he yelled.

"I wasn't. Must be why I didn't see you."

I know he had heard the old joke a million times before, but he laughed anyway.

"You tryin' to beat the heat by mowing at night?" I asked. I could tell he wasn't mowing since his deck was in the high position, but this was the only way I could think of to find out what the hell he was doing.

"Nope," he answered. "Headed down to DeWayne's for a little."

Then it hit me why he was driving the lawnmower. "The wife confiscate your truck keys again?"

"Yep," he said, bobbing his head up down and grinning sheepishly like a kid who got caught smoking behind the barn.

Hank was a big-time drinker. Everybody in town knew to steer clear of Hank's old Ford truck when they saw it out on the road. Rumor had it that he had his own set of jail keys so he could check himself in after the bars closed.

"The little woman says I cain't kill nobody but myself riding my lawnmower. But I think she's hoping I'll accidentally mow the yard."

That's when I noticed he was wearing a button-up shirt with cartoon pictures of cars and trucks. I didn't remark on it, though. Good irony is lost on most people.

"You headed out to DeWayne's?" he asked.

I nodded. "Going to Trudy's divorce party. I'm the Maid of Dishonor."

He laughed. "Seems like I was just at her last one."

"I know it. I think she gets divorced so people'll buy her drinks."

"Maybe I oughta try that."

I laughed and rolled my window back up halfway. "Don't run over Miss Pearl's petunias up ahead!"

He tipped his cap at me and shouted, "Tell your grandma I said hi!"

I putt-putted back onto the highway and watched Hank turn into a flyspeck in my rear view. I slowed down as I passed a brand-new city limits sign. Since the last time I was out here they had taken down the old sign with the shotgun pellet holes and put up a new one. This one even had a plastic owl nailed to the top of it to warn off roosting pigeons. I guessed Fat Matt had been at it again. Matt was my brother and I called him Fat Matt when I wasn't afraid he'd catch me and sit on me. He was the mayor of our town. His personal mission in life was to turn the town our ancestors founded into a tourist mecca like Branson, Missouri.

I turned around in my seat and read the front of the sign as I passed. "Welcome to Dooley Springs, Oklahoma! Birthplace of Carrie Underwood! Final resting place of Mr. Ed! Home of Bigfoot!"

That had Fat Matt written all over it. It was all bullshit, of course. Mr. Ed wouldn't be caught dead in this town, and Carrie was born some fifty miles to the east of here. The only thing that may have been true is the Bigfoot part. According to *Sasquatch* e-magazine, of which my rotund brother was sole-proprietor, editor and number one reporter, a whole tribe of Bigfoots

(Bigfeet?) lived in the Cookson Hills east of here. He claimed to have spent an evening with them sitting around a campfire eating beanie weenies and singing the best of Wham!

The new city limits sign was a sure sign that Fat Matt was off his meds. The sign was pretty harmless, though, unless you found too many exclamation marks an eyesore. It was beyond my comprehension how Matt got elected mayor. Yes, the town was founded by our great great great great grandpa, but electing Matt as a town official? Being mayor was only the second job he'd ever had. The first job was right out of high school when he worked over in Arkansas at a chicken factory. His job was to run around the fenced coop and catch the chickens, wring their necks and throw them on the conveyor belt. He got pretty good at catching them, but wringing their necks was something he didn't have the heart to do.

He quit after one day of work and put in for disability claiming he had PTSD from being forced to kill against his will. He didn't get any disability checks, but he did get his first script for meds. After that he earned a little money by opening an eBay business. He went around to the garage sales in town and bought up all the old baby dolls. He would roll the dolls in dirt, tie them up, drag them behind his car and pour lighter fluid on them, then light them on fire and sell them on eBay as demon-possessed dolls. He created biographies for each doll, saying they had murdered entire families in their sleep and their favorite movie was *Chucky*, stuff like that. He got as much as two hundred dollars for some of the dolls.

I think he won the race for mayor because he had the only truthful campaign slogan anybody had ever seen: "He's not handsome or popular. He has time to be mayor. Fat Matt Dooley."

I guided Betty around the hairpin turn, up the hill and jerked the wheel into the next right. DeWayne's was hopping and the lot was overflowing. I managed to squeeze into a too-tight spot right in front of the entrance between a bright yellow Mustang with a black racing stripe down the center of the hood and a brand-new patriotic blue Dodge Ram 1500 Quad Cab with hemi. Even before I turned off my engine I could hear Miley Cyrus's dad singing that song I hate that made the entire bar get up and boot scoot across the dance floor.

I was thinking that maybe I should order two drinks at once. That way I wouldn't have to make a second trip back to the crowded bar and who knows, maybe tonight I would finally meet my dream woman. Or if I had enough drinks, I'd just meet a woman.

Yeah, right. I'd have better odds of toasting marshmallows with Bigfoot.

If I ordered two drinks and made them doubles, that'd be like four drinks and tonight was ladies night, two for one drinks, so for the price of one drink I could get four drinks. Who could pass up a deal like that?

Crap on a shingle. All that mathematical calculating distracted me and I accidentally banged Betty's door into the Mustang.

I quickly closed my door, rolled down my window and leaned out to inspect the damage. The Mustang's door didn't look too bad. An itty-bitty ding. Hardly noticeable. Served somebody right for buying a fancy-ass car and driving it to a redneck bar in the first place. Everybody knows when you have a car like that you should park out in the back of the lot.

I lifted myself over to the passenger seat, but I saw right away that there was even less space between that door and the Dodge. I scooted back over behind the wheel (damn near impaling my ass with the gear shift) and decided to crawl through my driver's window. I could drop down into the ten-inch space between it and the Mustang and scooch my way out.

I climbed out my window head-first, twisted around and, by using my elbows on the Mustang's roof, managed to pull the entire length of my body out. I aimed my flip-flops for the space between the Mustang and Betty and let myself drop, hoping gravity would do its part.

It did its part all right, but my butt got wedged between the two cars with my skirt hiked up over my butt. I don't know what I was thinking. The last time my butt could fit into a ten-inch space I was in kindergarten.

My feet dangled about half a foot off the ground. I put my palms flat on the roof of the cars and tried to lift myself out.

Nothing doing.

I got tired of trying to lift up, so I tried pushing down.

Nothing doing.

I was stuck but good.

I wiggled my feet back and forth but that didn't help either. It made me have to pee and my shoes fell off.

I noticed the passenger window on the Mustang was rolled down. I came up with an idea. If I could stick my upper body in that car, then I could wedge my butt out, crawl through and let myself out on the other side the Mustang.

That was the plan anyway.

I got my head, shoulders and boobage inside the Mustang, but my butt didn't want to cooperate. It wanted to stay where it was. I was stuck worse than Winnie the Pooh going for the honey pot.

I reached out, grabbed the Mustang's steering wheel and pulled as hard as I could.

That turned out to be a not-so-bright idea because that made the car alarm go into hoot 'n holler mode.

Now I was half in-half out of the Mustang, bent over at the waist with my butt in the air and the car alarm was *whoop-whoop-whooping*.

I promised myself that if I ever got out of this predicament, I was going to treat myself to eight drinks for the price of two.

I kept pulling and praying, praying and pulling and working up a pretty good sweat in the process.

Beep beep.

The car alarm stopped. I straight-armed myself up high enough to see through the Mustang's front window. It was Kimmy the Hairstylist. She was standing there with her car keys in her hand and wearing another delectable little dress and looking downright delicious.

My stomach growled.

Kimmy was staring at my butt, which was hanging out of her car window. She looked confused. I didn't know what to say, so I said the only thing that made any sense. "Help me, please."

"Did I run over you?" she gasped. She clasped her hand over her mouth like movie actors do to show horror.

I shook my head, but she was wound up into panic mode. She dropped her hand and said, "Oh my God, I ran right over you! Are you okay? I don't have insurance. Please don't sue me."

"I won't sue if you can get me out of here," I replied. I wouldn't have sued anyway, of course, but I wasn't going to tell her that.

She whipped a cell phone out of her tiny purse and stared at the dial pad with a confused look on her face. She looked back to me. "I'm going to call Nine Eleven, okay? I'll get the fire department to bring the jaws of life."

"You don't have to call anybody," I protested. "I'm stuck."

She punched in a number, then stopped and squinted at the phone. "Where's the eleven on this thing?"

"There is no eleven," I said.

"I can see that," she said like I was the stupid one. "So, how do I dial an eleven? Do I dial a ten and a one or a one and a one? And why would they say to dial Nine Eleven for emergencies if there is no eleven? How stupid are they?"

"It's Nine One One, not Nine Eleven. You're getting the date mixed up with the emergency number."

"What date?" she asked.

"Remind me never to have a heart attack or bleed profusely around you. I'd be dead before you figured out who to call."

"You don't have to be hateful about it," she said. She edged closer and peered at my face through her front windshield. "Don't I know you?"

"Yeah. You cut my hair yesterday."

She looked from my face to my butt. "Your butt does look smaller."

"I know. Thanks. You did a good job."

An idea crossed her feeble mind. "Were you trying to steal my car?"

"No, I was not trying to steal your dang car. I was trying to crawl through your car to get out of my car but I got stuck. I need your help getting unstuck."

"Okay," she said. "What can I do?"

"I'm no expert, but I think if you get in your car, grab hold of me and pull, I'll pop free."

She stuck her phone back in her purse and got in the Mustang from the driver's side. I held my arms out to her and she grabbed me around both wrists and braced one of her high heel shoes on the seat.

"Give me a tug," I said.

She tugged.

"Keep pulling and don't stop," I said.

She pulled harder. And harder. And harder.

"Okay, stop," I said. "I think you dislocated my shoulders."

"I saw this exact same thing once on *America's Funniest Home Videos*," she said.

"What happened?"

"I'm pretty sure he died."

"That's not funny."

"I know, right? That's probably why they didn't win the grand prize."

"We need some leverage. Maybe you could lie on your back kind of under me, brace your feet against the passenger door, grab me under my arms and pull again."

She laid down on her back, stretching out under my upper body, put both feet flat on the door I was hanging over, grabbed my armpits and pulled.

I felt my butt give a little.

"Keep going! You almost got it! Use your legs!"

She gritted her teeth and pulled with all her might.

I felt the buttons on my skirt pop loose.

"Whoopsy doopsy," I said right before I slid out of my skirt and into the Mustang, face-planting myself right between her tits.

"You're out!" she yelled triumphantly.

"Yesth, I amth," I replied with a nose-full of her boobs, trying to decide whether I was going to laugh or cry.

She moved her hands down, brushing them across my underpants. She wrinkled her nose and asked, "Are you in just your panties?"

"I think so, yeah."

That was when Hank leaned down and peered inside the driver's window. He took in the sight of my ass with Kimmy lying under me and grinned. "Sorry to interrupt, Dana. I didn't realize that was you were in here with your girlfriend. I thought somebody was being coerced against their will."

"No, no coercion going on," I said.

"You going to introduce me?"

"Oh, sorry. Hank, this is Kimmy. Kimmy this is Hank. She's a really good hairstylist if you or the wife are in need of a haircut. She's working over at Wanda's place."

Kimmy smiled up at him. "Nice to meet you."

Hank smiled and tipped his hat. "You too." He stood smiling and made no move to leave.

"Can you go now?" I asked.

"Oh, sure thing. See ya inside," he said. I watched him mosey toward the front door. I looked back at Kimmy. I mumbled, "Sorry about that, but…"

She wrapped her hand around the back of my neck, pulled my lips to hers and kissed me. A real honest-to-God kiss too. She didn't use her tongue or anything, but she sure made good use of her lips.

She ended the kiss about the time I was getting good at it. She wormed out from under me, started the car, backed us out of the tight spot and watched me get out and fetch my skirt. I slid it on and hopped my way into my flip-flops while she tooted her horn and sped out of the parking lot.

I stood there for a moment with my lips tingling, then I walked inside DeWayne's like I had springs on the bottoms of my feet. I felt the stupid grin lighting up my face but was powerless to do anything about it.

```
Trudy walked up to the bar and looked me up and
down. "Did you just get lucky?" she asked.
    "What makes you ask that?"
    "Your skirt is on backwards."
```

* * *

After Dana and Ellen finished their sandwiches they moved to one of the wooden picnic tables. The table tops were scarred and pockmarked from the pocketknives of every teenage boy in Dooley Springs. Dana kept finding herself staring at one carving in particular. There were only two words: "tittie biscuits." She finally figured out what about the two words bothered her. She had always thought the word was spelled "titty," not "tittie."

"So tell me something about yourself," Ellen said.

"By yourself, I'm assuming you mean past relationships?"

"That too."

Dana traced her fingertip over "tittie biscuits," then said, "I've had five relationships. All with women named Lisa. Except this current one."

Ellen laughed.

"It's true. All Lisas except this one."

"You have a Lisa fetish?"

"Not consciously. Subconsciously, who knows? Maybe it's a real popular name." It suddenly occurred to Dana what was bothering her. The singular form was "titty" and the plural was "titties." There was no such thing as "tittie," there could only be "titties" with the s on the end. She had no idea, however, how many titties it took to make a biscuit.

Ellen said, "Tell me about your girlfriend now. The one not named Lisa."

Dana took a deep breath. "Well, for starters, she has an acute case of RPS."

"What's that?"

"You've heard of RLS, Restless Leg Syndrome?" Ellen nodded. "Well, she has RPS. Restless Pussy Syndrome."

Ellen laughed.

"Seriously, I think the only reason she stays with me is because she can live rent free." Dana smiled slyly. "Plus, I'm really good in bed." She threw that last line in there because it never hurt to advertise.

"Is that so?" Ellen asked coyly.

"I like to think so." She shrugged.

Ellen wadded up her empty chip bag and set it aside so she wouldn't have to look at Dana while she asked, "Do you love her?"

"No," Dana responded. "Now I'm wondering if I ever did."

Ellen breathed a sigh of relief.

"How about your girlfriend?" Dana asked.

Ellen smiled crookedly. "I don't love mine either. I think I mistook lust for love and only thought I loved her."

"Oh my God! That's what I've always said. What is it with us lesbians?"

"I don't know," Ellen said. "But it's true. One orgasm and that nesting instinct kicks in."

"How long have you been with your girlfriend?"

"Too long. How about you?"

"Seven dog years," Dana answered. She picked up all their trash, walked over to the trash barrel and threw it all inside.

Ellen laughed. "Using that formula, I've been with my girlfriend about three months. I mean, um…twenty-one dog months. What's her name? Your girlfriend, I mean."

"No," Dana said, "let's not say their names. I'd like to continue to objectify them. Once I know your girlfriend's name then she becomes real and I would feel guilty about imagining her dead." Dana sat on top of the table smack dab on top of "tittie biscuits."

"Oh, do you have those dreams too?"

"Yeah. Except mine aren't dreams, they're fantasies. My girlfriend breathes loud. She breathes so loud I want to kill her. I'll be upstairs and I can even hear her breathing downstairs. If she were hiding in the dark in a horror movie, the murderer would be able to find her every time. One night I woke up and she was sleeping next to me and I couldn't hear her breathing so

I thought she was dying, you know, in her sleep. So I whispered encouragement, 'Go to the light. Don't be afraid, walk into the light.' She woke up and saw me staring at her with my pillow in my hands. I think it scared her."

"No doubt. If I thought I could get by with it, I'd off mine for sure."

"Would you really?"

Ellen shrugged. "Maybe. If I thought I could commit the perfect murder, like stab her with an icicle and there'd be no murder weapon."

"My girlfriend will never die. She never does anything I want," Dana said morosely.

Ellen joined Dana on the table top. Ellen sat close, so close their thighs touched. If this wasn't a date somebody forgot to tell Dana's body about it. Ellen touched Dana lightly on the thigh and said, "You know, you're very beautiful."

Dana looked away. She didn't know what to say. A part of her wanted to contradict Ellen and another part wanted to say thank you and still yet another part wanted to throw her down and rut on top of her. Instead, Dana moved the conversation to neutral territory. "So why'd you move here and where'd you come from?"

"Oh, okay, subject change." Ellen took her hand off Dana's thigh. "Let's see. I got a job transfer to here. Actually, I asked for the transfer."

"What job?"

"It's pretty boring. I move little pieces of paper from one place to another."

"Where'd you move from?"

"San Diego. I got out of a bad relationship and even San Diego was too small after that."

"So then you came here and got into another bad relationship?"

"I didn't say I was smart. My current girlfriend isn't as bad as the last one though. At least this one goes to a little trouble to hide the fact that she's cheating on me."

"What're the odds, we both have girlfriends who are cheating on us? You know what would be weird? What if they were cheating on us with each other?"

They laughed at the outrageousness of it.

Dana said, "I wish I could catch my girlfriend with her fingers in somebody else's cookie jar. I want to throw her out of my house, but every time I try to break up with her...Well, suffice it to say the only time she sleeps with me anymore is when I break up with her."

"Sounds like my girlfriend," Ellen sighed.

Dana took a chance, "Can I tell you something?"

"Sure."

"I like you," Dana said quickly like it was all one word.

"I like you too." Ellen smiled. She took Dana's hand in her hands, which were calloused and strong. Dana wanted to rub lotion on them. She would rub Ellen's hands all night if given half the chance.

Ellen leaned in—close, so close—and Dana panicked. "You know what happened to the last girl I kissed in this park," she joked.

"I'll take that chance," Ellen said.

She leaned in again, but this time Dana stopped her by saying, "No."

"Why? Do I have bad breath?"

Dana smiled. "No, it's not that. I want to kiss you, you don't know how bad. But I don't want to be like our girlfriends. We'd be cheating too, and that's not what I want to do. So can we...? I don't know...? Can we...?"

"Catch their cheating asses, throw them out and then consummate our desire?"

"Well, I was going to say let's be friends, but I think that's an even better idea."

They laughed.

CHAPTER FIVE

The date that wasn't a date but really was a date lasted longer than Dana had planned. She hurried home and changed into her Slave Labor T-shirt and work jeans. She had about five minutes to spare or she was going to be late and that meant she'd have to suffer through another one of Wanda's clicking lectures about how all the evils of society exist because of people's inconsiderate tardiness or some such drivel.

On the way out the door, Dana almost stepped on the hind end of a squirrel that was laying on the welcome mat. Asscat had struck again. She ran to the garage and grabbed her trusty shovel. She scooped up the butthole remains and carried it into the backyard. She was digging frantically in the dirt and darn near jumped out of her skin when she heard, "What'cha doin', Dana Dooley?"

She whirled around with her shovel raised as a weapon. But it was only Old Man Pringle, her next door neighbor. He was peering at her over the privacy fence that separated their backyards, his large nose hooked over the boards and his rheumy eyes glaring at her.

She lowered her shovel. "Burying a butthole," she said a whole lot friendlier than she felt.

"Hmmm," he said. He scanned Dana's backyard, his eyes pausing at all the fresh mounds of dirt from her previous buryings. "You must have known a lot of buttholes."

"You can say that again," she said and dismissed him by turning her back and poking the shovel back into the earth. It took her exactly fifteen shovelfuls (a multiple of three) to dig a hole deep enough. She threw in the furry tail and kicked the dirt back on top. By the time Asscat's latest victim was buried, Old Man Pringle and his nose were gone.

Dana was twelve minutes late (another multiple of three) to clean the beauty shop. As soon as she opened the front door and saw the pinched look on Wanda's face, she knew Kimmy hadn't come to work. That meant Kimmy had been AWOL for at least twenty-four hours, maybe more like forty-eight.

Wanda slammed down the telephone and spat, "Where is she?"

"Who?" Dana asked, feigning innocence.

When Wanda was irate her clicking turned to clacking. "That girlfriend, *clack*, of yours. The one who used to, *clack*, work here."

"Kimmy?" Dana asked in an effort to buy time.

"Yes, Kimmy. Unless you have another girlfriend we don't know about," she snarled. "I've been rescheduling her, *clack*, appointments all, *clack*, morning."

"Kimmy's sick," Dana lied. "I thought she called you."

"Sick?" Wanda asked like she didn't believe her. She even squinted her eyes like she had x-ray vision and could peer directly into Dana's brain and see all the lies stored there.

"She's got that flu that's going around." Dana felt pretty safe in saying that because it always seemed like a flu was going around somewhere. As a writer she knew that the truth was in the details, so she piled on some. "It's coming out both ends. At the same time. I can't even be in the same house with her."

Wanda harrumphed and clacked but knew she couldn't say much to that. "Tell her to have you call me, *click*, next time."

Dana noticed that Wanda's irate clacks had turned into her usual clicks and that the danger of being fired by association was over. She retrieved the cleaning supplies out of the closet and wondered where Kimmy was keeping herself. At first she hadn't been concerned about Kimmy's whereabouts. Her not coming home was nothing unusual. But when she didn't show up to work, there had to be a darn good reason.

Wanda said, "Good thing you're cleaning today. *Click*. You're tracking dirt all over the floor."

Dana looked down and saw that she'd left a trail of muddy footprints from the door all the way to the back. "Sorry," she said, "I was digging a grave in my backyard right before I got here." She fetched the broom out of the closet.

"Kimmy that sick that you're already digging a, *click*, grave?" Wanda laughed at her own joke.

"If I was, I wouldn't tell you about it," Dana said with a chuckle.

"I dunno. *Click*. You might. To throw me off the trail. *Click*. I saw that in a movie once."

Dana swished the broom over her footprints and sighed. "You got me. I killed Kimmy and buried her in a shallow grave in my backyard."

"Not too, *click*, shallow, I hope," Wanda said. "Stray dogs'll dig her up." And then as an afterthought, she added, "*click*."

* * *

I met Lisa Number Two at Dr. Amos's office when I took Asscat in to get his yearly shots. Dr. Amos was the town vet. He loved animals and he hated people. When I was a little kid, I laughed every time somebody said his name because I thought it sounded like they were saying Dr. Anus. I must have been fond of scatological humor because I also cracked up when my third grade teacher said, "There's a ring of debris around Uranus."

Dr. Anus had a full waiting room by the time I arrived. So I lugged Asscat's wire cage over to the only empty chair and sat down next to an odd-looking woman. She was wearing all black and had big, sad eyes like a basset hound. She had an untamed Afro with pencils stuck in it haphazardly here and yonder. She also had pert boobs.

She smiled at Asscat and reached down like she was going to pet him through the wires of his cage.

"I wouldn't do that if I were you," I warned.

Asscat howled and hissed at her fingers. She quickly drew back her hand.

"Your cat is mad," she said.

I almost said, "Oh, yeah? How can you tell?" But for once I kept my smart-aleck remarks inside my head.

"My name is Lisa," she said. (She was only my second Lisa, so alarm bells didn't go off yet.) "I'm a pet psychic."

"Really?" I asked. This was getting more interesting by the second. "What defines a pet psychic?"

"I can communicate telepathically with animals."

"What number is my cat thinking of right now?"

She didn't laugh. I learned later that Lisa Number Two never laughed. She scrutinized instead. It was if she was picking the flesh off a funny bone to see what it tasted like.

"You probably won't believe me, but I can talk to animals," she said, defensively.

I asked, "Are you like Dr. Doolittle or do you see the pets move their mouths like Mr. Ed and Babe?"

She ignored my question and forged ahead with her lecture.

"You should be more serious about your feline companion. Cats are natural healers, you know. Their chakras are clean naturally so they can channel energy to a sick human. Have you ever noticed how cats cuddle up next to you or sit on your lap when you're sick or depressed?"

"My cat doesn't," I said. "He hates me to be happy. If I even so much as smile, he shits in my shoes."

"He's trying to tell you that he loves you, but you aren't listening. He wants to get your attention."

"Hmmm," I intoned. "Can you perhaps communicate telepathically to my feline companion that the next time he shits in my shoes, I'm going to shit in his litter box?"

She shook her head like she'd just heard the saddest thing in the world. She looked over at the big yellow dog sitting on his haunches next to her and watched as he slurped at his balls. "We should be more like that dog," she said. "If all men could do that, the world would be a better place."

I laughed. She looked at me sternly. I guess she wasn't trying to be funny.

"Yeah, but if all men could do that we'd still be living in caves," I countered.

"What's his name?" she asked.

"I don't know."

"You don't know your own cat's name?"

"Oh. I thought you meant the dog that's licking his balls." I had my mouth open to tell her that if she was truly a psychic she'd already know my cat's name, but I took it back because I liked her boobs. "His name is Asscat."

She looked like I'd shocked her in the butt with a cattle prod. She immediately said, "Poor kitty, poor, poor kitty," reached down, unlocked the cage and pulled Asscat into her arms. He nuzzled in between her boobs, turned on his purring engine and, while I'm no pet psychic, I was pretty sure I knew what he was thinking.

"Cats are people, you know," she said while scratching behind his ears.

"Actually," I said, "soylent green is people."

She shot me a dirty look. "Animals are people in animal bodies like people are animals in people bodies."

I pretended to consider this, then said, "So what is Catwoman? Is she like...a woman inside a cat who's inside a person inside a cat or what?"

"Don't be absurd," she replied. I took that to mean that she didn't understand what I said any more than I had understood what she said.

I nodded and pretended to watch Asscat knead kitty dough on her breasts when in reality I was watching her breasts. She continued, "Your cat is like a mirror image of you. He is the receptacle for your own hostility. When his human companion is upset, nervous or angry, so is he. He is a reflection of your inner feelings and desires."

"Ahhh," I said. "That's why he's always horny."

She almost smiled. I actually saw the corners of her mouth quiver a tiny bit.

"Can you read human minds too?" I asked.

"No."

"Good." Then I invited her over for dinner at my house so she could show me some meditative exercises to remove my hostilities. All in the name of helping subdue Asscat, of course.

She showed up later that night and promptly cleansed my chakras. Doggy-style.

We never went out on a date. We never moved in together. We never saw each other in broad daylight. But every night around ten o'clock she appeared on my front porch and told me that Asscat was telepathically summoning her. She would whisper to Asscat for a while then we would find our way to my bedroom where we had wild, primal, feral, animalistic sex. She insisted on role-playing different animal couplings every night. That's not as out-there as it sounds because basically all animals do it doggy-style, they just make different sounds.

Monkey sounds made me laugh too much to come. And I wasn't too keen about all the scratches on my back when she was a badger. But other than that, I thought we were very compatible.

In only one week, I was less hostile because my sexual energy was being tapped and even Asscat had stopped shitting in my shoes.

The beginning of the end happened one night when I was lying in bed with Lisa Number Two and she was lightly teasing me with her fingers. "I have a dream," she said, licking the curve of my ear.

I squirmed against her fingers and begged her to tell me more.

"It's a petting zoo," she said, stroking my fur. "You know, like a real petting zoo."

"Uh huh," I moaned, moving against her petting.

"Except it's opposite."

"Opposite," I repeated, not really listening. I rolled onto my stomach and she knelt behind me.

"It's a reverse petting zoo. Humans will be in the cages and all the animals will stroll by and pet, sniff and pat the humans."

"Pet, sniff, pat," I panted.

"Cows, horses, goats, chickens, geese, all petting the humans, see?" She moved her hips against my ass and flicked a finger at my most vulnerable flicking spot.

"Yes," I intoned. "Petting, yes."

She pressed her boobs on my back and snuffled softly into my ear. "All I need to open the petting zoo is a thousand dollars. That's all." She teased me more with her fingers and her breath burned hot in my ear. "Will you give me the money?"

She thrust her fingers deep inside me and I gasped. "Yes, oh God, yes." She oinked and I wrote her a check.

The next morning I found her in the living room. She was red-faced and mad as a wet hen. She pointed her finger at me like it was a loaded gun and accused, "Your cat is a lying bitch!"

"I beg to differ," I said calmly. "He's a he, so he's actually a bastard, not a bitch."

She hollered, "Where is he?" She ran around the living room, looking under the sofa, the sofa pillows and the coffee table. "Where is the furry bastard?"

I calmly sat on the couch and patted the cushion next to me. "Let's calm down," I said. "Chillax and tell me what's going on."

"You chillax! I'm not going to calm down until I wring the scrawny bastard's neck!"

I leaned back into the cushions, the picture of serenity and asked, "I don't know what's going on. Did he leave a squirrel butthole on the porch again?"

She sucked in a deep breath, then slowly exhaled. "He built up my trust. He confided in me. Told me he was unhappy. Unhappy, he said!"

I nodded like it was perfectly normal for my cat to be holding a conversation with this woman.

"He suckered me in. Told me how he was mistreated. Told me you kept him locked up in this house and wouldn't let him go outside to play with friends. You never bought him any pretty things…"

I thinned my lips into a grimace. I did that so she couldn't tell I was on the verge of apoplectic laughing.

She continued, "I bought it all. He told me, or rather *pretended* to tell me, his deepest dream and desires."

"Go on, please," I urged. This was getting good. I leaned forward on the edge of the couch waiting for the punch line.

"I brought him treats. Every night. I brought him little presents, you know, catnip, cat toys, things he told me he wanted."

I nodded. "Uh huh, sure."

"He was thankful. Said I made his life worth living. He said he didn't know what he'd ever done without me."

I had a woman once tell me the same thing about a week before she packed all my CDs and walked out the door. But I didn't tell Lisa that.

"He told me the thing he wanted most was a friend."

"Aha," I said. I also had a girlfriend once who told me the blond she was texting 600 times a day was her friend. I found out the hard way that different people have different definitions of "friend."

"And I brought it to him," she cried. "I brought him the special friend he wanted."

"Special friend?"

She bobbed her head up and down. Tears leaked out of her big, sad, hound dog eyes and ran down onto the neck of her shirt. "He wanted a mouse friend. A little mouse friend like Stuart Little."

"You brought him a pet mouse?" I asked. I didn't know if I wanted to know the answer to that, but I already had several minutes invested in this story and I had to know the outcome.

She bobbed her chin up and down, slinging tears like a cartoon character with those little teardrops and squiggly lines drawn all around its head.

"Then I found this!" she bellowed. She held up something between her thumb and forefinger that looked like a tampon string. "I found this in my shoe!"

"Is that a tampon string?"

"It's a mouse tail! Asscat ate his special friend!"

This was the part where I laughed. I couldn't help it. And maybe that makes me a really bad person, but I don't care because this was too rich. "He didn't eat all of him," I sputtered. "He left the butthole."

"You're sick," she hissed at me. "An animal lost its life! He died a horrible cruel death due to deception and fraud!"

My laughter faded to hiccups and I managed to spew, "Let me get this straight, you gave a cat a mouse and now you're upset because he ate it?"

Asscat chose that moment to waltz into the room. I tried to telepathically warn him, but he rubbed his backside against the coffee table leg and jumped up onto the window sill. Either he couldn't hear my secret brain waves or he was ignoring me.

"You lying son-of-a-bitch," Lisa Number Two screeched at my cat. "You made me love you! Then you broke my heart!"

She ran to the front door, threw it open and dramatically turned to Asscat with these last words: "We're breaking up! I never ever want to see you again as long as I live!"

Then she was gone. From his perch on the window sill, Asscat watched her drive away. He turned to me with lazy, indifferent eyes. And, I swear, I heard his thoughts: "Easy come, easy go."

"I know," I thought back at him, "but you shouldn't have flaunted the tail by putting it in her shoe."

"I couldn't resist," he said. He turned his attention back to the window where he watched the squirrels play in the yard. I made a pot of coffee and called the bank to put a stop payment on the check.

* * *

Dana couldn't sleep. She was sprawled on her sofa with Asscat purring on her lap, spooning Rocky Road ice cream right out of the carton and into her mouth. One half of her brain was watching a TV show about tracing rich and famous peoples' ancestry and the other half was thinking about Ellen's cute butt in Levi's and the remaining half was in an ice cream delirium.

She heard a strange noise. It sounded like a vibrator. Like a vibrator tingling her left boob. No, wait, it was her cell phone. Dana dug it out from under her boob and, figuring it was Trudy, she put it on speakerphone. Without looking at the caller ID, she said, "Talk to me. And make it fast 'cause *Hoarders* is on next."

"Dana?"

She dropped her ice cream spoon. "Ellen!"

"It's not too late to call is it?"

"No, it's perfect!" Dana lowered her voice so Ellen wouldn't think she was easy or something. "Hey," she said again, softer. "Uh…I couldn't sleep anyway. What's up with you?"

"What's *Hoarders*?"

Dana laughed. She reached down and picked her dropped spoon up off the floor. She wiped it on her T-shirt. "It's a TV show. Reality TV where they film these people that're hoarders, you know, they collect massive amounts of crap, and they go in their house and throw it all away for them."

"Sounds interesting…"

"It makes me feel better about myself. And it usually gives me the impetus to clean house."

Ellen chuckled.

Dana found the remote control buried in the sofa cushions. She muted the TV and the program switched to captions.

Dana continued, "But right now I'm watching this show where Lionel Richie is tracing his roots."

"Oh, yeah? So what's up with Lionel these days?"

"He found out he's black." Dana realized she was babbling, but she also realized she was powerless to stop the babbling. She wondered what Ellen was doing. Was she eating ice cream too? Was she sitting around in her boxers? Was she as nervous?

"So…What're you up to?" she asked and took another bit of ice cream.

"I couldn't sleep. I was debating whether or not to call. I didn't want you to think I was easy."

Dana laughed. How weird and symbiotic that they were thinking the same thing. It's like they shared a brain. And by that, Dana meant that it was like they were a brain squared or a brain to the second power, not that each of them had only half a brain.

"You still there?" Ellen asked.

"Yeth, I'b hereth," Dana said with a frozen tongue. Time to set the ice cream down. She held her tongue between her fingers, warming it up.

Ellen continued, "But if I didn't call, then you might think I'm playing hard to get. I don't know which is worse—too easy or hard to get."

"Are you hard to get?" Dana asked. Were they flirting? Dana thought it sounded like they were flirting.

"I called, didn't I? That means I'm easy."

Dana laughed. Yep, there was definitely a flirt vibe happening.

"How about you? Are you easy?" Ellen asked.

"Definitely not. I like to get to know a person first." *Like for about fifteen minutes*, Dana thought, but thankfully, did not say.

"Hmmm—playing hard to get. Okay, so let's get to know one another. Tell me something about yourself."

"Like what?" Dana asked and took a big bite of ice cream.

"Make it good," Ellen said, "this is a crash course tour into each other's psyche. Tell me something you never told anybody else."

"Okay, let's see. In high school…" she stopped. She tapped her spoon on the ice cream carton and contemplated what she was about to divulge. She didn't know if she should share her past. It was embarrassing. It might cause Ellen to run. But that isn't necessarily all that bad. If Ellen didn't want to have anything to do with her, wouldn't it be better to find that out right up front?

"C'mon, out with it," Ellen urged.

Dana took a deep breath and decided to bare all. "Okay…In

high school the other kids made fun of me. 'Cause of my weight. You know, the fat. They called me names and…you know, stuff like that. My senior year I was voted 'Most Likely to Eat Dooley Springs.'"

Ellen laughed, then choked it back. "Oh my God…Sorry for laughing, but that is kind of funny. You know, unless you're the one they're making fun of."

"It's okay. It only hurts when I think about it." Dana held out her spoon and let Asscat lick it.

"So what happened?" Ellen inquired. "How'd you lose all the weight?"

"You're so sweet."

"What d'ya mean?"

"I haven't lost the weight. I'm still fat," Dana said.

Ellen gasped. "Oh my God, no, you're not! You're perfect! How could you even think that?"

"You don't have to be nice to me. I know what I am."

"No, you obviously don't. You're gorgeous! Hasn't anyone every told you that before?"

"No," Dana said truthfully. She set the ice cream carton on the coffee table. "And you just said it because you're trying to get into my pants."

Ellen laughed. "Yeah, I am. But you're still beautiful. Or I wouldn't even want into your pants."

Dana looked at the TV and watched Lionel Richie talk to some older white woman. He wiped away a tear and the old lady smiled and touched him on the shoulder. Dana didn't know if she was projecting Lionel's sadness or if it was her own melancholy, but regardless she forged ahead with her soul-baring. "A therapist would say that overeating is my way of filling the hole my mother left when she abandoned me."

"You're in therapy?" Ellen asked.

"God, no," Dana snorted. "That's not the Oklahoma way. We're supposed to pull ourselves up by our bootstraps with no help from anybody else. Besides, you ever looked at the word 'therapist'?"

"What d'ya mean?"

"The word itself," Dana explained. "Therapist. The. Rapist. Coincidence? I don't think so."

"I never thought of that," Ellen chuckled.

"Oh my God!" Dana exclaimed when she read the crawl across the bottom of the TV screen. She leaned forward and punched the volume up on the TV. She listened for a moment, then hit the mute button again.

"What's going on?" Ellen asked. "You still there?"

"Lionel just found out he's white," Dana said.

"That sucks," Ellen says.

"Yeah, now he has to rethink his entire career." Dana muted the TV again. "Okay," Dana said, "it's your turn. Tell me about you."

"Hmmm…I'm white as far as I know," Ellen said.

Dana laughed and sat up. She hugged her knees to her chest and whispered, "Tell me a deep dark secret about yourself."

"Deep and dark. Okay…" Dana could practically hear Ellen thinking. "I'm scared of insects," Ellen said.

"That's lame. Tell me something good." Dana closed her eyes and concentrated on Ellen's voice. The timbre, the cadence, the tone. It was a good voice, Dana decided. A voice that could wrap you up and carry you a million miles away.

Ellen continued, "No, I mean I'm really scared. Like phobic. I see a spider, I scream and jump on a chair. I even have nightmares sometimes about spiders roosting in my hair or crawling in my ears and eating my brain."

"Spiders don't roost."

"Well, whatever they do. It scares me."

"Okay, I'll keep the spider thing in mind. I'll protect you. Any other fears?"

"I have an irrational fear of standing in front of a microwave while it's running."

"I have an irrational fear of Gary Busey movies."

"Don't even get me started on Christopher Walken."

"Or Dick Clark."

They laughed.

"So ask me something. Anything," Ellen said.

Dana knew you could tell more about a person by the questions they asked than by the questions they answered. For instance, if she asked about something sexual, like when did you lose your virginity, then Ellen would know that this was a physical thing for her. That it was more about lust than love. So, Dana tried for something more substantial. "What's your favorite book?"

"My favorite of all time?" Ellen asked.

"Yeah, of all time."

Ellen didn't hesitate. "*Go, Dog. Go!* By P.D. Eastman."

"I had that book when I was a kid!" Dana said. "I loved it!"

"Yeah, well, I still read it now. A couple of times a year."

Dana said, "Okay, now you have to tell me why it's your favorite."

"It's a great metaphor," Ellen said.

"How so?"

"Eastman was a genius. He did this whole take on relationships and put it in the context of a children's book. You know how there's two dogs, a boy dog and a girl dog? The girl dog keeps trying on new hats, wanting to please the boy dog. I keep hoping the boy dog will like the girl dog's hat, but he never does and the girl dog keeps changing hats, trying so hard to get him to love her. She keeps saying, 'Do you like my hat?' But he keeps saying, 'No. I do not like your hat.' Finally at the end, he likes her hat and they go off, riding in a convertible toward the sunset, and live happily ever after in the party tree."

"That's very romantic in a 1950s retro 'woman has to please the man' kind of way. Can I ask you another question?"

"Shoot," Ellen said.

"No, never mind."

"Ask. I said ask anything."

"You probably don't want to talk about it. And it's really none of my business," Dana said.

"You Midwesterners and all your manners. Ask me. If I don't want to answer, then I'll lie."

Dana laughed. "Okay...How long have you been an alcoholic?"

"Since I was in high school. But I think what you really want to know is, how long since I've had a drink?"

"Okay. How long?"

"Two years, three months and sixteen days."

"And you're okay with it?" Dana asked.

"Most of the time. Sometimes it's hard, you know, it'll always be hard. But I'm done with drinking."

"What made you stop?"

"Long story."

"Give me the edited version."

There was a long pause, and Dana thought Ellen wasn't going to answer or maybe she was thinking up a lie. Ellen paused long enough that Dana reconsidered wanting to know the answer. Maybe it was a story that would make her look at Ellen differently. Maybe it was something she didn't want to know. Then Ellen said, "I was at Ralph's, the grocery store, and was stocking up on booze. My week's supply, you know. I had my cart filled with bottles—and by bottles I mean the great big ones, the half gallons—a bottle of Absolut, two bottles of Southern Comfort, a bottle of Maker's Mark, a case of Dos Equis and a bottle of Dom. That was always my treat—a bottle of Dom on Sunday morning. So, I go up to the cashier with this cart full of booze and she says, 'Oh, are you having a party?'"

Ellen paused so long that Dana urged, "And?"

"And I lied. I told her yes, that it was my birthday. Because, you know, I was embarrassed that I was buying all this and it was a normal week. So when I go to pay with my credit card, it's declined because I'd been drinking too much to make any bill payments and so I go to write a check. And, of course, the cashier asks to see my ID. I get all nervous but have to hand it over. She checks it out and writes the birth date on my check. Of course, she sees it's not my birthday or even my birthday month and she looks at me all weird like I lied to her. It was really embarrassing and awkward and...stupid. That made me stop and realize that I had a problem, you know. Most people don't ingest a whole grocery cart full of booze in one week. I didn't quit drinking right away, though. Not that week or even the next. But that's when I realized I had a problem. Took me about six months before I tried to quit."

Dana was glad she asked. And she was even more glad that Ellen trusted her enough to talk about it. "You're very brave."

"Thanks," Ellen murmured. "Drinking was one of the reasons I moved here six months ago. To start over clean, you know."

Dana closed her eyes and listened to the sound of Ellen's breathing. Finally, she said, "I want you to know—I like your hat. You don't have to change it for me."

Ellen didn't say anything. But Dana could hear her breath even out and become long and steady. It felt good not to talk, to be connected by breath over an invisible wave. It was so tenuous, yet strong at the same time.

"'K, bye then," Dana said.

"Bye."

Dana had her thumb poised to hang up when she heard, "Dana?"

"Yes, Ellen?"

"G'night."

"G'night."

Dana didn't hang up until she heard the dial tone. She put the phone down and smiled at Asscat. He had never seen her smile at him before. Confused, he showed his fangs, then buried his head in the ice cream carton and pointed his butt at Dana.

"Go ahead and eat it all, Asscat. I don't want it."

CHAPTER SIX

I was lying in bed that next morning after I got stuck in Kimmy's car when my cell phone rang and jarred me out of my fantasy. I took my hand out of my panties but didn't answer the phone because a call at eight a.m. can only mean one of two things: Fat Matt needed help again or somebody was calling to offer me a dirty job they didn't want to do. Both those things were unappetizing, so I let it ring through to voice mail. After a moment, my phone beeped and I pressed 1.

After Sylvia told me I had a message (Sylvia was what I named the automated female voice that told me how many voice mails I had.) I listened to somebody suck in some air and breathe it out over their receiver. Then a coarse-grit sandpaper voice scratched, "I need to hire you all to pick up dog turds out of my front yard. The neighbor's cockamamie dog keeps on doin' its business in my front lawn and I can't even walk in it for fear of hitting a land mine." Pause, then, "Do you all charge by the turd or by the hour?"

The woman left her address, Sylvia instructed me to save the message by tapping the 3 button, and I buried my head back under the covers and thought about Kimmy's boobs.

By the time I got out of the shower, I could hear Maw Maw in the kitchen banging around pots and pans and I smelled maple sausage frying. Maple sausage means biscuits and gravy and biscuits and gravy means it's Saturday.

As I walked downstairs, I heard my brother, Fat Matt, talking to Maw Maw. Could this day get any worse? First dog turds and now my dog turd of a brother is at my breakfast table.

I picked my way through all Maw Maw's taxidermy experiments in the living room. The room was stuffed (pardon the pun) with opossums, raccoons, armadillos and a deer. They lined the walls and stared at me like I was in a cage at the zoo. I ignored their glassy-eyed stares and weaved my way to the kitchen.

A few years back Maw Maw took a correspondence course that she found advertised in a magazine and got her degree in taxidermy. Ever since then she's been picking up roadkill and experimenting on the dead animals. However, stuffing them wasn't enough. She wanted to embalm them with her own special embalming juice. Supposedly, she was going to patent an embalming juice that repelled insects and moths. She wanted to make taxidermal history.

As a creative sideline, she also used some of the roadkill she picked up to create Christian art installations alongside the same highways where she found the animals. She fancied herself an artist and liked to say she resurrected the dead and was giving them a second life so that they didn't die in vain. As Maw Maw was fond of saying, "It's the perfect melding of art and science."

And Maw Maw was the normalest one in our family tree.

When I walked into the kitchen, Maw Maw was at the stove and Fat Matt was sitting at the table in his boxers with a heaping plate of biscuits and gravy in front of him. He had gravy dibbled in his beard and all over his hairy chest and big, hairy belly. He was so hairy he looked like he was wearing the bottom half of a bear costume. Or like a bear wearing men's boxers.

"You're the reason I'm a lesbian," I said sitting down at the table across from him.

"Be nice to your brother," Maw Maw said without conviction like she'd said it a million times before, which she had. She was stirring a big pot of brackish foulness on the stovetop. For a moment, I thought she was making us a stew for dinner, then I smelled it and realized she was working on perfecting her embalming recipe.

Matt paused in his mouth-shoveling long enough to say, "At least I wasn't the one dry humping some woman in the parking lot of DeWayne's last night for all the world to see."

"How do you know about that?"

Matt grinned. "I'm the mayor. People feel obliged to tell me when my sister is tarnishing my good name by committing public indecencies."

Maw Maw turned from the stove and looked at me. It wasn't the kind of look you want aimed at you.

"I wasn't humping her. I accidentally kind of fell on her is all."

"Without your pants on," Matt added.

"You're jealous. You haven't dry humped a woman since Wanette in the seventh grade who was blind and in a coma and was trying to win a bet…"

"Shut up!"

"And had no sense of smell."

"Shut up!"

I laughed. "Why are you even here? Shouldn't you be out cutting some ribbons or leading a parade or something?"

"It's Saturday," Maw Maw said. "He's a busy man, but he still takes time out to visit with his poor ol' grandma." In other words, I live here but don't pay enough attention to her is what she was saying.

"That doesn't explain why he's wearing his underwear at the table," I said.

Maw Maw turned and looked at him. "Why don't you have some clothes on?"

"I didn't want to get my mayor costume dirty. It's in the car."

Only my brother would call a three-piece suit a costume. "You drove over here clear from the trailer park in your underwear?" I asked.

He grinned.

"You're friggin' disgusting."

"Yeah, but I'm the mayor and you're not," he said.

Maw Maw handed me a plate of biscuits and gravy. I scooped up a forkful and almost had the first bite in my mouth before I noticed something wasn't right. "Maw Maw?"

"What, darlin'?"

"I don't think this is gravy on my biscuits."

She looked at my plate and wrinkled her nose. "Well, hell's bells and angels," she said. "I mixed up my pans. Good thing you didn't eat that," she said with a laugh. "It's my newest recipe. I've got some fresh animals out in the freezer to try it out on today. Matt, after you eat, I need you to bring them in from the ice cream truck."

Maw Maw drove an old ice cream truck that she bought off the Blue Bunny Man when he retired. The deep freeze in the back was perfect for her to stow her roadkill until she could get it home and embalmed or put in one of her artistic dioramas. The truck even came equipped with a megaphone apparatus on the roof so you could play music and the whole neighborhood would hear you coming. Unfortunately, the music player was stuck in the ON position and everywhere she went the speaker blared "Jesus Loves Me, This I Know."

I scraped Maw Maw's newest recipe into the trash can and watched it curdle the plastic milk container it landed on. What the heck was in that concoction?

I put the empty plate in the sink while Maw Maw loaded me up another with biscuits and real gravy. I got my appetite from Maw Maw. I also got my genes from her. She was big-boned and strong as an ox like those pictures of pioneer women in history books. She had

wild gray hair that she hadn't combed since Paw Paw
died twenty years ago. He used to brush it out for her
every night and since he died she can't bear to do it
herself. Her long gray mane hung halfway down her back
in natural dreads and she liked to put "pretties" in
her hair. Buttons, ribbons, shells, anything bright
that caught her eye. Her hair resembled a blue jay's
nest. She wore all tie-dye dresses and the only shoes
she ever wore was a pair of old Converse with the toes
cut out. In the winter she wore them with wool socks.

Maw Maw handed over my new plate and I dug in.

"Maybe Matt could bring you a Bigfoot to embalm,"
I said.

"Shut up," Matt said.

"In fact, you look like a Bigfoot, Matt."

"Shut up, Double D."

"Maybe those photos in the *National Enquirer* were
actually pictures of you roaming the woods naked."

He mouthed a silent, but fierce, "Shut up."

I giggled. "So tell me the truth. The night you
spent around the campfire with those Bigfeet, you didn't
mate with one, did you?"

"Maw Maw!" Matt squealed like he was five years old
again.

"Ow!" I yelped when Maw Maw thumped me on the head
with her wooden spoon.

"Don't pick on your little brother," she said.

"Little, my butt. He's two hundred pounds bigger
than me." I rubbed my head. There was going to a knot.

"Yeah, but you're a bully," Matt said. "I'm going
to pass a law in this town against bullying. Then I'll
have you thrown in jail."

"Mayors don't pass laws. All they pass is gas," I
said around a mouthful of food. "And then have a parade
to celebrate it."

"Your mother called last night," Maw Maw pronounced.

Matt and I stopped our quibbling. We sat still with
our mouths open. Maw Maw stood at the stove with her
back to us as she stirred the goo in the pot. "Said
she misses you two something awful," she said like she
were telling us what was for supper.

"Yeah right," I said.

"It wouldn't hurt you to give her a call." She turned and looked at me. "I think she was hinting that she'd like to pay us a visit."

This news sat heavy on my stomach. I felt like I was going to upchuck. "What if we don't want to see her?"

"I want to see her," Matt blurted.

"Well, I don't," I said, pushing my chair back and standing up. "I've gotten along for all this time without her, I think I can last a little longer."

Maw Maw shook her spoon in my face. "She's your mother. You should be grateful to even have one. Plenty of kids don't, you know."

"I'm grateful she ran away and left us," I said.

"She didn't run away," Matt said, defending her.

"What do you know? You were too young to know the difference and now you're too crazy to know."

"End of discussion," Maw Maw said, turning her back again.

I let it go. When Maw Maw said "end of discussion," she meant it.

"I'm going to work," I said, kissing Maw Maw on the cheek. I said to Matt as I left, "And when I get home you better not be here." I stuck my tongue out at him on the way out the door.

I thought about my mother while I drove. I can't believe she had the nerve to pop back into my life after that disappearing act she pulled when I was six. I hadn't seen her since the night she pushed me and Matt out of the car with a cardboard box full of our clothes and our stack of Little Golden Books and told us we were going to live with Maw Maw now. I remember smelling the exhaust from her old Thunderbird as it drove away. I pulled Matt along by his hand and kicked our box up the sidewalk. Maw Maw came out on the front porch, ushered us in and pretended that she'd been expecting us all along. She served Sugar Smacks for breakfast and she and Paw Paw made over us like it was Christmas Day and they'd gotten the present they'd always wanted.

It took Maw Maw the better part of a week to coax little Matt away from the front window where he stood with his nose pressed against the glass awaiting the return of a mother who wasn't coming back.

My mother might be able to buffalo Matt and Maw Maw into letting her back in the door and into their hearts, but not me. No sir, I didn't want to be on that welcome committee. Even the thought of her made me so mad, I could eat nails and spit rust.

I steered Betty into the driveway of a newly built duplex. I double-checked the address to make sure it was where dog-turd woman lived. It was a pretty nice place as duplexes go, with all red brick siding and two garages in the middle separating the residences' front doors. One door was marked A and the other was B.

The most noticeable thing about the duplexes was the disparity between the two units. The A side was clean and well-kept. But the B side lawn had brown grass and dirt patches showing through. Weeds had overtaken the flower bed and spider webs were strung between the porch posts and grimy windows. There was a chain looped around one of the posts and on the end of the chain was a brown toy poodle panting in the heat. On second glance, the dog wasn't brown. It was white and dirty.

The woman hadn't told me in which place she lived, A or B, so I scanned the yards and looked for poop piles. A's yard was immaculate except for the abundance of landmines.

I approached Door A and had my knuckles ready to knock, but it flew open before I could. A skinny woman with big round glasses, brown, curly hair like the poodle's and a cigarette dangling from her lips, thrust a wad of plastic Walmart bags at me. "Pick it all up and I'll pay when you're done."

She slammed the door in my face.

I set about picking up dried white turds while the poodle stared at me. He had a superior look on his face and I didn't appreciate it.

"You look like something my cat spit up," I sassed the dog.

He yipped at me and bared his pointy teeth. "Yeah, well, who's picking up whose poop," the dog said.

"At least I don't poop outdoors," I said back.

"You don't see me picking up your poop," he said.

"I don't like you," I said because I was all out of argument-winning material.

"You have a college education and you're picking up dog doody," he taunted.

"And you're on chain, sitting outside, with no water or food," I retorted.

"Fuck you," he said.

"Eff you back."

Why is it that all poodles have foul mouths? I turned my back on Mr. Sassypants and worked steadily until the lady's yard was doody-free.

I walked back up to Door A and had my fist all poised to knock when the door flew open and revealed the same lady as before. She was at the door so quick, she must've been peeking out her front window watching me the whole time.

Before I could say a word, she ordered, "Take all that poop and go hand it over to Miss So-and-So next door. It belongs to her."

The door slammed in my face.

I sensed a Hatfield-and-McCoy type feud going on here and I was caught in the crossfire. The way I saw it I only had two options: Accept the fact that I had worked for free or go next door and hope I got my twenty dollars.

Demeaned and demoralized, I walked up to Door B. Mr. Sassypants snarled as I got closer, but I held the bags out like I was going to hit him upside the head with his own feces if he got too near. He backed off and growled down deep in his throat like he was gargling. I knocked on the door.

I heard feet approaching and the door opened a crack. It was so dark inside the apartment that I couldn't see anything but a slice of black. "Hi!" I said with fake cheer. "I'm Dana Dooley with Slave Labor and your neighbor over there said…"

A throaty voice interrupted. "What's that smell?"

The voice tickled my brain and I knew that I recognized it but couldn't place exactly where.

"That smell's not me," I said. "Well, it may be partly me. But what you're most likely smelling is your dog's doody in these bags." I held the two bags up close to the crack for her to see. Or smell. Or both. I thought of my best friend Trudy and how she wanted me to be more assertive, so I sucked in a big breath of air and said without pausing, "Your neighbor hired me to pick it all up out of her yard then she sent me over here to collect the payment. You owe me twenty dollars."

There was a long silence, probably because the person behind the door was putting spaces in between all those words in order to figure out what I said.

Then the door opened and Holy Crapola! It was Kimmy. The woman who cut my hair. The woman who kissed me. The woman who was going to be my future wife. The woman who was wearing a lingerie teddy thing like in the intimate apparel catalogues for women that lesbians masturbated to. (At least I hoped I wasn't the only one who did.)

I felt so ridiculous. Here she was looking like she was starring in a really hot Hollywood sex scene—the tasteful kind with Vaseline smeared over the camera lens—and I was thrusting bags of doody under her nose.

I lowered the bags and averted my gaze.

It was dark behind her, but now that the door was open, I could see into the grayness of her living room. It was bare. And by bare I don't mean that there wasn't hardly anything in it, I mean there was nothing at all in it. No furniture. No lamps. No rugs. Nary a book. Not even a TV.

She looked me up and down. I was painfully aware of the sweat stains under my boobs and my hair plastered to my skull. Her eyes focused on the Slave Labor logo on my T-shirt and she said, "Is that for real?"

"Yeah," I answered. I unplucked the front of my shirt from my sweaty chest and held out the logo for her to examine. "I own the company. It's real."

"No," she chuckled and flapped her hand at me. "I meant your boobs." She pointed a red polished nail right at my girls and asked, "Are they real?"

"Oh...uh," I stammered. "Sure. They're real." I laughed and threw out a feeble joke. "Wanna feel for yourself?"

Okay, that was my version of a joke, but she didn't get it. She extended that same red polished fingernail and poked my right boob a couple of times. My left nipple instantly got hard. I've always been that way, kind of cross-wired. If you touch my right nipple, my left nipple gets hard and vice-versa.

"They're so firm," she said.

"I'm wearing a sportsbra," I replied. "That kind of packs them in."

"What size are they?"

"Um…" I hesitated. This was really weird. Exchanging bra sizes like recipes. "Double D."

"Wow."

"Yeah," I said. "I've had them since I was twelve. I think that's why I'm so klutzy. It's a weight distribution problem."

Okay, that was probably too much TMI (was that redundant?), but I always talked too much when I was nervous.

"Feel mine," she offered. And, by offered, I mean she bent at the waist, placed her hands under her boobs and hefted them up under my nose. "I got them redone six months ago and they're hard as concrete."

She didn't have to ask twice. I dropped the doody bags, stuck out my finger and poked. They felt fine to me. I poked again because I could. They still felt fine. So I grabbed her boobs in my hands and gave them a squeeze. They were hard. But if they were cantaloupes in a grocery store that I was testing for ripeness, I'd buy them. I squeezed again to make sure.

A horn honked and I turned in time to recognize Hank driving his riding lawnmower down the street. He took off his ball cap and waved it in the air at me.

I almost waved back before I realized that would mean letting go of Kimmy's boobs and I wasn't ready to do that yet.

She placed her hands on top of mine and said, "You can stop squeezing now."

"You sure?" I asked.

She laughed and I took my hands off her boobs to be polite.

"What'd you think? Hard, right? And I have no feeling at all," she said. "Not a thing. You could bounce on them with both feet and I still wouldn't feel a thing."

Good to know. But to test her theory, I reached up and tweaked her right nipple.

"Okay, that I definitely felt," she giggled. "How'd you do that?"

"Well," I replied with a shrug, "I am a professional."

She noticed the poop bags at my feet. "How much did the old douche-bag pay you to pick that up?"

"She didn't. She told me it was your dog, so you had to pay me the twenty dollars."

Kimmy tilted her head and smiled mischievously. She looked left to right, then whispered, "I'll pay you double to go dump it back in her yard."

"Tell you what, I won't charge you anything if you let me feel your boobs again."

She laughed harder. She must've thought I was joking.

"Okay," she said. "It's a deal. Come back at seven tonight to collect." She took a step back, winked and shut the door.

I was feeling so good about my impending date that I strode into the other yard and before I could think too hard about what I was doing, I swung the bags around and around like a helicopter propeller and let it all fly.

Dog turds rained down like manna from heaven.

The door to A opened and the douche-bag lady stepped out onto her porch yelling, "What the H. E. Double Hockey Sticks are you doing?!"

"You should've paid me!" I yelled. I humped it for the street, jumped into Betty, and sped away.

CHAPTER SEVEN

By Thursday evening, Dana still hadn't heard from Kimmy. She knew Kimmy was coming home when she wasn't there because she saw the telltale signs of Kimmy's hair in the bathtub drain. And her dirty clothes kept magically appearing in the hamper.

Dana drove by The Best Little Hairhouse for the umpteenth time and didn't see Kimmy's car parked out front or in the back lot. She checked her cell phone for the thousandth time, hoping there would be a text or voicemail from Ellen. She hadn't heard from her since Lionel Richie found his roots. Maybe Ellen was busy with work. She thought about sending her a "Hi, how ya doing?" type of text, being friendly and all, then she stumbled upon an even better idea. If the mountain wouldn't come to Mohammed...

Dana made it out to the VFW in record time. She parked Betty next to Hank's riding lawn mower. He had obviously discovered that holding an AA meeting in a bar was a good thing. Now he could tell his wife he was at the meeting and not at the bar drinking.

Dana waved to Hank on her way through the bar to the meeting room in back. This time she made sure to step high over that metal strip that had a tendency to jump up and bite flip-flops. She moved over behind the rubber tree plant hoping to be inconspicuous. She looked over a big, green leaf and scanned the crowd for any signs of pokey hair.

She found Ellen on the other side of the room. Ellen saw her and smiled. So much for the camouflage of the rubber plant. Dana moved toward the refreshment table, acting like that was where she had been headed. If Ellen were to come over and ask her why she was there, Dana didn't know what she'd say. She wasn't an alcoholic, so she didn't have any reason to be here.

Great. She's gonna think I'm a stalker. Not even a very good stalker.

Too bad stalking had gotten such a pejorative meaning. Ever since that whole John Hinckley/Jodie Foster thing, people freaked out about being stalked. Before that girls used to think stalking was romantic. John Cusak could stand outside your window all night long holding a blasting stereo above his head, wearing a creepy long overcoat, and that was romantic. Nowadays if Cusak did that, he'd end up in the county pokey.

Dana gnawed on a Styrofoam cup and tried to think up a good spin story on why she…

"Glad to see you here," said Ellen's voice from behind her.

Dana's heart jumped into her throat. No, wait, that wasn't her heart, it was a chunk of Styrofoam. It was going down the wrong way. She gulped for air, but that lodged the Styrofoam more securely in her throat. She felt like she had swallowed concrete.

She forced a cough, but it came out more like a wheeze. When she tried to inhale, the bit of Styrofoam wedged in even deeper. She gasped for air to no avail and vainly tried to eject the cup by pounding on her chest. Her eyes started tearing and her fingers involuntarily clawed at her throat.

Ellen's eyes widened. She jumped up and down, flapping her hands in front of her, not sure what to do or how to help. She finally came to her senses and pounded Dana on the back, saying over and over, "Can you breathe, can you breathe?"

Dana shook her head. If she could breathe, she wouldn't be turning blue and making sucky noises with her mouth.

My Gosh-All-Mighty, my premonition is coming true. I'm going to choke and die like Tennessee Williams. But at least he went out knowing he had created a body of work that immortalized him. All I have is my lesbian pulp fiction that I can't even finish.

Dana used the last of her breath to whisper, "I...can't breathe...oh...my...God...I'm going...to die..."

I'm too young to die. I haven't even experienced true love yet.

Dana reenacted a scary impersonation of Mama Cass with the ham bone. Time slowed down and she realized the woman she saw standing before her doing the chicken dance was her true love and she was going to die a slow, horrible, cruel death before she got to tell her that.

I love you, Ellen. I really, really love you, Dana tried to convey with her eyes.

"Her eyes are bulging!" Ellen screamed at the room in large. "She's dying!"

Dana blinked rapidly six times (a multiple of three), then closed her eyes and saw a series of romantic snapshots of a future with Ellen: Sharing spaghetti noodles from the same plate, *Lady and the Tramp* style; Ellen and Dana freezing to death in the Atlantic Ocean, lying on an ice floe while Rosie O'Donnell's cruise ship sinks in the background; Ellen seated at a pottery wheel while Dana tantalizes her from behind...

Ellen pounded Dana's back with her fist, interrupting her visions.

Dana quickly made a promise to her higher self...if she did ever manage to draw another breath, she would use that last breath to tell Ellen that she loved her.

Note to self: Good line. Put that in my book.

"Somebody help, she's choking to death!" Ellen yelled.

Everybody in the room turned and looked at Dana. Dana smiled and waved, shaking her head and flapping her hands like she was all right, but her blue face probably gave her away. The next thing she knew, she was surrounded by people. Most of the people didn't have the foggiest notion of how to help a choking person, but they didn't want to miss the show. After all, it wasn't every day that somebody expired right in front of you.

Pearl Drowningbear, a big Indian lady with gray streaks in her long black hair and big dreamcatcher earrings, pulled a Bic pen out of her flannel shirt pocket and yelled, "Give me room! I'll do a tracheotomy!"

"You know how to do that?" Ellen asked.

Pearl pulled the pen apart with her teeth. She spit the ink tube onto the floor and said, "I saw it in a movie once. You jab the tube into the windpipe is all." Pearl narrowed her eyes at Dana, held the empty shell of the pen in her fist and raised it above her head like a hatchet.

Dana squeaked and covered her neck with her hands. When Pearl walked toward her, Dana panicked. She bent over and butted Pearl with her head. She was trying to do that head-bashing move she'd seen in all those action movies, but instead she rammed Pearl's belly like a drunken goat. It had the same effect, though. Pearl *oomphed*, dropped the Bic and before she could find it again a big, bearded man wearing camouflage and smelling like deer piss grabbed Dana from behind and squeezed so hard that she coughed and the Styrofoam shot out of her mouth like a cork out of a champagne bottle.

The man gently set Dana down and patted her on the head like she was a good dog.

Dana sucked air into her lungs and the color returned to her face. "Thanks," she wheezed at the big, stinky man. "You saved my life."

"Not a problem, little lady."

Dana looked at Ellen and smiled feebly. "Somebody should put a warning label on those cups."

* * *

As soon as I left Kimmy's duplex after what I soon dubbed as the "Dog Doody Incident," I drove straight over to Engleman's Funeral Home. Trudy worked at Engleman's as the makeup and hair lady for all the dead bodies. She took a lot of pride in her work and most people in Dooley Springs had locked in Engleman's to do their funerals because of how good Trudy was with a makeup kit. Trudy's motto was "Just because you're dead doesn't mean you have to look it."

Her daddy owned the place and it was a family operation. Her mom did the embalming and laying out of the bodies and her daddy sold the caskets and did the handshaking. Trudy did the corpse fluffing.

Trudy and I practically grew up in the funeral home. We played hide and seek in the coffins, passed out cookies and punch during the viewings and did our math homework with naked, dead bodies. I brought my first girlfriend in here when I was fourteen and we made out inside a silk-lined casket. Trudy didn't mind because she was making out with the girl's brother in another casket.

We learned how to drive on the hearse. We used to load up the back with our friends and go to the drive-in movies. Trudy would pick me up for school in the hearse. When we were late, she'd flip on the headlights and cars would pull over to the side of the road for us.

The only time we ever got in trouble was when her mom caught us playing pin-the-tail on dead Mrs. Coates. We didn't see the harm—old Mrs. Coates was dead and was going to be buried bottom side down anyhow.

I walked down the basement steps and through a series of small hallways until I got to the big room where Trudy did her thing. When I walked in she was bebopping around the floor with her MP3 player and swiping some makeup on Mr. Peterson, who had died of heart failure a few days earlier. He was laid out on the cold, steel table with a sheet draped over his lower half. He looked greenish. I hoped Trudy could fix that. I leaned in the doorway and watched Trudy move to the music only she could hear. I shook my head and laughed to myself. Trudy moved like a white girl wearing brand-new Wranglers.

I could faintly hear screechy music coming from her earbuds. She was wearing her orange wig with its ringlets piled up high on her head. She wore a rhinestone-studded tube top and tight black stirrup pants with high heels. A person might not like her style but there's no denying that the woman *had* style. I'd never had any and probably never would.

I walked farther into the room and waved my arms through the air like one of those guys who direct airplanes where to go. Trudy saw me and unplugged her earbuds. She looked me up and down with wide eyes. "DD, did you lose weight?"

I shook my head. "I got my hair cut a couple days ago."

She walked a tight circle around me. "Your butt looks smaller."

"So I've been told."

"Wanda cut it?"

"That new girl working there, Kimmy."

"She's a goddamn miracle worker."

"That's what I wanted to talk to you about, Trudy. I kind of sort of have a date with her tonight."

"No shit." She sat in a metal folding chair and wrapped her earbuds around the MP3 player.

I crossed my arms. "You say that like you're surprised I could get a date."

"It's not that I don't believe you," she said, "but I don't believe you. I saw her the other day at Walmart looking at lipstick and she looks awful straight to me."

"How do you know that by looking at her?"

"She was carrying a purse."

"So you're saying lesbians don't carry purses?"

Trudy shrugged. I wanted to prove her wrong, but I wasn't carrying a purse. Instead, I took a defensive tack. "So, in other words, you think I'm too ugly or too stupid to get an actual real-live date with an actual real-live woman who wears lipstick and carries a purse?"

"No, that's not what I meant and you know it," she said. "And don't take this the wrong way…"

I hate when people begin sentences with "don't take this the wrong way" or "don't get mad, but…" You know good and well that they're getting ready to piss you off, but now you can't get mad because they already took your mad rights away by saying that.

Trudy continued, "I don't want to sound..."

She hesitated long enough that I jumped in with, "Stupid?"

"No..."

"Like a butthole?"

"No..."

"Mean?"

"No..."

I rapid-fired a selection of adjectives: "Bitchy? Grumpy? Jealous? Obnoxious? Uptight? Unbelieving?"

"That's the one!" She poked the air in my direction. "I don't mean to sound unbelieving, but is this a date or is it a date-date?"

"She asked me out."

Trudy sighed. "Straight women ask each other out too, you know. I could ask a woman to go to lunch or the movies or shopping because I wanted to go out with a friend, not because I wanted to boink her."

"Okay, first," I began, "lesbians don't boink. I find your word choice offensive, and third, she didn't ask me to go shopping with her. She asked me to come over to her house."

"You forgot second," Trudy said.

"And second—she touched my boobs."

"Oooh, now we're getting somewhere."

"I touched her boobs too."

"You already got to second base?" she asked.

"Boobs are second base? I thought they were first base."

"No, silly, they're second. If they were first, that would make the woo-hoo second. And then where would third be?"

"The butthole?"

"Ewww!" Trudy screeched. "Don't tell me you do the butthole thing! That's an exit, not an entrance!"

"Well," I stammered, "I don't want anything big like a penis up there. But a pinky..."

"Stop!" she yelled and put her fingers in her ears. "I don't want to know!"

"Okay, okay," I said and then couldn't help but add, "if you'd been more willing to experiment with the butthole thing then you might've been able to save your marriage with Bruce the Fag."

Anybody who has ever said black people can't blush has never seen Trudy when she's embarrassed. She turned the color of an eggplant and shuffled her feet. After a moment, she regained her composure, waved the air in front of her like she was getting rid of a fart and said, "Moving on…Tell me about the boob-touching incident."

I hopped up on the table and sat next to Mr. Peterson. I swung my feet back and forth and told Trudy about it as she applied pancake makeup to his bulbous nose. "She gave me her boobs to feel. She actually *offered* them to me. See, she has fake boobs and she wanted to know if mine were real and she touched mine to test their firmness and then she let me squeeze hers like I was Mr. Whipple and they were Charmin 'cause she wanted my opinion on how fake they felt."

Trudy pooched out her bottom lip and wrinkled her nose like she didn't believe me.

I explained further. "She got them done a few months ago and they put too much air in them or something and I think they're kind of like car tires, you always have to check the air pressure and rotate them and stuff. She wanted me to check her air pressure." I paused. "I think."

Trudy considered my story, then said, "Sounds more mechanical than romantic."

"Why would she feel up a known lesbian unless she was putting the moves on me?"

She looked up from Mr. Peterson and asked, "She felt your boobs too?"

"Yeah, I told you that. She felt mine first. She made the first move."

"Did she feel them like this?" She held her palms out and moved them in little circles like she was washing a window. "Or did she feel your boobs like this?" She held her palms up and weighed the air like she was getting ready to juggle.

"Kind of half and half," I said.

"Show me," Trudy said.

I reached out to grab Trudy's breasts, but she deflected my hands with a slap of her hand. "Not on me, doofus. We've known each other way too long to be boob-feeling each other."

"I wasn't going to enjoy it," I said.

"Yeah, right," she said like a woman who thought everybody always wanted to feel her up. She stood behind the steel table and propped Mr. Peterson up into a sitting position. She slid her arms under his and locked her hands around his big belly. "Here," she said, "pretend he's got your big boobs and you're her and show me exactly what she did to you."

I wasn't going to have to do much pretending. He did have some pretty good-sized man boobs. In fact, his moobs were bigger than those of lots of women I'd dated.

I was aware that to a lot of people, okay, most people, this would fall into the "you're sick and need professional help" category. But remember dead bodies weren't icky or even unusual to me or Trudy. Most little girls had stuffed animals. We had dead people. So I didn't think twice about reaching out and demonstrating on Mr. Peterson's moobs. "She poked me a couple of times with her finger and then she did this." I did a rendition of "wax on, wax off" that Ralph Macchio made famous in *The Karate Kid*. "That pretty much sums it up."

Trudy nodded and put Mr. Peterson back to rest. "It's a date-date for sure. I would never do that to another woman's boobs unless I was going to give her some."

"You think?" I asked excitedly. "You think she's planning on giving me some?" I hopped off the table and grabbed Trudy's hands. "You have to help me, please, please, please, please. Please do my makeup and hair so I don't show up looking like me."

Trudy nodded and let out a deep sigh that said "It's a dirty job, but somebody's gotta do it." "Okay,

Double D, I'll come over at five-ish. I'll bring my box
of magic, you bring a box of wine."

"I love you, I love you, I love you!" I shouted,
hugging her close. "You're my bestest friend in the
whole wide world!"

"I'm your only friend, girl, now get a friggin'
grip."

* * *

The crowd dispersed once they realized Dana wasn't
going to choke and die. Dana felt like she'd disappointed all
the alcoholics by living. She had taken away their Thursday
night entertainment and now they were going to have to find
somebody else to talk about. They went back to their cup-
gnawing like she hadn't been an example of the dangers of
Styrofoam chewing.

Ellen took Dana by the elbow and steered her over to an
empty folding chair at the back of the room. Dana plopped
down into it, grateful and embarrassed.

Ellen gently wiped the tears off Dana's face, and as soon
as her breath evened out, Dana sheepishly looked at her and
offered a weak smile. "Sorry," Dana said. "I really pulled a
Dooley, didn't I?"

Ellen accepted Dana's smile and gave one of her own. "It
was my fault for sneaking up on you like that."

"I thought I was a goner, for sure," Dana said. "I even saw
my future flash before my eyes."

"Future? I thought you were supposed to see your past.
Most people who have survived near death experiences have
said that their past flashes before their eyes."

"Really?" Dana asked, sinking into Ellen's gorgeous browns.
"Guess I'm not most people."

"You can say that again."

"Guess I'm not most people," Dana and Ellen said at the
same time.

They laughed.

"You know, I was hoping you'd show up," Ellen said.

Dana gulped and came precariously close to choking again. But this time it was on her heart, which had jumped up into her throat. "Well, here I am. I'm here," Dana said. "Actually, I didn't know whether I should come or not."

"Why?" Ellen asked. She reached out and gently laid her hand on Dana's knee.

"I didn't want you to think I was stalking you. I mean stalking you in a bad way like Glenn Close in *Fatal Attraction*. Not in a good way like John Cusak in *Say Anything*."

Ellen laughed and wrapped Dana's hand in hers. She traced light circles on Dana's knuckles, then said, "You're very brave, you know that?"

"You think? What's so brave about sucking Styrofoam into your windpipe?"

Ellen explained. "It's hard to come to your first AA meeting. It takes a lot of courage to admit you have a problem and need help."

Dana jerked her hand away.

A drinking problem? She thinks I'm an alcoholic? She thinks I came here to attend the meeting? Cheeses, Mary and Joseph.

Ellen interrupted Dana's thoughts. "This is the hardest part. But believe you me, we've all been through it. I'll be with you every step of the way."

"You'll be with me?" Dana echoed, a plan slowly taking shape in her mind.

Ellen nodded. "Day or night. Anytime. Doesn't matter. You can call me any minute of the day and I'll come running, I promise you. We'll get through this. Together. You'll never be alone again."

Dana smiled. If she had heard Ellen right, all she had to do was admit to being an alcoholic and she could see her anytime she wanted. She could even see her all the time if she so desired. And Dana knew, *she knew*, that if Ellen spent enough time around her, she would fall in love with her.

All I have to do is pretend to be an alcoholic. It can't be that hard. I saw Meredith Baxter-Birney-Baxter do it in that one TV movie.

Dana counted the cracks in the linoleum flooring. She made a pact with herself. If the total of the cracks came out to be a multiple of three, then she would be an alcoholic. If not, she would tell the truth and let Ellen disappear.

One, two, three, six, nine, twelve, fifteen…

Ellen put her hand on Dana's thigh.

Twenty-one, twenty-four…

The warmth of Ellen's seemingly innocent touch seeped through Dana's jeans, into her skin, into her muscles, into her bones, into her blood, getting hotter and hotter, until it boiled over in her brain and that was when she blurted, "I'm an alcoholic."

I'm absolved of all guilt. There were thirty-three cracks. It's fate.

"I'm an alcoholic?" Dana said again, this time more like a question than a statement.

Ellen grabbed Dana in a hug. Dana snuggled into the embrace, feeling Ellen boobs against her own. She inhaled and smelled ocean mist-scented dryer sheets and watermelon-flavored Jolly Ranchers. From that one delicious second on, Dana embraced Ellen and her faux alcoholism with open arms.

"I need you," Dana muttered. Those words, at least, were true.

"I'm right here," Ellen reassured, hugging her closer. "And I won't let you go."

That's what I'm hoping.

CHAPTER EIGHT

Dana sat still as a statue in back of the room and listened as a parade of alcoholics got up, stood at the podium and related their hard luck stories. She had to pee really bad, but she was afraid that if she moved, Ellen would take her hand off her thigh. So, she listened as Pearl Drowningbear went on and on about how the white man had got her people hooked on evil firewater. Next was the man who saved her life with the bear hug. He told a story about how he knew he had hit rock bottom when he woke up in an abandoned car down in El Paso wearing women's underwear. Then a man with no legs and dozens of medals pinned to his army jacket drove his electric wheelchair up to the front of the room. He introduced himself as Stumpy and then he preached about how every man in a foxhole is a good Christian. But all Dana could concentrate on was the warmth of Ellen's hand.

Suddenly, Ellen stood and announced, "We have somebody new here tonight. Let's show Dana how much we appreciate the courage it took her to come to our meeting."

Everyone applauded. Horror-stricken, Dana stared back at their expectant faces.

"Would you like to share your story, Dana?" Ellen asked.

"No."

Ellen coaxed, "It's okay. I'm right here with you."

"I don't have any good stories to tell. I have legs, I'm white and I wear women's underwear every day."

Everybody laughed.

"C'mon," Ellen coaxed, "tell us your story. We're all friends here."

Crapola. Where's a drink when you need one?

* * *

The one and only time I stayed in a hotel was when I hid out at the Best Western on the outskirts of town. I was hiding from my girlfriend, Lisa Number Three, whom I had broken up with.

Our relationship began and ended because of the couch. It began when I bought the couch on a clearance sale at Poor Boy's Furniture. Lisa Number Three was one of the deliverymen. Let's just say that one day she delivered more than a couch.

We'd been living together for six months and I had gotten back from work (cutting Mrs. Poteet's standard poodle's curly pelt—the poodle's name was Hillary and she was trained so that if you said "Obama" she growled) and I will readily admit, I wasn't in the best of moods. I grabbed a Pop-Tart out of the kitchen cupboard and walked into the living room. Lisa Number Three and Asscat were watching TV.

"What happened to the couch?" I asked.

"What d'ya mean?" Lisa Number Three asked back.

I pointed at the back cushions of the couch and said, "Has Asscat been clawing at the cushions?"

At the sound of his name, Asscat shot me a "Who, me?" look, then went back to licking his butt.

Lisa Number Three let out a cry of pure anguish, flopped back on the couch with her arm across her face in a bad imitation of Greta Garbo doing the final scene from *Camille*. She buried her face in the crook of her arm, sobbing pitifully. "Now you know," she cried. "I'm a bad, bad person."

I grabbed the remote and turned off the TV. "What exactly do I know?" I asked, patting her on the shoulder and stuffing the rest of the Pop-Tart in my mouth.

She looked up at me through her tears and sputtered, "I eat the couch. I can't help myself. I get stressed out and eat the couch."

I looked at Asscat for clarification, but he was more interested in performing his ablutions than in helping me out.

I did the only thing I could think to do. I laughed.

"You think it's funny?" she said in a voice that was half-angry, half-relieved, and all-crazy.

"Yeah, that was a good one."

She swiped at her tears with the back of her hand and smiled tentatively. "You don't think I'm a weird person?"

I shook my head. "Nah. That was funny." I snickered. "You eating the couch…"

She forced a chuckle of her own. "I thought you'd think I was weird. And bad." She snuffled up her snot and tears.

I mustered up as much sympathy as I could and said, "It's okay. Now tell me what really happened to the couch."

She sat up. "I did tell you."

"No, really, tell me. I won't get mad, I promise."

"I ate it," she said, crossing her arms.

I said, "Let me explain the rules of comedy. Saying something once is funny. I laughed, okay? And twice is still a little bit funny. But if you say it three times, then it's not funny anymore and it's creepy-weird."

"I ate the couch."

That was the third time. It gave me the same willies as seeing a tight-faced Joan Rivers on *Celebrity Apprentice*.

I looked at Asscat. He took a final lick and walked out of the room.

Lisa Number Three reached behind me, grabbed a handful of the yellow foam sticking out of the ripped cushion and stuffed it in her mouth. She chewed. And swallowed.

"See?" she said.

The Pop-Tart threatened to come back up. To my credit, I didn't yell or scream or swear. I simply walked into my bedroom and locked the door behind me. I sat on the bed, put my head between my legs and hyperventilated.

After a few moments, Lisa Number Three knocked on the door. When I didn't answer, she tried the doorknob. Then she rapped on the door again. "It's a sickness," she said from the other side of the door. "It's like an OCD thing. It's a real disease. It's called trichotillomania and it's real."

I put my hands over my ears and did my own rendition of Edvard Munch's *The Scream*.

Even with my ears covered, I could hear her talking, "Are you telling me you never noticed my bald spot? You never noticed in all the time we've been together that I pull out my own hair and eat it?"

I puked a little in my mouth. I buried myself under the covers and didn't come out of my room for twelve hours. She slept out on the couch. I guess if she wanted a midnight snack, she wouldn't have to get up.

Over the next few days, I surreptitiously shadowed Lisa Number Three around the house. I caught her eating the couch, her own hair, a hot pad, the ironing board cover and the lint out of the dryer.

I suspected that my cat wasn't the one who was coughing up hairballs under the bed.

I broke up with her the day I noticed Asscat was sporting some bald patches. And to think I'd been blaming him for eating the neighborhood squirrels. Now, I wasn't so sure.

I didn't so much as break up with Lisa Number Three as I threw all her shit out the front door and yelled, "Go away! Get out of my life!"

She stood in the middle of the front yard in a rainstorm of her own panties and shouted, "Is this because I can't have an orgasm?"

I screamed louder and threw all her CDs onto the lawn.

"Is this because of your inability to arouse me?! A lot of couples have that problem! We can work on it!" she yelled.

I ran out the door, across the yard and jumped into Betty. I squealed her tires out of the driveway and left skid marks on the street. I drove in a fugue state until I reached the Best Western and locked myself inside the sanity of a room where nobody ate the hair out of the bathtub drain.

I drove home the next morning intent on conducting a civil break-up. I pulled Betty into the driveway in time to see Lisa Number Three sitting inside her truck. The truck's bed was heaped with garbage bags full of her belongings. The engine was idling and she was sitting behind the wheel studying a road atlas. I noticed she had highlighted I-40 straight to Los Angeles. She couldn't get lost unless she made a turn.

I rapped on the window. She rolled it down halfway.

"You all packed up then?" I asked.

"Yeah," she mumbled.

It was weird, but ever since she ate her eyebrows, I couldn't read her expression. I couldn't tell if she was sad or mad.

"Sure you don't want to take Asscat? You might want a snack on the way," I said.

She flipped me off and backed out of the driveway.

I guess she was mad.

* * *

"My name is Dana and I'm an alcoholic."

"Hi, Dana!" the people shouted back.

Dana opened and closed her mouth a few times, but no words came out. She knew she was supposed to tell them a sob story. They were expecting her to tell them about guzzling mouthwash for her next high and giving handjobs for a sip of beer and sleeping in alleys with her shoes as a pillow, but nothing near that exciting had ever happened to her.

She wracked her brain trying to remember any good TV movies about alcoholics, but the only sordid story she could think up was an urban myth she'd heard as a kid. So before she could talk herself out of it, she said, "It all began, I guess, when I was six years old. It was Christmas Eve. Daddy had gone out of town on a business trip. Mama and I lit a fire in the fireplace that night and that's when we smelled something funny. Something bad. It smelled like singed hair and charred flesh. We put out the fire and I looked up inside the chimney."

Dana threw in a few sniffles to make her story more realistic. She continued, "It was Daddy. He was wearing a Santa suit and had a bag of presents. He had cancelled his trip and was going to surprise us Christmas Eve by coming down the chimney, but he broke his neck in the fall and was stuck. He died trying to make me happy."

Dana held her breath and blinked.

Everyone had their mouths open, staring at her. After a moment of thick silence, some of the people shifted in their chairs. Others looked at each other. Some whispered behind their hands and Dana could make out a few words: "Awful... horrific...My God Almighty..."

Dana summed up her story quickly with, "That's when I had my first eggnog. I've drunk ever since. Especially around Christmastime." She paused, then added, "I'm terrified of chimneys."

"When you were six years old?" said an old woman who was wearing a plastic Walmart bag tied on her head like a shower cap. "You started drinking that young?"

Dana hadn't thought about that. That did seem a tad young to start a life of alcoholism. But now that she had told the story she had to stay committed. She nodded at the raincap and said, "Yeah. Sixish. Thereabouts."

"That's awful young to start drinking," said a man with fingerless gloves. He stroked his long gray beard and said, "I didn't start up till I was nine."

"I was six, but...I looked seven."

The legless man in the wheelchair said, "That's the awfullest story I ever heard. And, believe me, I've heard plenty."

All the people nodded and made "Bless your little heart" faces at Dana. She stole a look in Ellen's direction. She was beaming at Dana. Encouraged, Dana ended her story by saying, "That's also when I stopped believing in Santa Claus."

She stepped down from the podium and was surrounded by all her new friends. They hugged her and fussed over her and patted her and squeezed her and she had never felt so loved in her whole life.

Dana hated to admit it, but she was happy. She belonged.

* * *

Trudy showed up right on time. I unplugged the box of red wine as she walked through my front door carrying a big fishing tackle box and an oversize photo album. I poured wine from the box's spigot into two of my vintage Jetsons juice glasses while she opened her fishing tackle "Bodacious Box of Beauty" (that's what she had bedazzled across the top of it) and set her supplies out on the counter like a surgeon getting ready to operate.

Trudy sniffed the air and wrinkled her nose. "What's that god-awful smell?"

"One of Maw Maw's new recipes. It's stewing in the Crock- Pot. So, how come you don't have a date tonight?" I asked, handing her a glass of wine.

"I did have. I cancelled," she replied. She held out her glass of wine and made a gimme-more gesture with her hand. "Don't be stingy. Fill it up to Elroy's eyes, please."

I held Elroy back under the spigot. "Why'd you cancel?"

"My best friend needed me," she said much too sweetly.

"Yeah, right. Why'd you really cancel?"

"It was with Bob Wyer." She rolled her eyes. "You were a good excuse to cancel."

"Wait a minute! You finally told Bob Wyer you'd go on a date with him?"

She took the glass from me, downed half of it in one gulp, then shrugged. "I had a moment of weakness."

"You know, he's probably a pretty nice guy if you'd give him half a chance." I was trying to put a shine on Bob Wyer. He'd been declaring his love for Trudy ever since the eighth grade. "You could do a whole lot worse than him, you know." I refrained from saying "You *have* done a whole lot worse than him." Besides his unfortunate name, he didn't seem that bad.

Trudy downed her Elroy. "He's boring as all get-out. His idea of a big Friday night is playing dominoes with his mother."

I sipped from Rosie the Robot. "So he still lives with his mother. That's nice if you think about it. It means he has respect for women." I didn't voice that I was really thinking it was little too *Psycho* for my taste. "And he plays dominoes, which means he's very good at adding."

"I don't like his bow ties." She handed Elroy back to me, saying, "Hit me again."

"That's not exactly a deal breaker." I poured her another. "You married Jeffrey and he wore black dress socks with white tennis shoes."

"Bob Wyer's too quiet," she said. "I work with dead people all day long. I don't want to be dating them too."

Not a week went by that Bob Wyer didn't ask her out at least once. And not a week went by that Trudy didn't turn him down. "You got to admire his perseverance," I said. And his creativity. Every week he invited her to do something different. I guess he thought that if he came up with the right thing to do, Trudy would say yes. "What did he invite you to do this time?"

"One of those SCA things."

"What the heck is a SCA thing?"

"Society for Creative Anachronism. It's where all these geeky people get together and the men dress in tights and sword fight with these big foam noodles. They pretend they're in the Middle Ages and beat the crap out of each other. I think the women sit around and watch them and drink homemade wine."

"Noodles?"

She nodded. "It's symbolic of their peckers."

"That could be…interesting," I said dubiously.

"Besides, I don't have anything Middle-Agey to wear."

I took another sip and considered her vast collection of wigs. "What kind of wig would you wear?"

"I don't know. I think they wore fox tails on their head," she said between gulps. "Besides, there were no black women in the Middle Ages."

"Sure there were," I said. "They were called Moors."

"Well, Bob Wyer ain't getting no *more* of this *Moor*, I can tell you that. Besides," she said, "I already married one man who wore panty hose, I'm not going to marry another one just because he calls them tights and stuffs a codpiece in 'em."

I changed the subject. "What's that?" I pointed Rosie the Robot at the big book she'd brought in with her.

"It's my book of faces. I've been trying out new makeup styles and taking pictures of my models all done up. You know, for when I open my own makeover business. I brought that for you to look through so you can pick out a new face."

"A new face?"

She nodded. "Then I'll make you over to look like it."

"What's wrong with my old face?"

"Nothing if you like librarians."

"Librarians look smart."

"Yes, they do. But nobody wants to have hot sex with one. I was under the impression you wanted to have hot sex tonight. True or false?"

"True."

"Then look through there and pick out a new hot, sexy face."

"What defines a face that you want to have hot sex with?"

Trudy said, "Pick one out that makes you want to sit on it."

I spit the wine out my nose and into my lap. It burned so bad tears streamed down my face. Trudy laughed. "Just kidding. Sort of. Find a face whose eyes you want to gaze into. Lips you want to kiss. That type of thing."

I opened the book and skimmed through a few pages. "All the people in the photos have their eyes closed."

"They're all dead, silly."

"Oh." I flipped through several more pages. I pointed at a photo of an older woman whose eyes were bulging. Upon closer inspection I noted that her eyes were painted on top of her closed eyelids. "That one looks a little like our old third grade schoolteacher," I said. "Remember Mrs. Anthony?"

"That is her."

I looked closer. "How'd you get rid of her wart?"

"Putty and a spatula."

"I like how you painted on her eyes."

"That's one of my newest creations. I call them 'Lady Gaga eyes.'"

"Good job," I said.

Trudy fast-flipped through a couple of pages and pointed. "That's Mr. Gilbright. Remember our grade school janitor?"

"I never would've recognized him."

"I call it 'Geisha Girl.'"

"What did his family say when they saw him like that?"

"Closed casket."

"Oh." I flipped through more pages. "I like this Peter Pan look you have on Mr. Dunphree."

"That's a 'Forest Nymph' and green's not your color."

"How about this Marilyn?"

"Nah…" She flipped a few pages back and tapped her fingernail on a photo. "I think we should do this Lindsay Lohan. I've been wanting a model to perfect it. LaFonda Duke was the right age when she died, but her bone structure was wrong."

"I don't know," I hedged, "Which Lindsay are you going to do? Before *Herbie* or after *Herbie*? 'Cause I don't want to look like I'm on drugs."

Trudy said, "Before. I'll make you look like Lindsay in *Freaky Friday* except with big boobs."

"Okay," I said. "Let's get started." I closed my eyes and pointed my face toward her.

"Lie down on the table."

I opened my eyes. "Huh?"

"Lie down on the table on your back."

"Why?"

"I only ever do makeup when they're lying down. I don't know if I can do it when you're sitting up."

"Do I have to cross my arms over my chest?" I asked.

"Yes. To make sure, you know."

I sat on the edge of the table and lay back with my arms crossed over my chest. After a moment, I opened one eye and saw her open a jar of stinky goop and smear it all over her palms. "What's that for?"

"Gel for your hair. To lift it off your face." She rubbed her hands through my hair like she was drying them on a paper towel in a public restroom. "Did you mow your front lawn?"

"I pay the kid down the street to mow."

"I meant, did you, you know, weed your garden." She wiped her hands on the tablecloth. I made a mental note to throw it in the washer later.

"Weed? I don't have a garden this year. Maw Maw planted some tomatoes in that old metal pig trough out by the back fence but that's it."

I opened both eyes in time to see her dip a rubber spatula into a pot of beige goop. She aimed the spatula at my face so I closed my eyes again. "I was talking about trimming up your woo-hoo. You're the one with the English degree, haven't you ever heard of a euphemism? Keep your eyes shut."

My eyes popped open. "Oh, that garden. The euphemistic garden of delight, I get it." I closed my eyes and tried to keep my face supple while she rubbed the goop all over it. "No, I didn't weed the garden, but I did walk the dog."

"What dog? You don't have a dog."

"I also washed the car. And cleaned the gutters."

She pulled one side of my face up two inches higher than it's supposed to be and slapped more stuff in the taut flesh. "What the hell're you talking about, DD?"

"I don't know. I thought we were playing a euphemism game. But to answer your question, yes, I mowed my front yard a couple of weeks ago."

"Better mow it again. If you plan on anybody seeing it tonight."

I snickered. "You mean, you won't weed my garden of delight for me?"

She snorted like a horse. "I'd have to drink a dozen Elroys to even consider it," she said.

"You really think I should do it again? Isn't twice in one month a little excessive?"

"Honey, I've seen you naked. Your woo-hoo grows faster than a chia pet."

"Okay," I said. "I'll mow."

"Don't want to scare the poor woman off."

"I said okay, no need to harp on it." I felt weird talking about my chia pet even if Trudy was my best friend, so I changed the subject. "What're you going to do with your famous faces portfolio?"

"That portfolio is my ticket out of this dump. I'm not going to work at the funeral home forever, you know. I'm going to move to Tulsa or Fayetteville, some big city, you know, and open my own business doing specialized makeup and hairstyles for the deceased."

"I don't get it."

"Say a woman who dies always had the fantasy of being Marilyn Monroe. She can hire me to make her look like Marilyn for her burial and her entrance into the afterlife."

"How's she going to hire you if she's dead?"

"No, silly, she'll hire me before she's dead. Then when she dies I'll do the makeover."

"How's she going to know you did it if she's dead? You could sell her the makeover and when she dies, say screw it and she'd never know."

"I'm not that type of person."

"Okay, just saying. It wasn't meant to be a slander on your morality."

"I know you're always going around trying to concoct the perfect crime and the perfect murder, but that doesn't mean that everybody in the world thinks like you do. Some people don't cheat at Trivial Pursuit."

"Good God, Trudy, that was over twenty years ago. I already said I was sorry."

Trudy muttered under her breath, "Staying up every night for a week to memorize the answers to all those cards."

"Drop it, okay? You know good and well I'm not going to commit those murder schemes. I like to think them up for when I start writing my magnum opus. In case the plot turns out to be a mystery. Ouch!" I rubbed my nose where she poked it with a paintbrush.

"Sorry. I'm not used to working on live people." She re-aimed the brush for my lips.

An hour later I looked like a hungover Lindsay Lohan on her way to court. I had on my best pair of jeans, the black ones that I saved for funeral-going and dates (sometimes it's hard to tell the difference). I sincerely hoped that I didn't have to pee anytime soon because I had had to lie down on my back and suck in my gut to get them zipped. I couldn't go through all that again. (I swear I was the only person in the civilized world who gained weight by eating at Subway.) I chose my favorite blouse—a peasanty-type thing that gave my nondescript eyes a hint of blue and hid my muffin-tops. My boobs were going to be too big no matter what I did, so I deemphasized them by tying up the strings around the collar and hiding the cleavage. I had to wear flip-flops because the too-tight jeans wouldn't let me bend over to tie any other shoes.

I took one last look in the mirror and grabbed a box of Kleenex. I could wipe all the crap off my face on the way over to Kimmy's duplex.

Trudy was pretty zonkered on the wine by the time I was ready to leave. She was lying back on the couch, sound asleep and making ZZZZ noises. She looked like Cleopatra waiting to be fed grapes. Asscat was perched regally on her belly with his paws stretched out in front of him like the Sphinx.

I was halfway out my front door when Trudy yelled from behind me, "Oh my God!"

"What?" I spun around. She was sitting up ramrod straight with an agog expression. Or maybe it was more of an aghast expression. Yes, it was definitely aghast.

"Nothing," she said way too sweet. She affected a tone of nonchalance. "I was thinking—can you make sure to always keep her in front of you?"

I touched the back of my head. "Why? What's back there? What'd you do?"

She sighed. "It's one of the hazards of working on the dead. I've never actually done the back of somebody's head before."

"It looks bad?" I put my hand back there and patted. It felt like a hard rat's nest.

"Nope," she said with a tiny grin. "Not if she doesn't see it."

I'd try to brush it out on the way over there. I could brush and drive a stick shift at the same time. I hoped. "Okay, wish me luck," I said.

"Wait!"

I stopped halfway out the door and turned back. "What now?"

She suppressed a grin. "Maybe you should take Asscat with you."

"Why?"

"He might be the only pussy you get tonight."

"You're so not funny, Trudy."

"I'm a little bit funny." She grinned.

"No," I said. "You're most definitely un-funny."

She stuck out her bottom lip like a tipsy toddler. "A wittle? A teeny tiny wittle bit funny?"

"Nope."

"Aren't you even going to say goodbye to my pussy?" she fake-pouted and waved Asscat's paw at me.

"Get that cat off your lap and I will," I retorted. I closed the door and headed toward my car. I heard Trudy's guffaws all the way to the driveway.

* * *

"I'm so happy you're an alcoholic," Ellen said.

Dana playfully socked Ellen in the arm.

"I mean, I'm not glad you are, I'm glad you admitted it."

After the AA meeting Dana and Ellen met up at the city park. Dana led Ellen back to the monkey bars, but this time they were hanging upside down by their knees. Dana looked at Ellen hanging upside down next to her and giggled.

"What?" Ellen asked.

"Our hairs match," Dana said. "Now mine is sticking straight up too."

"Maybe it's sticking straight down because you're upside down."

"Or maybe we're sitting straight up and the world is upside down," Dana said.

Ellen was quiet for a moment. "That's a strange thought, but it is a familiar feeling," she said.

"Yep," Dana agreed. "Most of the time I feel like the world is going one way and I'm going the other. Like I'm always walking upstream."

"Me too. Except when I was drinking. Then I felt like the world and I were in sync. That's the only time I fit in. Or maybe the alcohol numbed me so much I didn't care." Ellen reached over and wrapped Dana's fingers in her own. "You feel that way too?"

Dana looked away from Ellen's searching eyes. "I'm glad you're here to help me through this." Her words tasted metallic and false. She changed the subject. "This is my thinking place. You know how Winnie the Pooh has his thinking place? This is mine."

"You always hang upside down when you think?"

"Yep. It increases the blood flow to my head and my best ideas always happen when my brain is engorged."

Ellen chuckled. "Engorged. That's a weird word."

"So…" Dana said. "Have you caught your girlfriend cheating yet?"

"No. Have you?"

"Not yet. I can't find her, let alone find her cheating." Then Dana voiced what been scaring her the most lately. "What if… our respective girlfriends aren't cheating? What do we do then?"

Ellen frowned. At least Dana thought she was frowning. She could be smiling and Dana was seeing her smile upside down.

"I don't know," Ellen uttered softly. "All I know is that I don't want us to end before we've even begun."

"I guess we could be friends," Dana said without conviction.

"Yeah, we could," Ellen said half-heartedly. "Or we can both get out of our relationships anyway. It's just messier. We'd have to admit why—that we didn't love them and we wanted to be with each other and...you know. We have to be the bad guys."

Dana nodded, which is harder than you think when you're hanging upside down.

A sudden crack of thunder underscored the mood. Dana scanned the sky and saw rolling thunderheads obscuring the moon and the stars. "Crapola. It's going to rain."

They didn't move. Dana didn't care if an F5 ripped through the city park, she didn't want to let go of Ellen's hand and she sure didn't want to go home all by herself. There was nothing quite so lonely as lying in bed and listening to the rain hit the roof, counting seconds between thunder claps—all alone.

The first drop of cold rain splunked right into the middle of Dana's forehead. Ellen laughed and wiped it away with the cuff of her shirt. Within seconds, the sky opened and cold, hard pellets of rain battered them. Still, neither one moved.

Ellen uncurled herself from the monkey bars and landed nimbly on her feet. She helped Dana unhook a leg, but before she could help with the second leg, Dana slipped from the bars and kerplunked head-first into the mud.

"You okay?" Ellen asked, kneeling on the ground with Dana.

Dana grabbed Ellen, pulling her into the mud beside her. They laughed. Ellen sat up, wrapped an arm around Dana and pulled her close. They sat that way for a moment, their faces tilted up letting the rain wash away the mud.

"It could be worse," Dana said, shivering against Ellen. "We could be struck by lightning."

"Oh God, don't even say that."

"I believe that if you say bad things out loud, they don't come true. Only unvoiced fears ever materialize."

Ellen pooched out her bottom lip and thought about it.

"Or maybe it's the opposite, I never can remember," Dana amended.

"I knew a lady once who got struck by lightning," Ellen said. "She was washing dishes at her kitchen sink, the lightening shot inside, hit her on top of her head and blasted out her butt."

Dana laughed.

Ellen said ultra-seriously, "It's not funny. It completely burnt out her sphincter."

Dana laughed harder.

"She had to get an asshole transplant."

"Stop," Dana sputtered around waves of laughter. "You're killing me."

"It's true," Ellen insisted. "They gave her a pig's asshole. You know, since pig parts are the closest things to a human's."

Dana laughed so hard she snorted. "I snorted," Dana giggled. "Like a pig."

"I haven't even told you the funny part. Instead of sending her flowers at the hospital, people sent her pig figurines. Now she collects little pig statues. She has thousands of them."

"Oh my God!" Dana managed to gasp. She snorted again and this caused her to break into renewed hysterics.

"True story," Ellen said uber-solemnly, holding up two fingers in the Girl Scout salute. "You can look her up in the Guinness Book of World Records."

Dana caught her breath and asked, "For what? She break the record for pig collecting?"

"Nope. She's the only living pig asshole recipient."

"I have one question. When she farts does it smell like…" A small laugh escaped and Dana stuffed it back down. "Does it smell like…" She broke into gales of laughter.

Ellen finished the sentence for her, "Does it smell like bacon?"

"Yes!"

They fell backwards under a tidal wave of laughter, rolling in the mud. They laughed for a good five minutes. Each time one stopped, the other mumbled, "Bacon," and they were off and running into more bouts of laughter.

Laughed dry and sopping wet, Dana managed to say, "You're hysterical. And to think I once hated you."

Ellen was shocked. "Hated me?"

"Yeah," Dana said. "I hated you from the second I saw you."

"Why?"

"I hated that you were you and I was me and I was stuck being me in a life that was mine and I didn't like it because you weren't in that life. Like, you know, when you're watching an infomercial for the ab cruncher or that Bowflex thing and you want a stomach and butt like hers but your credit card is maxed out because you spent it all on fattening foods at the grocery store so you realize you can never have her butt or stomach or even have her…Okay, maybe it's not like that at all…What I meant was I hated you because I could never have you."

Ellen stared at Dana. There was a long silence. Long enough that Dana got nervous. Finally, Ellen said, "Well, as long as we're being honest, I hated you too."

"Why?" Dana whispered. She was pretty sure Ellen was going to say she found her unattractive. It was the whole fat thing again. Or maybe it was her hair or the way she dressed.

"Because I wanted you, too," Ellen said.

Dana searched Ellen's face for any trace of insincerity. And when she didn't find any, she allowed herself to hope. One tiny sliver of shining hope leaked through the cracks. "You wanted me?" Dana whispered.

Ellen nodded. "I wanted you and I hated you for that because you weren't mine. You belonged to somebody else."

Dana knew that her heart didn't belong to anybody else. As far as she was concerned her heart was a free agent. She opened her mouth to tell Ellen she loved her, but what came out instead was, "Well, I hated you first."

Ellen smiled. "No, I hated you first."

"I hated you way before you hated me."

Ellen countered, "I hated you before I even knew you."

"That's impossible."

"I hated the very idea of you."

"You're making stuff up," Dana said. "I hated you first and you're mad that I beat you to it."

"I hated the idea that somebody like you even existed."

Dana replied, "I hated your mother before she gave birth to you, therefore, I hated you first."

"Big deal." Ellen rolled her eyes. "I hate you more."

"I hate you the most."

Ellen wrapped her fingers around the back of Dana's neck and leaned in until their lips were only a breath apart. "I hate what I'm about to do," Ellen said.

"Stop talking and do it already," Dana breathed.

Ellen touched her lips to Dana's. They kissed deeply and Dana felt time freeze like in that *Twilight Zone* episode starring Burgess Meredith where he's the only man on earth.

Dana was so lost in the kiss that she didn't even bother to count the twenty-seven raindrops that fell on her head.

Ellen pulled back. She smiled, then rested her forehead against Dana's, muttering, "I hated that."

"I hated it too."

"I hated it so much, I want to do it again." Ellen pressed into Dana and kissed her again. This kiss was deeper and more insistent than the first. This kiss was full of the promise of things to come. Ellen's lips beamed Dana out of this world and transported her to a place where she wasn't fat or cold or being rained on. Suddenly, Dana found herself sitting on a beach with warm sand under her butt and ocean waves tickling her feet. No, wait, she was in a mountain cabin on a bear skin rug in front of a roaring fireplace. No, on second thought, she was in her bed with Ellen, wrapped up in a quilt, skin-to-skin, exploring with her mouth and fingers and—

Ellen pulled away from the kiss, leaving Dana shaking. And not from the cold, either.

"You know what we have to do next, don't you?" Ellen asked.

"Consummate our hatred?"

Ellen laughed.

"I was being serious," Dana said with a straight face.

"I want us to get rid of our girlfriends first," Ellen responded. "What we have—what we will have—will be better if they're out of the way and we're not feeling guilty about cheating on them."

"I wasn't going to enjoy it or anything," Dana said. "After all, I hate you."

Ellen planted a popcorn kiss on Dana's lips.

"How do I hate you?" Dana recited.

Ellen popped another kiss on her lips.

"Let me count the ways," Dana continued.

Popcorn kiss.

"I hate thee to the depth and breadth and height my soul can reach."

Kiss.

CHAPTER NINE

That night, Dana lay in bed by herself. This time instead of leaving room for Kimmy, she sprawled across the whole bed. But she couldn't sleep. She felt all pent-up like there was something about to bust loose inside her. She thought about masturbating but somehow that seemed like cheating on Ellen. She thought about ice cream, but she didn't even think sugary gooeyness could soothe her.

So for the first time in over a year, she got the old Smith-Corona out of the closet and started typing. The words flew fast and furious. She didn't even care if they were good words, she was ecstatic that her fingers were dancing on the typewriter keys again.

* * *

I did a last-second booger-check in the rear view mirror before I got out of the car. I had wiped off Trudy's makeup job on the drive over. She did a pretty good job if I had been a dead person. I quickly swiped on some watermelon-flavored lip gloss, but then licked it off before I could even get out of the car. That's the trouble with flavored lip glosses, they taste so good that I keep licking them off. It's a good thing they don't make bacon-flavored gloss or I'd chew off my own lips.

I sucked in a breath of courage, grabbed the handle on the box of wine I'd bought (I had scored a two-for-one sale) and headed for the B duplex.

The front door opened before I even got to the porch. As soon as I saw her I stumbled over a crack in the sidewalk that only my feet could detect. This stumble set into motion a whole series of events: My right toe slapped against the back of my left calf, I pitched the box of wine forward and followed its trajectory with my face. Somehow Kimmy managed to not only catch the box of wine, but using her magnificent and expensive breasts, she also softened the blow for my face.

It was a Dooley for the record books.

This wasn't the grand entrance I had envisioned, but it did get her full attention.

I reluctantly pried my nose out of her cleavage and stepped back, but as anybody knows who's ever worn flip-flops before, they are not the best shoes for backing up. I stepped completely out of my left one and tripped again. This time there were no cooshy cushions and I clunked the left side of my face against the porch post.

I ended up on my tookus with my hand clasped over my left eye. I could feel it swelling. I looked up at Kimmy with my one good eye.

"You look amazing," I said.

She was too busy laughing to register what I'd said. I took the approach that she was laughing with me, not at me, and smiled back at her.

"Sorry," she said. "I know I shouldn't laugh, but that was funny."

You know how cats slip and fall, then get up and pretend that they meant to do it that way all along? That's what I did. I got up and smiled. "I meant to do that."

For some reason that made her laugh even harder.

I brushed off the back of my pants until she caught her breath.

"I've never seen anybody do that without a banana peel," she said between chortles. "Sorry. I've always found it funny when people fall down."

"Well, then, you should find me constantly amusing."

"Winter is my favorite season. All that ice is better than a Three Stooges movie." She held up the box of wine and examined it. "Wow. I didn't know they made wine in boxes." She winked at me. "Let's go have a glass."

She didn't know wine came in boxes? What was she, born in a barn? She pranced through the apartment (she really did prance too). I followed her through the bare living room and into the kitchen. I said the living room was bare, but I only assumed it was bare like it was this afternoon because, to be truthful, I wasn't looking at the living room. I was looking at Kimmy's shapely butt. It was swinging back and forth like a hypnotist's pendulum. And she was rocking that tube top and cut-offs like nobody's business. She had a golden glow from head to toe and no visible tan lines. That must mean she sunbathed in the nude. I wondered if she did that in her backyard. I wondered if her backyard had a privacy fence. I wondered if I did a slow drive-by down the alley if I could see her sunbathing in the nude.

"Ouch!" I stubbed my left toe on a kitchen chair. I blamed it on the blind spot I now had out of my left eye, but it might have been because I was too busy picturing Kimmy nude to actually see where I was going.

I gritted my teeth, clenched my toe in my hand and hopped through the pain.

"Maybe you should sit down," she said, pulling out a chair.

Good idea. I sat down at the kitchen bar and gingerly touched my swollen eye. "Do you have any frozen peas?"

"Peas?" she asked like she couldn't have heard me right.

I nodded. "Yes. Peas, please."

She opened the freezer half of the fridge and looked inside. "I hadn't planned on cooking peas…" She bent over and rummaged around in the freezer, pointing her butt in my direction.

I was busy enjoying the view when I felt something wet brush against my foot. I looked down. It was that ugly little poodle from this afternoon. The one with the Leroy Brown attitude. It rubbed his/her nose all over my foot. I shook it off my foot and went back to admiring Kimmy's butt. That's when the little dog wrapped its front paws around my shin and started humping away. I tried to shake it off, but it gripped harder. Shaking my leg made the dog even more excited.

I stood up and kicked like I was a punter going for the winning point.

It sounded like a squeak toy when it hit the wall.

I quickly sat back down. Kimmy had her head inside the fridge and didn't notice.

The dog peeled himself off the wall and bared his teeth at me. I bared my teeth right back at him.

"No peas, sorry," Kimmy said.

I turned my teeth-baring into a tight smile and aimed it at Kimmy. "You have corn." I pointed at the bag in the freezer door.

Kimmy turned her back to me again and looked inside the freezer, muttering something that sounded a lot like, "What the hell does she want with vegetables?"

The damn dog was back in attack mode. He stuck his wet nose between my legs. I squeezed my legs together and got him in a knee-lock. He tried to twist away, but I vise-gripped him with my thighs. That would teach him to stick his nose where it didn't belong.

"Are you a vegetarian?"

I looked at Kimmy and smiled way too big. I swiveled on the barstool, hiding the wrestling lock I had on her dog. "No, I need a cold compress for my eye. So it won't swell so bad," I said.

"Oh. Why didn't you say so?" She pulled out the bag of corn. I loosened my death grip on the dog and he backed away, shaking his head like Wile E. Coyote after he was hit on the head with a falling anvil.

Kimmy pranced across the kitchen floor and gently pressed the bag of corn over my blackening eye. It hurt like a summabitch. She moved in a little closer, pushing her right boob mere inches from my nose. My eye started feeling better. I don't know if she was putting her boob in my face on purpose, but it was my experience that women never do anything even remotely sexual by pure accident.

The damn dog sensed that I was vulnerable and moved back in for the kill. He stuck his nose directly into my crotch again.

"His name is Snickerdoodle," Kimmy said. "Isn't he the cutest thing you ever saw?"

"He sure is," I said with gritted teeth.

If you think Rosemary's baby is cute.

"He likes you," she said.

"He's liking me a little too much for my taste."

Kimmy laughed. I pushed the dog back (gently because Kimmy was watching) and crossed my legs.

She scooped the dog up and said, "Aw, you hurt his feelings." She rubbed her nose against his nose and I made a mental note to not go anywhere near her nose tonight.

Kimmy sat the dog on top of the table. She pranced to the other side of the room and opened one of the kitchen cabinets. I gave Snickerdoodle my most evil eye. He didn't seem threatened. I used two fingers to point to my eyes and then point to him in that "I've got my eyes on you" gesture. He was unimpressed. I finished off with an evil eye like the one Miss Celie gave to Mister in *The Color Purple*.

Kimmy interrupted out staredown. "I don't have any wine glasses yet. I just moved in and haven't really had any time to shop or decorate. I usually eat out, so…" She pulled a dog bowl out of the cabinet. I knew it was a dog bowl because "Snickerdoodle" was painted on the side. "This is the only dish I have."

She has to be kidding. She wants to drink wine out of a dog bowl?

"We could put our mouths under the spigot and drink it that way."

"We could," she said. "But that's so white trash."

A dog bowl would be classier?

"But what about the dog?" I asked.

"It's okay, he loves wine. He gets drunk and passes out after a while."

That explains it. The dog's not only a butthole, he's a drunken butthole.

I pulled the plug on the wine box and Snickerdoodle licked his lips and drooled.

On a scale of one to ten with ten being the best, I'd rate this date so far as a negative three. In under ten minutes, I'd gotten a black eye, a throbbing big toe, a bag of frozen corn, a dog bowl of wine that I was going to share with the dog, and the only time I made her laugh caused me great physical harm.

This was good news. There was nowhere to go but up.

Kimmy placed the brimming bowl of wine in front of the dog.

Now would be a really good time for me to quit drinking.

Maybe half an hour later, Kimmy poured the last of the wine into the bowl. I bet your average person didn't know that there were approximately ten dog bowls in every box of wine. Instead of liters, a wine box can be measured in dog bowls. Ten of them. Or maybe twelve. I kind of lost count after six or five.

Snickerdoodle, aka evil personified, was passed out on top of the table with his tongue lolling out the side of his mouth and his eyes rolled back in his head.

If I sit him out on the side of the road Maw Maw could have him stuffed by morning.

I stopped lapping wine and jerked my attention back to Kimmy. She'd been talking for a really long time.

"So when the hand modeling went tits up, I moved here," she concluded.

"Hand modeling?"

She posed her hands in front of my face like she was a queen and I was supposed to kiss them.

"Pretty," I said because it was all I could think to say.

She took her hands back. "You ever see a dishwashing commercial?"

"Uh huh, sure," I said between laps.

"Or a glove commercial? Or a close-up of a movie star's hands?"

"Uh huh."

"Or somebody's hands holding a box of Hamburger Helper?"

I lapped the last of the wine out of the bowl.

"Me, all me," she said, pointing to her own chest.

"Really?"

"Not only commercials either. Movies too. I doubled the best of them. Julia Roberts. Angelina. Meg Ryan? All me."

"Wow." I bent my head over the dog bowl and was disappointed to see all the wine was gone.

"I made over one hundred commercials and fifty movies in my career. The only woman with better hands than me was Barbra Streisand. Then the economy went bust and the first thing Hollyweird got rid of was the hand and feet models. Now stars have to do their own hands. And, believe you me, they have some butt-ugly hands."

"I bet," I said for lack of anything better to say.

"Now, I'm still making a living with my hands only I'm styling hair with them."

I nodded.

"Money's not as good, of course, but what the hey. What can I do?" She looked forlornly at her hands.

I looked forlornly at the oven. "When are we going to eat?" I asked. I was going to have to either eat soon or end up on the counter next to Snickerdoodle.

Kimmy looked at her watch. "Soon."

I broke open the bag of frozen corn and tossed back a few kernels. They weren't too bad if you didn't think about it.

"Straight women like cunnilingus too, you know," she said.

"Is that so?" I shoved in another fistful of corn.

She crossed her arms and tilted her head like she was accusing me of something. "All you lesbians think you have the market cornered on the eating-out thing," she said like she was talking about going out to dinner at *Olive Garden*. "Us straight women like it too, but it's hard to find a man who will do it. I've even considered being a lesbian so somebody would go down on me without me having to ask them to do it."

"I can't believe you have to ask," I said.

"Well, there was my first husband. He went down on me. The first time he ever went down there, I made him stop."

I had my mouth halfway open to ask why until I remembered it was full of corn and I shut it.

She continued. "I was young and prudish, I guess. All those feminine hygiene commercials had me feeling self-conscious. Which is why I refused to work in a douche commercial. You ever see somebody holding up a box of Summer's Eve, it's sure as shit not me."

"You have principles."

"You bet I do. Then when I tried to get Marty, that was my first husband, to go back down there, we already hated each other, so it was too late. The French man I dated between marriages, his name was Jock, would go down there and stay all night if I wanted him to. He liked to pleasure me. I think that's the thing with French men. They may smell like warm chicken broth, but they love to make a woman feel good. Jock had a big dick too."

"Is that important?" I asked because I really wanted to know.

"It sure doesn't hurt any," she said. "I broke up with him because he was stupid and now I wish I hadn't. I mean, what's a little stupidity when a guy will do that? You can ignore stupid, but you sure can't ignore a guy who's bad in the sack. My second husband was horrible in bed. But he was smart. And he had a good job. I figured two out of three, right? I figured I could teach him the bed part."

Wrong. The bed part is a natural ability. Like a superpower. You either have it or you don't.

"Wroooong," she echoed my thoughts. "And he had an above-average dick. The problem with him was that he was fat. Not all over. Just his belly. His belly stuck out further than his dick. Which meant I always had to be on top. Which wasn't a problem because I like to be on top anyway."

More good news. I preferred the bottom. Not because I was passive in bed. Because I was lazy.

"You know how bad he was?" she asked.

I shook my head.

"One time I got on my elbows with my ass in the air and he couldn't even find the right spot. I mean, seriously, it's not like my pussy moved around independently of my other body parts or anything. I thought I was going to have to paint a damn bull's eye on it for him. I asked him once if he would like to watch me masturbate. I thought a sexy show might liven things up, you know?"

I nodded.

"Would you like that? Watching a woman touch herself for you?"

Hell, yes. "Sure."

"Well, *he* didn't. He got all indigent about it." (Yes, she said "indigent," not "indignant.") She continued. "He said if I could do it myself then why was he there."

"Oh. That's too bad."

"And when I brought up the idea of cunnilingus? Forget it."

"He wouldn't?"

"Nope. Wouldn't even consider it. Said it wasn't natural. I said, 'Fucking doggy-style is about as natural as you can get and you wouldn't do that either.'"

"Is that why you divorced him?"

"Yes, but we're still friends."

"How many men have you...been with?" That was a tricky question and I knew that. If her number was too high, it would be a definite turn-off for me. Too low and it would make me nervous because I'd wonder why it was so low when she was obviously very sexual and attractive. Like maybe there was something wrong with her that I couldn't smell.

"Six."

Okay, that's a good number (a multiple of three.) A middle-of-the-road number, not too low, not too high.

"And out of that six, four of them wouldn't go down. I should never have broken up with stupid Jock. Those French women don't know how good they've got it." She put the tip of one finger in the middle of her chin and squinted her eyes like she was thinking real hard. "Makes you wonder about French lesbians, doesn't it?"

"*Oui oui*," I said and giggled.

She put both her hands under the table where I couldn't see them. I heard a snap unsnap.

I eat when I get nervous, so I grabbed for the bag of corn and tossed another handful of niblets in my mouth.

I heard another snap unsnap.

Maybe Kimmy was getting comfortable. I'd never been good at reading signs from women. I didn't want to assume she was making sexual advances.

I distinctly heard a zipper unzip. Okay, maybe she was getting *really* comfortable. Because of the counter, I couldn't see her from the waist down, but when she kicked her shorts up in the air and they landed on my head, I was pretty sure that was all the sign I needed.

My nervousness skyrocketed into the stratosphere of panic. And when I'm panicking I can't be held responsible for what comes out of my mouth. "You know, there's a town in Indiana called French Lick. I always wanted to go there. For the heck of it." I threw back another handful of cold corn and chawed. Her jean shorts drooped down over my forehead.

Kimmy had both hands under the counter, her eyes closed, sucking on her bottom lip and she was wiggling.

I continued my nervous diatribe. "I think it'd be cool to have a fridge magnet from there. One that said 'I've been to French Lick.'" I crunched on more cold niblets and concentrated on breathing.

Kimmy lifted one leg up above the counter. Her purple silk panties, the thong type, were hanging off her ankle.

"Or maybe a snow globe. You shake it and it snows. And it says French Lick inside the globe." I crunched corn faster.

She kicked her leg and the panties flew across the bar and hit me smack dab in the middle of my chest. They stuck there, dangling off my boobs.

I kept talking, "They might even have bumper stickers that say something like 'I went down to French Lick.' I wonder if they have an airport there. That's where you buy stuff like that."

Crunch, crunch, crunch.

"Are you going to sit there eating corn all night?" she asked. "Or am I going to have to do this all by myself."

I swallowed. I ran my tongue over my front teeth. It wasn't the best time to ask for a toothpick.

Kimmy stood and pranced around the bar toward me. I gulped. She was bare from the waist down. And I do mean bare. As in bald, as in hairless. I'd never seen a real live bald one up close before—outside of the girls' bathroom when I was about seven years old. I couldn't wait to tell Trudy about this. Her Lindsay Lohan makeover was really working.

I wondered if Kimmy was a nympho or a sex addict or something? She was coming on awful strong. Then I wondered if I cared. I didn't have time to wonder too long. She grabbed me by the ears and tugged my face right into her crotch.

So much for foreplay.

I wiggled my nose a little and she moaned. I tentatively stuck my tongue out and she wiggled her hips a little and moaned louder.

"Your tongue is ice cold," she gasped.

"Frozen corn" I tried to explain, but it came out sounding more like "Fuzzy kore."

"Right there. Oh, baby, right there," she said, plow-reining my face with my ears.

I put my hands on her bare ass and pulled her closer. I figured if I was going to do this thing, I might as well do it up right. I kneaded her ass and flicked with my tongue.

What was that?

I flicked again and distinctly felt something hard.

Oh my God, she's pierced.

My tongue found the barbell thingee and I speed-flicked at it like it was a punching bag. Each time I flicked her hips jerked and she made noises in her throat like water boiling inside a tea kettle.

I decided I liked the piercing. It sure made my job easier. It was like an X marking the spot on a treasure map.

I flicked and nipped and sucked and after only thirty seconds, she boiled over and I heard a teakettle whistle.

She held me by the back of my head and screamed. Screamed loud, too.

Oh geez, I hoped I didn't hurt her. I tried to wiggle away, but she had a death grip on my ears and I heard her say, "Smoke! There's smoke!"

Seriously? We had enough friction going to cause smoke?

That was when she stumbled backwards and because she still had me by my ears, I tumbled out of the chair along with her and we fell to the floor. I was nose-deep in her bald crotch when I heard the door crash open.

I snapped my head back and this time Kimmy let go and all I could see was black smoke everywhere and that was when a stream of water hit me in the chest, threw me back against the wall and pinned me there. I held my arms over my face and sputtered, "What the heck is happening?" over and over.

The water stream moved from me to Kimmy lying on the floor and the force of it sent her rolling to the other side of the kitchen.

I wiped my face and saw the living room was filled with firemen and they had their water hose turned on and were dousing everything in the apartment. Black smoke was pouring out of the oven, and that wasn't Kimmy I heard screaming, it was a smoke alarm shrieking.

A fireman aimed the hose at the smoke alarm up on the wall and it burst into tiny pieces.

Silence.

It took me a good ten seconds to put it all together: Dinner had burned in the oven and the smoke had set off the smoke alarm and we were so busy getting busy we didn't even know it or know when the fire department had arrived.

Finally, one of the firemen had enough sense to turn off the hose and they all stood there staring at half-naked Kimmy lying on the floor and me, sopping wet, huddled against the wall.

I made up the only excuse I could think up spur of the moment and said, "The smoke made her faint. I was giving her mouth-to-mouth resuscitation."

The firemen grinned and one of them said, "You were working on the wrong end, darlin'."

That's when Kimmy stumbled to her feet, looked at me and said, "That was fucking incredible."

* * *

Dana had been walking on air ever since she'd hung upside down on the monkey bars the night before and it had nothing to do with an engorged brain. She had stayed up the better part of the night writing and didn't even feel tired. She didn't even bitch about cleaning out Mrs. Olsen's garage all day. It was a sure sign that love was invading her body like an airborne infectious disease.

She had a renewed sense of well-being that she usually was only able to achieve after watching *It's a Wonderful Life* or reveling in the dopamine rush of an orgasm. This sense of all's right with the world gave her a new lease on life. Yesterday she wanted to kill herself, or at the very least lock herself away until she grew fingernails as long as Howard Hughes', but today she was all about exploring her potential with Ellen. Her mission, should she choose to accept it, was to climb out of the hole of Kimmy, figuratively speaking, and dive into the hole of Ellen, literally speaking.

All this thinking about climbing and missions made Dana ravenous. As soon as she got home, she rushed to the kitchen and opened the fridge door to see what there was to eat. There were stacks and stacks of unlabeled Tupperware containers. Maw Maw never threw anything away. If you so much as left one pea on your supper plate she packed it away and you'd find it back on your plate at the next meal.

Dana grabbed the first Tupperware she saw and popped the top.

Ick and double ick. It looked like one of Maw Maw's experiments. She put it back in the fridge and opted for two slices of bologna, a slice of white bread and a couple of hunks of Velveeta. She was going to make what she called an inside-out sandwich. An inside-out sandwich was exactly what it sounded like: a piece of bread in between two slices of bologna and Velveeta. Whenever Dana got some spare time she was planning on selling this idea to the Oscar Mayer or the Velveeta people. She was sure they'd pay her to put the recipe for her inside-out sandwich on their packaging. The recipe could be her golden ticket out of Dooley Springs. Dana's only concern was that the bread people might be sore. If her inside-out sandwich was as big as she thought it would be, bread sales would be cut in half. She hoped the bread corporations didn't send Mr. Slugworth after her like in *Willy Wonka*.

Dana took a big bite of sandwich and scanned the to-do list she had posted on the fridge door one day when she was under the influence of *Hoarders*. All she had accomplished was writing the list, but according to the show's certified professional organizers, that was at least a step in the right direction.

The to-do list read: "Wash windows. Clean top of fridge. Dust ceiling fans. Lose ten pounds."

Somebody (her butthole brother, judging from the handwriting) had X'ed out the "ten" and written "one hundred" above it.

Dana picked up the pencil on a string that was hanging from a magnet and added to the bottom of the list, "Get rid of Kimmy." She was fully aware that Kimmy might see this and she would have to pay the consequences. But on the plus side maybe she would see it and then Dana wouldn't have to tell her to leave. She would see how unwanted she was and leave of her own accord.

Writing down those four words made Dana feel better. They were like the death gurgles of her relationship with Kimmy, signifying the end was near.

She shoved the last of the bologna in her mouth, got a rag and cleanser out of the cupboard, stood on a chair and attacked the top of the fridge. She scrubbed until she could see her own reflection smiling back at herself. Satisfied with that job, she put a check mark beside number two on the list. Only three more to go.

That accomplishment felt so good Dana allowed herself a Pop-Tart to celebrate. She bit off all the corners of the pastry as she walked upstairs and into the bathroom. She turned on the hot water in the shower and sat down on the toilet lid, eating her dessert while the water heated up. She listened to the old water pipes groan. The pipes sounded a lot like Kimmy when she was in throes of an escalating climax. That was a sound she wouldn't miss.

Dana considered her options for finding Kimmy cheating on her:

1. Follow her and catch her in the act
2. Find written proof
3. Ask her point-blank

Since Dana was a chicken and avoided all confrontations and Kimmy would lie anyway, that ruled out number three. She wasn't sure that Kimmy could write so that meant number two was out. That left Dana no choice but to follow Kimmy and catch her making water pipe noises with somebody else.

She swallowed the last of the Pop-Tart, stood up and stepped on something yucky. What the heck? She sat back down on the toilet lid and examined the bottom of her foot. A blob of something that looked like wax was stuck to her heel. She pried it off and sniffed it. It even smelled like wax. She rolled it between her thumb and forefinger, booger-style, and flicked it into the waste basket.

She had no earthly idea how wax could've gotten on the bathroom floor. She hadn't burned any candles. She got down on her hands and knees and took a closer look at the linoleum. The entire bathroom floor was dotted with little blobs of wax. That's when it hit her—dripping wax, Kimmy's bald whoozit—she'd been waxing her whoozit and walking around the bathroom while she did it and it dripped and left burn holes where the hot wax had landed. Son-of-a-gun! Kimmy had ruined the linoleum.

Dana was furious. That was just like Kimmy to drip her pussy wax all over the linoleum and not even notice or care or take the time to scrape it up. In Kimmy World, the sun revolved around her pussy.

Unable to stand another second of pussy wax blobs on her floor, Dana ran downstairs to the kitchen, pulled the utensil drawer out of the cabinet and dumped its entire contents on top of the table. She picked a metal spatula out of the jumble of silverware and ran back the way she came, taking the stairs two at a time.

She threw open the bathroom door, dropped to her knees and began using the spatula as a lever to pry the blobs of pussy wax off the linoleum. One by one, the blobs popped off, leaving tiny burned pockmarks behind. The entire time she worked, Dana chanted a mantra under her breath, "I hate Kimmy I hate Kimmy's bald pussy I hate Kimmy I hate Kimmy's bald pussy."

Behind the chanting words Dana's brain kept sane by concocting the perfect plot for her book. It would be a revenge fantasy. The antagonist, Kimmy (she would change her name, of course), would meet her demise in a cruel death caused by her tragic flaw. In the final climatic scene of the book, Kimmy would meet a horrible and gruesome death. She would be run over by a train. No, that was too quick a death. Maybe Kimmy could jump from an airplane with a defective parachute. That would give her plenty of time to realize the wrongness of her ways. No, that might make the reader empathize with Kimmy, and Dana didn't want to create pathos. Maybe she could have Asscat gnaw through the brake lines on Kimmy's car and she would spiral out of control, fly off a cliff and smash to the ground.

"What're you doing with my pancake spatula, young lady?"

That question sucked all the air out of Dana's revenge fantasy and she looked up to see that the bathroom was clouded with steam from the hot water she had forgotten to turn off and Maw Maw was standing over her with her hands on her hips. Maw Maw's face was a putrid shade of green and she had a huge wart on her chin. She was wearing a black filmy dress and a pointy hat, and she was holding a broom.

"Did you let Trudy have her way with you?" Dana asked.

Maw Maw ignored the question by asking one of her own, "What're you doing with my best spatula?"

"Trying to pry this dried wax off the floor."

"How in the tarnation did you get wax all over the floor?"

"I didn't do it," is all Dana said.

"Kimmy?"

Dana didn't answer, which was as good as an answer.

"What the heck was she waxing in here anyway?" Maw Maw asked next.

Dana raised one eyebrow, giving her the "did you really have to ask" expression.

Maw Maw pursed her lips. "Remind me not to make pancakes with that spatula." She turned and headed for the door, mumbling, "I can't have anything nice in this house with you kids." She stopped, whipped around and poked the air between her and Dana with the bristly end of the broom, saying, "I put your new costume on your bed. Get dressed. You have five minutes." She sighed and all the bravado leaked out of her and her shoulders sagged. She walked away, dragging the broom behind her like a very sad, dejected witch. "I don't ask for much. One spatula. One measly little spatula and even that is…"

Crapola.

Dana totally forgot that it was Halloween. No wonder Maw Maw was so upset. Halloween was Maw Maw's favorite holiday and every year she made Dana dress up with her to hand out treats. Dana could forget Christmas or even Maw Maw's birthday, but if she was five minutes late for her annual Halloween candy handout, there would be hell to pay.

Dana's house was the highlight of the town's trick-or-treaters. Maw Maw thought the kids loved her costumes and sound effects recordings that she piped over the speakers she set in the windows. Dana knew better. The kids lined up halfway down the block for the full-size candy bars Maw Maw handed out.

Dana furiously bent back over the spatula, working on a big blob. She leaned her weight on the handle, hoping to get more leverage. The spatula curled under the extra pressure. She held it up and examined the damage. The spatula was completely bent in half. In a fit of anger, she threw it as hard as she could. It clanked off the wall and splashed into the tub.

Dana swiped her stringy hair out of her red, sweaty face and sat back on her haunches. The bathroom was like a sauna. She pulled on the front of her shirt, unplastering it from the sweat rings under her boobs. She closed her eyes and inhaled the hot, humid air.

She thought of an even better ending for her book: Kimmy could be using hair spray on her hair and smoking at the same time and her head would catch on fire *a la* Michael Jackson. Then her head would be as bald as her pussy. She would have a matched set. Her scalp would be so burned she'd have to have skin grafts. Doctors would take the skin from her butt and put it on her head and the next time Dana called her a butthead, it would be the truth.

* * *

After the firemen, Kimmy's entire apartment was smoke-filled and water-logged. There was no way she could stay there, so I gallantly offered my place. It only took one trip to pile everything she owned into the backseat of Betty—two suitcases, one passed-out dog, a toothbrush, a flat iron, a dog bowl, a blowdryer and half a bag of thawed corn. It all smelled like a campfire. Especially the dog.

After the cold shower I got from the fire department, I was stone cold sober and not sure I wanted to be. I knew that with Kimmy I was in over my head, but I didn't know what to do about it. I didn't even know if I wanted to do anything about it. All I knew was I wanted to get Kimmy out of my head and into my bed.

I drove with my hands on the wheel and one eye on the rear view mirror watching for any sign of life from Snickerdoodle. He was stretched out on top of the suitcase in the backseat. The only way I knew he was alive was because he hiccupped every other beat.

"It's so nice of you to offer me a place to stay," Kimmy said all formally-sounding like I hadn't gone down on her and given her the orgasm of her life. (Her words, not mine.)

I waved away her words with a devil-may-care toss of my hand. "I have lots of room. It's a big house, old, but big. Maw Maw lives with me, but in the mother-in-law house out back. She only comes in to cook, do laundry and stuff. You can stay as long as you want, you know, as long as you need to get back on your feet."

I pulled into the driveway of my house and shut off the engine. Betty's headlights were a little cockeyed and they shone eerily at the turret on the side of the house. My old house was built by my great-grandfather, Daniel Dooley. Daniel was a carpenter by trade. Unfortunately, he was missing his left arm. He was fond of telling anybody who would listen that he got caught in a bear trap and had to chew off his own arm to escape. That was a lie, but it was a good one, and most people believed it. He didn't let having only one arm stop him from building things. His career soared after he said he ate off his arm. People either liked the novelty of hiring him or they felt sorry for him. Either way, half the town hired him to build their new homes. Which explained why most of the houses in town listed several feet to the left.

My old house not only leaned several feet port side like a drunken sailor, but it sunk some in the middle too. It looked like a soufflé that had fallen in the oven.

"What's that thing?" Kimmy asked, pointing up.

"That's called a turret. They were originally designed as defensive fortification during the Middle Ages. You could shoot a gun from it and still be…" I could tell Kimmy had stopped listening because she was putting on a fresh coat of lipstick using a lighted compact mirror and humming to herself. The way the light shone up from the compact under her chin reminded me of the way kids shine a flashlight on their faces to tell a ghost story. I continued with my history lesson in a smaller voice, "It's decorative now. A little circular room. It's part of my bedroom."

"It looks like a giant penis," she said, snapping her compact shut.

I nodded. Maybe she was listening after all. "It's a phallic symbol. I've often thought it was designed as part of the house to symbolize power and virility…"

"I knew a guy once who had a dick like that. It kind of curved to the left."

Okay, so maybe she wasn't the smartest woman I'd ever met. But she did have redeeming qualities (*quali-titties?*).

"This is the historic district. There's lots of old architecture over here. Most of these houses were built in the early 1900s." Kimmy reopened her compact and this time she started powdering her face. I knew I would always be able to tell how bored she was by the layers of makeup she was wearing. To see if she was listening, I threw in, "There's a garage two doors down that looks like a vagina."

She clicked the compact shut again and looked at me. "Really?"

"Well, if you think about it," I said, "all garages resemble vaginas." There was a joke in there somewhere (*two-car garages? remote-controlled door?*), but I was too tired to excavate the funny out, so I changed the subject. "Do you mind if I ask you a personal question?"

She tossed her compact back in her purse and said with sigh, "I'll save you the trouble. I'm bisexual. Emphasis on sexual." She waggled her eyebrows up and down on that last part. "I don't have any debt. I don't have any emotional baggage. I like you, I don't know why except you're cute. And you're honest. And you're really good at the lesbian thing. I'm thirty years old. I've been married twice. I don't have any kids. I have a job. I like to party, but not too much. My favorite color is red. My parents are dead and I have no siblings. I'm not an axe murderer so you don't have to worry." She crossed her arms and raised her eyebrows. "Does that answer your question?"

"No, actually, I was going to ask if you had to remove your clit piercing to get through airport security."

She laughed and whapped me on the arm with the back of her hand. "Let's go in." She winked at me and licked her freshly coated upper lip. "I believe we have some unfinished business."

The lower half of my body woke up and cheered.

She climbed out of Betty, then leaned back in. "Get all my stuff, would you? And don't forget Snickerdoodle."

She gave me a big smackaroo of a kiss which involved a tiny bit of teasing with her tongue. She pranced toward the house. I quickly grabbed Snickerdoodle by the scruff and hauled him out of the car. "Asscat's going to love you," I said under my breath.

CHAPTER TEN

Dana didn't have a floor-length mirror in her house because she wasn't masochistic enough to want to see all of herself at the same time. So she balanced in her knee-high red vinyl boots on top of the toilet lid and looked into the mirror over the sink. (The boots came with the costume and they weren't real. They were shin-high spats that you wore over your own shoes, but if you squinted they looked almost real.)

All she could see in the mirror was the reflection of her strike zone—her knees to her shoulders. She twisted from side to side but still hated what she saw.

Dana liked her knees fine. She almost liked her shoulders. It was all the fat parts in between that nobody in their right mind would find appetizing. Unless you liked blue-ribbon hams. In her darkest hours, Dana always thought that she should marry a butcher. He would undress her on their wedding night and mutter seductively, "Nice marbling."

Maybe if she bought a taller mirror she wouldn't hate her reflection so much. She definitely looked better when you could also see her head. She'd always thought her head was her best feature.

She squatted until her head entered the frame of the mirror. She practiced smiling at herself. She looked like she was grimacing. From this vantage point she was all teeth and boobs.

She didn't know where the costume's cape was. That was one of her unwritten fashion rules: she didn't wear a costume unless it had a cape. (Maybe she should write it down.) That way her butt was hidden from view. Kind of like that giant head in the *Wizard of Oz*. Don't look behind the curtain.

It suddenly dawned on Dana what to do. She could wear her fuzzy blue bathrobe as a jimmy-rigged cape. It was even the same blue hue as the shorts.

She hopped off the toilet and grabbed the bathrobe off the hook over the door. She hurriedly tied the arms of the bathrobe around her neck and climbed back up on the toilet lid.

She checked herself out in the mirror again. Uh huh, exactly what she figured. The bathrobe-cape was working its magic. It completely hid her butt and draped down over her abundant thighs, disguising them as well. Dana discovered what full-figured women had known for years: this was the real reason superheroes wore capes.

If only she could do something about the tights. They were stretched so thin over her thighs that the red material looked pinkish. The tights' crotch was a good five inches below her own crotch and making her shorts ride too low. She pulled and stretched on the tights, trying to get the crotch up somewhere in the vicinity of her own but gave up when she realized she'd pushed the spandex to the breaking point. The package the costume came in said "One Size Fits Most."

Really? Most what? Most anorexics? Most nine-year-olds? Most Asian women?

Dana scratched her boob under the gold lame corset and then hefted both her girls skyward. The corset was tight enough to keep her boobs aloft for all of three seconds. Her boobs dropped and she gave up. She stuck her cell phone back in its hiding place under her left boob. She dismounted the toilet, faced the door and squared her shoulders. She took a deep breath and struck a heroic pose with her feet shoulder-width apart and her fists on her hips.

She heard the rip before she felt the draft of air on her butt. *On second thought, maybe this is why superheroes wore capes.*

Undeterred, Wonder Woman threw open the bathroom door and headed for the stairs.

* * *

As it turned out, Kimmy wasn't so bad at the lesbian thing either. In fact, she was good at it three times in a row. I was lying sprawled on my back, cross-wise on the bed in a post-coital daze, half-afraid that my clitoris was blistered. Kimmy had her arm and leg draped over me and I had this sudden crazy thought that she wasn't really cuddling, she was actually holding me down.

I turned my head and saw Snickerdoodle and Asscat lying at the top of the bed. Asscat had his front leg draped over the snoring dog. To the casual observer, it looked like they were in love. But I knew better. As soon as I fell asleep, Asscat would devour the unsuspecting poodle and in the morning all that would be left was a dog butthole on the pillow.

Kimmy leaned up on her elbow and looked down at me. Her face was close up, like I was sitting on the front row of a movie theatre. I could see straight up her nose.

"What're you thinking?" she asked.

I didn't want to tell her I was thinking about how I could see up her nose, so I said instead, "Umm…I was wondering why they call it coming when it really feels like you're going."

She laughed. "You know what I'm thinking?"

"Seven?"

"Huh?"

"I'm trying to guess what you're thinking. Is it a number between one and ten?"

"You're funny," she said. She lightly traced her fingernail around my left nipple. My right nipple got as hard as one of those bells on the counters at motels that you ding-donged for service.

"I'm thinking this could work," she said.

"What d'ya mean?" I squeaked in a Minnie Mouse voice.

"Us. I like us together. Don't you?"

"Uh huh," I said, thinking more about what she was doing to my body than what I may or may not have been agreeing to.

"Good," she said. She lowered her head and sucked my nipple into her mouth.

"I love us," I echoed. She slipped her thigh between my legs and my hips moved with a mind of their own.

She moved her mouth to my other nipple and murmured, "I could do this the rest of my life."

"Please do…"

She thrust her fingers deep inside me and I think she said, "Let's get married."

"God, yes," I said as I was going.

* * *

"Trick or treat, smell my feet, gimme something good to eat."

Dana thumped her forehead against the closed door and wished the trick-or-treaters standing on her front porch would go away. Far, far away.

She was one of those people who didn't think that children dressed up in costumes were cute. She also didn't think they were cute naked. She didn't think they were cute with birthday cake all over their faces. She didn't think they were cute when they ate out of the dog bowl or took baths in the kitchen sink. She didn't even think they were cute when they actually were cute.

Dana didn't like children. Children had problems metabolizing sugar and as a result they ran around the house, bouncing off the walls, screaming and flapping their arms. Children spun themselves in circles until they got so dizzy they fell down. Children wiped their noses with their shirt sleeves.

They ate their own boogers. They pooped their pants. They thought knock-knock jokes were funny. They thought farts were funny. (Well, okay, farts *were* pretty funny.) They made fun of other kids who were fat and called them names like Fatso and Fatty Patty and Two-Ton Dana.

But to be honest and completely fair, Dana didn't like grownups too much either. She knew some adults who ate their own boogers and told knock-knock jokes. Heck, she'd even gone to prom with a guy who had pooped his pants on their first date.

His name was Steve Snackenberger and he was an All-State linebacker. He asked her out on a date and Dana said yes because she was going through a rough patch of adolescence. She thought maybe she had decided at too early of an age to be homosexual and maybe she should give bisexuality a try. Steve had glasses that sat crooked on his face and the lenses were always smeared and greasy. Dana wanted to clean his glasses. That was her goal for the evening; get his glasses off his face and give them a good cleaning.

Steve took her to Long John Silver's. It was awkward and was glaringly obvious that the date was going to suck ass. In fact, that was exactly what Steve said while they waited on their order. "This date sucks ass." Dana agreed even though she was polite enough not to say it out loud.

As soon as they sat down at a table with their paper boats of fried food, Steve glared at her through his dirty glasses, got up and, without a word, walked away. Dana waited on him to return. She nibbled at her meal while she waited. Fifteen minutes of nibbling later, she'd eaten her chicken planks and fries. After another ten minutes, she picked up Steve's paper boat and walked out to the parking lot, halfway expecting to see that he'd left her behind. But his Camaro was still there.

Dana walked up to the car. Steve was sitting inside with his forehead resting on the steering wheel. She rapped on the windshield. "Steve?"

"Huh," he grunted.

She held the paper boat out toward him. "Here's your Super Sampler and corn cobbette."

He glanced at her and rolled the window down two inches. "I crapped my pants," he said.

"What?"

He looked away. "I think I must be sick or something. I sharted," he said louder.

"That's what I thought you said."

"I'm going." He started the engine.

"Okay," Dana said, "but can you drop me home first?"

He snapped his head in her direction and screamed, "What part about 'I sharted' don't you understand!" His spittle dotted the window. Dana took a step back. Steve threw the car in reverse and backed all the way out the lot, swerving onto Main Street. He threw the car into D and peeled out.

Dana watched him drive away. She walked home, nibbling on his Super Sampler until it was nibbled away. She threw the overcooked, mushy corn cobbette into a rain ditch.

The next Monday at school Steve walked up to her in front of all his jock friends and asked her out to the prom. "Yes" jumped out of her mouth before she even thought about it. She didn't want to be the only girl in the school who didn't go to her own senior prom. Even Wacky Jackie had a date to the prom and the doctors kept her unstable mind so doped up there was a permanent wet streak down the front of her shirt from her drool.

Prom wasn't all it was cracked up to be. All Dana did was dance a couple of times with Trudy, drink a cup of spiked punch, throw up in the girls' room and start her period. Steve left her halfway through the evening to go cow-tipping with his drunk friends. She didn't get a chance to clean his glasses. A couple of days later, she heard a rumor that she had jacked off Steve in the backseat of his Camaro during prom. She tried to start a revenge rumor that he had sharted in his pants at Long John Silver's, but nobody believed her.

Dana hated trick-or-treaters almost as much as she had hated high school. After she thumped her head against her front door thirty-three times, she opened it and found a sugar-crazed mob of children in costume. They were dressed as ballerinas and princesses and a couple of OU football players and an army man, and there was even a teenager that looked like Paris Hilton. Dana couldn't tell if she was in a Paris costume or if she had dressed normally and looked like Paris. Either way, she didn't like her.

She put a Tootsie Roll in each paper sack and all the kids put on their frowny sad faces. One of the princesses even squeezed out a moan and a tear. A football player wiped his snotty nose on his sleeve. The camouflaged army man pushed his way to the front of the mob and asked, "What happened to the big Snickers candy bars? You always give out Snickers."

"Not this year."

"I waited fifteen minutes in line to get up here! I want a Snickers!"

"I'm saving them for me," Dana said, shutting the door in his face.

"You have an assface!" he shouted through the door.

Dana leaned her back against the door and popped a Tootsie Roll into her mouth.

Maw Maw hustled into the room with another big bowl of sugar-inducing hyperness for the little trolls masquerading as trick-or-treaters. Dana grabbed for bag of peanut M&M's and Maw Maw slapped them out of her hand.

"Your brother called," she said.

"So?"

"He's in trouble again," she sighed.

"So?"

"You can either go rescue him or hand out candy. Your choice."

"Where's he at?"

"Tanner's field."

The doorbell rang. And rang. And rang. Dana peeked through the peephole and saw the red-faced army man. He screamed, "I want my Snickers bar! This is the Snickers house where the lady gives out full-size Snickers and I want my freakin' Snickers!"

Dana quickly grabbed the squirt bottle full of water from the side table (she used it to spray Asscat when he scratched the side of the couch or when she got bored and wanted to see him run around the room) and opened the door.

"Make my day," Dana said to the green army man.

"I want my Snickers!"

Dana shot a stream of water right into his assface.

Army man fell on his butt, wet and sputtering. She aimed and shot another stream of water at his crotch for good measure. "Don't mess with Wonder Woman," Dana said.

She closed the door and smiled at Maw Maw. "I'll go get Matt."

* * *

When I woke up the sun was bright and I was alone in bed. I could hear the shower on in the bathroom. I was lying on the bed with my feet at the top and my head at the bottom. The entire room smelled feral.

The door opened a crack and Maw Maw stuck her head in. I pulled the covers over myself.

"Breakfast is ready," she said.

"I think I'm engaged," I blurted. "Or maybe even married."

"Married? To a man?"

"No, silly. To a woman. And I know two women can't get married in Oklahoma, but I think somebody forgot to tell her that."

Maw Maw looked toward the bathroom, registered that somebody was in there and then looked back at me. "Don't be making important decisions when you're naked, Dana. Take it from me, it never works out the way you think it will."

"But Paw Paw and you got married after only one week of knowing each other."

"Exactly." She closed the door behind her as Kimmy emerged from the bathroom wrapped only in a towel.

"Do you love me?" I asked in that needy tone that I hated when other women used it on me.

"I used your loofah sponge, didn't I?" she said like that was an answer to my question. She dropped the towel and I immediately forgot about everything else.

Seven days and thirty-five orgasms later, I asked Kimmy, "Are you sure you love me?

She replied, "I gave you half my tuna fish sandwich, didn't I?"

One month later, I asked, "Do you really love me?"

She smiled, patted my hand and said, "You got a free haircut, didn't you?"

Three months later, "Do you love me?"

"I'm home, aren't I?"

Six months went by and I asked again, "Do you love me?"

She said offhandedly, "You ask too many questions."

A couple of weeks ago I asked her again and she said on her way out the door, "I'd love you more if you'd do a load of laundry for me.'"

What a difference a year made. Kimmy didn't come home all the time or even most of the time. She stayed out all night three, maybe four, times a week. She had headaches and backaches and we never had sex.

She began charging me for haircuts and never offered me half her tuna.

I was beginning to think she didn't really love me in the first place.

* * *

Judge Tanner's cornfield didn't have any corn and hadn't as long as Dana could remember. It was actually a makeshift airport landing strip. (Judge Tanner had his own airplane and used his field as he pleased.) The location was also used for traveling carnivals to set up their midway and rides every spring. By the time Dana drove Betty out onto the field, half the town had already beat her there.

She parked as close to the crowd as she could get without running over anybody. She squeezed through the mob, bumping people out of her way with her shoulders and hips to could get a good look-see. She craned her neck and saw Fat Matt, wearing what looked like a diaper, standing in the middle of an enormous mowed-down circle with his cell phone in one hand and a blue light saber in the other. He was swinging the saber around like

Han Solo on speed. Or maybe more like Chewbacca with a bad case of mange.

She wasn't at all surprised to find the mayor of Dooley Springs wearing only an adult diaper standing in the middle of a corn field waving a light saber. Dana knew what most other people didn't. Fat Matt wasn't crazy. He was not only sane but was a card-carrying member of MENSA. In high school he was voted "Most Likely to Succeed." Instead, the summer after he gave the valedictorian speech (and the day after his one day as a gainfully employed, chicken neck-wringing citizen), Matt stayed in his bedroom for three months without coming out. Maw Maw brought him meals on a tray and dumped out the Folger's can he used as a bedpan three times a day. At the end of his self-imprisonment, he had typed out a seventy-five page, single-spaced thesis aptly titled *Matt's Manifesto*. In it he detailed how he was going to "beat the system" by "never working for The Man." He vowed that he would always "suck off the government's teat."

Dana knew that Matt was a misguided genius with a brain the size of Jupiter living inside a hairy, fat man's body. The psychiatrist who prescribed him drugs diagnosed Matt as SICK (Sensitive, Intelligent, Creative and Kind). Matt had never worked a day in his life (okay, he did work that one day at the chicken plant) and was elected mayor by a vote of 13,526 to 89. Nobody ran against him because he kept talking about "taking them to the mattress" in a professional wrestler's voice. Not very many people in town were up on Italian mob lingo, and they thought taking them to the mattress meant he was going to mate with them or something. (The 89 votes against Matt were write-ins, ranging from Daffy Duck to Oprah Winfrey. Dana herself had voted for Ellen Degeneres so Portia could be first lady.)

Before he was elected mayor, Fat Matt sucked on the government's teat for a while—as a guinea pig for the FDC. They gave him new drugs and tested him; most of those drugs never made it out of the lab and onto drugstore shelves. He did that job for three years and was never quite the same. Since then, however, Matt felt he owed his full head of luxurious hair (and a body covered with the same thick pelt) to something he called "Rogaine gone rogue."

Matt viewed his only job as mayor was to put Dooley Springs on the map. He did have a modicum of success seven years ago when he climbed a tree and said he wouldn't come down until David Letterman asked him to be a guest on his show. Mr. Letterman ignored him until one day after three weeks, Matt accidentally fell out of the tree and broke his tailbone. Then David Letterman officially announced that his home office was in Dooley Springs, Oklahoma, and made Matt's mishap #1 in his top ten list of "Ten Stupid Ways to Get on National TV."

Dana knew that whatever Matt was up to in the cornfield with the light saber was another prank designed to create a buzz for the upcoming mayoral election. She watched for a few moments. Some of the braver souls were throwing hard candy at Matt. The woman next to Dana threw a Dum Dum; it hit Fat Matt square in the middle of his belly and bounced off.

Dana tapped the woman on the shoulder and asked what was happening. The woman threw another Dum Dum like she was playing third base and a runner was trying to steal home. The sucker hit Matt in the butt and he yelped. The crowd laughed.

"Excuse me," Dana said again, "but what's going on?"

The woman looked Dana up and down. She tossed a Dum Dum up in the air several times and caught it without looking at it. "Who you supposed to be?"

"Wonder Woman."

The woman gave Dana a judgmental look before she said, "He says that aliens landed here. He says that's a crop circle he's standing in made by one of their spaceships. I heard about it over my police scanner and called up some people."

"Oh." Dana digested this and watched Matt bat away hard candy and Tootsie Pops with his light saber like he was Babe Ruth. "Why's he wearing a diaper?"

The woman unwrapped the Dum Dum and stuck it in her mouth. She sucked on it for a second, then plucked it out of her mouth with a loud pop. "He says the aliens beamed him outta his own bed while he was sleeping. He says they looked like Star Wars characters. Then Princess Leia probed him a couple of times and set him back down here. He wrapped that sheet around hisself so as not to offend the children with the nakedness of his violated orifices."

"Violated orifices?"

"His words, not mine."

"But why're you all throwing candy at him?"

She shrugged. "'Cause it's funny."

It was funny, watching him get pelted with Jolly Ranchers. Especially when they dinged off his butt and made him jump. Dana pushed through the mob, working her way toward Matt.

"You mowed that circle yourself!" shouted a man from behind.

"I most certainly did not, sir!" Fat Matt shouted back, holding his saber skyward like the Statue of Liberty. "This circle is what is left of the UFO landing."

A man in front shook his fist at Matt. "You mowed it! I ain't no idjit! There's the tractor you did it with!"

Dana's eyes followed to where the man was pointing. Sure enough, there sat a tractor with a thresher hooked up to the back and some damning, freshly mowed grass stuck between its blades.

The same man shouted again, "How do you explain that?"

"Yeah!" the crowd shouted in unison.

Matt took a moment to scratch under one arm. "The aliens mowed it?"

"Fraud!" people shouted.

"Liar!" others yelled.

The crowd was growing a mind of its own and its mind was turning ugly.

Dana knew about herd behavior and mob mentality because she had seen the movie *The Accused* where Jodie Foster got raped on a pinball machine by a pack of frat boys. She didn't want the same thing to happen to her brother even though the nearest pinball machine was several miles away, so she pushed people out of the way and ran toward him, screaming, "Don't rape him! Please, please don't rape my brother, can't you see how homely he is!"

A brilliant, blinding flash of white light stopped Dana as she grabbed the back of Fat Matt's diaper. For one frozen moment, Dana was pulling on the diaper and Matt's giant heinie was all bright and shiny. He looked like a grotesque version of that old Coppertone commercial with the dog pulling down the little girl's panties.

Dana caught a glimpse of CeCe White. She was in another one of her Hawaiian print mumus and popping off flashes with her camera. Fat Matt saw her too and quickly morphed into celebrity mode. He struck poses with his saber as if he fancied himself as a modern-day Errol Flynn.

Matt's posturing seemed to enrage the herd, and they stampeded forward with thundering hooves and gnashing teeth. Dana grabbed Matt by the elbow and propelled him on a circuitous route toward her car. CeCe snapped photos until the crowd blocked her view.

Fat Matt dove headfirst into Betty and Dana jumped in the driver's seat. She pulled her cape safely inside the car, then slammed her door shut.

"Let's go!" Matt shouted.

"Mind the hole in the floorboard!" Dana hollered. Matt picked up his feet and Dana mashed down on the gas pedal. Betty's rusty frame bounced over pasture bumps as Dana honked and swerved around the mob.

Dana reached the far end of the pasture before she looked behind her. The crowd had mostly given up; only a few young ones were still giving chase. She wheeled through a ditch, almost sending them topsy-turvy, but Matt leaned against his door and that extra weight kept them upright. They bounced out of the ditch and onto the gravel road. They rode in silence for a moment.

"What the hell, Matt?"

"I bet ol' CeCe will have that in tomorrow's paper," he said gleefully, rubbing his palms together.

"Tell me this is some harebrained publicity stunt and you don't think Princess Leia really put anything up your butt."

He grinned. "Election's comin' up. People will reelect me to have something to talk about."

Dana glared at him. "What if I hadn't been there? What if I didn't rescue your big, hairy butt? What if this whole thing had backfired and they'd stoned you with Jolly Ranchers?"

"But they didn't," he said as if that made sense to anybody but himself.

"You're an idiot."

"No, you are," he taunted.

"No, you are."

"You are."

"You."

"I know you are, but what am I?" he sing-songed.

She doubled up her fist and socked him as hard she could. She was aiming for his chin but got his shoulder instead.

"Ow!"

"Shut up," Dana fumed.

"You shut up."

"You shut up."

"No, you shut up!" He socked Dana in the arm.

She let go of the wheel and threw a couple of wild punches at him, connecting with only air.

"Watch out!" he yelled.

Dana grabbed the steering wheel and jerked it hard to the left, almost but not quite careening into the rain ditch.

As soon as the car was traveling on a straight path, Dana elbowed Fat Matt in his ribs.

"Ow! Quit hitting," he whined. "Or I'm gonna tell Maw Maw."

"Don't make me stop this car," she warned, tapping on the brakes.

He crossed his arms and leaned against his door where she couldn't elbow him. After about two miles of silence, he said, "I was thinking that after this Kimmy thing was over for you…"

"You mean after I find her cheating on me and throw her butt to the curb?"

"Yeah that. I was wondering if you could put the lesbian thing on hold for a while?"

"What d'ya mean?"

"Maybe you could pretend to be straight for a while? Like go out with my friend Doobie a couple of times or something?"

"Doobie? Are you serious?"

"He told me once that he's really a woman trapped inside a man's body. So, that makes him kind of a lesbian too."

"He sells tie-dye clothes at the flea market for a living and smells like horse manure."

"He's into organic farming is all. And the deal is...my reelection is coming up and I figure I'd have a better chance without a lesbo for a sister. You know, since I ran on the Republican ticket..."

Dana screeched Betty to a stop and if the dashboard hadn't stopped him, Matt would've sailed through the front windshield. She leaned over him, popped open his door and used her feet to kick her brother out of her car and onto the side of the road.

"What'd you do that for?" he asked.

"You're lucky I stopped the car first."

She zoomed off with the passenger door flapping open and shut, open and shut. When she squealed her tires around the next left, the door slammed closed on its own.

CHAPTER ELEVEN

After giving her brother the heave-ho, Dana took the long way home so she could do a drive-by of all the local bars. She drove through the lots of every one of them, but still there was no sign of Kimmy's Mustang.

She slowed down as she drove by The Best Little Hairhouse. There was a light on inside the building. Weird. It was nine o'clock at night and Halloween to boot. Either somebody was working late or Wanda had left a light burning, which, knowing the tightness of Wanda's wallet, was highly unlikely.

Dana guided Betty around the block and parked in the alley. She reasoned that she better investigate the light because if the beauty shop was being burgled and she didn't stop it, she would never forgive herself. And, hey, Wanda gave her a key and wouldn't it be the Christian thing to stop and save Wanda a little on her electric bill?

Dana closed Betty's door real quiet-like, pulled her bathrobe-cape around her shoulder and crept down the alley toward the beauty shop. The first thing she ran into was Kimmy's Mustang.

Literally. She didn't see it until she banged into it and Dooleyed over the hood.

Dana hadn't been expecting a car to be parked in the middle of the alley. Interesting. Kimmy chose not to park her car in the beauty shop's parking lot, which meant she didn't want anybody to know where she was.

Didn't take a Stephen Hawking to figure out why.

Dana slid off the car and placed her hand on the hood like how they do in mystery movies. It was cold. Kimmy had been there a while. Dana squatted down so as not to be seen and duck-walked around the car and up to the back window of the building where the light was burning.

She raised up slowly and peered through the window. She saw Kimmy reclined in her beautician's chair. Her mouth was moving like she was talking to somebody. There must be somebody in the back room.

Dana sneezed. The force of the sneeze snapped her neck forward and she banged her forehead on the window pane.

Kimmy quickly swiveled in her chair and looked at the window. Kimmy and Dana's eyes met for a split second, then Dana ducked.

Dana wasn't sure whether Kimmy saw her or not. And if she did see her, did she recognize her? Impossible to tell.

Only one way to find out. Dana slowly, ever-so-slowly, raised back up and looked through the window. She found herself face-to-face with Kimmy.

They each yelped and ducked.

This was exactly what Dana was afraid of. Kimmy had caught her, instead of the other way around. And since Kimmy had obviously seen her, Dana stood back up. No sense in hiding now.

Dana didn't see Kimmy. Odd. She pressed her nose against the glass and looked as far to either side as she could. There she was. Kimmy was standing near the back storage room. She was shouting something, Dana could hear her voice, but she couldn't make out the words. Dana was a pretty good lip reader though, because once her TV set went on an audio fritz and she watched it for three whole months without sound before she finally figured out that Asscat had sat on the mute button on the remote. Dana watched Kimmy's lips move and was pretty sure she was saying something like "Call the police! There's a mad woman outside trying to kill me! She has a chainsaw!" Of course, the part about the chainsaw might be her over active imagination.

I might have an overactive imagination, but Kimmy has an overactive vagination.

A blast of bright light hit Dana from behind and pinned her to the brick wall. She quickly turned into the light and had to shield her eyes with her hands. She heard a siren "Wooooot" like a slide whistle. Dana peeked between her fingers. Red and blue lights flashed up and down the bar on top of a police vehicle.

A voice boomed over the speaker mounted on top of the police car. "Step away from the window! Put the weapon down!"

Weapon?

"Put the weapon down!"

Dana looked down and only then did she realize that she was holding a big chunk of concrete in her hand. She had no recollection of picking it up. Maybe somebody put it in her hand, trying to frame her. Maybe that somebody was Kimmy. But wouldn't she know if Kimmy had put something in her hand?

Oh my God! Dana realized what was happening. She was going insane. The flashing lights tap danced across her vision and she blinked. She could hear her own rapid breathing inside her head. Or was that her heart pounding? She was going to pass out. She could make out the silhouette of a police officer, but it was like looking down a tunnel.

The megaphone roared. "This is the Dooley Springs police! Put down the weapon!"

Dana dropped the hunk of concrete. Unfortunately, she dropped it on her right foot. "Shoot a brick!" she shouted, grabbing her foot in her hand and hopping up and down. "Dang, dang, dang!"

The cruiser door opened and Officer Drumright climbed out. He hitched his pants up, hooked his thumbs through his belt loops and stared at Dana.

Dana recognized her old nemesis and stopped hopping. She put one hand on her hip and affected a casual, yet superior stance. "Hey ya, Puddinhead. Slow night?"

Puddinhead's God-given name was Wilson Drumright. He and Dana had been enemies since grade school. Dana was responsible for giving him the moniker Puddinhead. She was a big Mark Twain fan, even in grade school. Puddinhead didn't like the nickname and he didn't like Dana either.

It didn't help matters when she got him drunk on Everclear and Mountain Dew at their senior class graduation party and talked him out of his pants. Once he was sporting only his tidy whities, Dana gave his pants to Steve Snackenberger. Steve and the football team made Puddinhead put his pants on backwards and walk around backwards all night.

Dana feigned a sudden interest in her fingernails and muttered, "Got your pants on right tonight, I see."

Puddinhead pulled his gun and aimed it somewhere in the general vicinity of Dana's kneecaps. "Dammit, Dana Dooley, how many times I got to tell you to call me Officer Drumright?"

Dana decided to play by his rules. Seemed the most sensible thing to do when a gun was aimed at you. "Officer Drumright," she smiled in what she hoped was a genuine fashion. "I saw a light burning in the beauty shop and stopped to check it out. Wanda's one of my customers. Didn't want her to get robbed or anything. You know Halloween's kinda crazy…" Her voice trailed off and her smile twitched nervously.

He took a menacing step toward Dana. He kicked the hunk of concrete she'd been holding. "What were you planning on doing with that rock?"

Dana was at a loss. Even she didn't know why she was holding it in her hand while she looked through a window at her cheating girlfriend. Puddinhead was notoriously stupid, but even stupid could connect those dots. "I was…I wanted to… self-defense?"

He looked past her head at the window. "I don't see no light burning in there."

"She turned it out when you drove up?" It came out sounding more like a question than the statement that Dana intended. She cleared her throat and tried again. "She turned it out. It was on. Then out. She turned it out to make me look guilty."

Gosh, why can't I shut up? I'm acting guilty and I haven't even done anything.

"She?"

"Kimmy. My girlfriend." Dana was struck with a sudden inspiration. Well, okay, it was more female instincts than it was inspiration. She stuck out her lower lip and forced it to wobble. She tried for a quiver, but it came out more like a wobble. She made her voice sound all soft and trembly. "My girlfriend's cheating on me."

"Hell, everybody knows that." Puddinhead snorted.

Dana's anger lit up. She quickly put a lid on it and croaked, "Okay, I was spying on her, all right? I was trying to catch her, you know. Then I could tell her to get lost. I need to know who she's cheating on me with."

Puddinhead stowed his gun back in his holster and blew hot air through his lips, making them do that raspberry thing that sounded like a fart but only with his mouth. "Better question might be who *ain't* she cheating on you with."

That was exactly what Dana didn't want to hear. "Will you go in there?" she asked. "Can you at least help me out that much? Go peek inside and see who she's in there with. I can't bear to look."

"She inside?"

Dana nodded.

"I got no good reason to go in there," he said. "I'm not in the habit of stopping two consenting adults from doing whatever they want to do as long as it ain't hurting nobody."

"It's hurting me," she said. Two tears leaked out of her eyes. She didn't plan for that to happen. Her bottom lip quivered for real, and she swiped at her tears with the hem of her bathrobe-cape.

"Karma's a real bitch, ain't she?" he said.

Why did he say "she?" Why is it men think everything bad like karma and tornadoes are she?

A bell jingled. Dana recognized it as the bell to the front door of the beauty shop. She panicked.

She's getting away!

Dana sprinted for the front of the building and rounded the corner in time to see the back of somebody disappearing around the far corner. The bells jangled again when the front door closed on its own.

"Hold it right there! I'll shoot, Dana Dooley, you know I will!"

Dana looked over her shoulder and saw Puddinhead aiming his gun at her and looking like a B-film version of Robocop. This time his gun was pointed at her chest.

Dana decided to call his bluff, see what he was made of. "You gonna shoot me?" she asked.

"Run away again, you'll find out."

"This isn't about tonight, is it?"

The questions seemed to confuse him. His gun wavered.

"It's about you. It's about me and you."

"I don't know what you're getting at," he said.

"It's about graduation night. It's about trying to get in my pants and ending up with your pants on backwards."

"And wrong side out," he added.

"You going to shoot me 'cause of what happened years ago?" Her nose itched. It must be because of that English Leather smell he emitted. She rubbed at her nose with the back of her hand and sniffed twice. "You going to shoot me dead 'cause your pride got hurt?"

"No," he said, grinning. His tiny rabbit teeth gleamed in the dark. "I'm going to arrest you first. I won't shoot unless you resist arrest."

He looked for all the world like he meant what he said. Dana rubbed harder at the itch in her nose and wiped at it with the sleeve of her bathrobe-cape. She knew that Puddinhead had been spoiling for a fight with her since they were seven years old. "Okay, then," she said. "Let's get this over with. Cuff me." She held her wrists out in front of her.

He reached around behind him for his cuffs, letting his aim drop and that was all the opening Dana needed. She twirled and ran.

Pop!

He was shooting at her! The gravel in front of her jumped like popcorn in a microwave.

Pop! Pop!

A brick in the wall in front of her exploded. A second later gravel jumped and bit her in the ass. Instinctually, she lifted her feet one after the other, quickly, like she was doing her own version of *Riverdance*.

Dana knew her choices were to either be a sitting duck or she could run, so she chose to run. She darted back and forth, zigging and zagging like in the old Westerns.

Pop! Pop! Pop!

Dana rounded three corners of the building until she was back where she began. She needed to get back to her car. She quickly changed directions and ran into the alley.

Honk! Honk!

Dana flung herself headfirst out of the oncoming car's way. She ended up doing a forward diving roll that would have made an Olympic gymnast proud. When she got back to her feet, she saw the rear end of Kimmy's Mustang tear around the corner.

Dana sneezed.

Next, she spun on her heels and…

Puddinhead tore around the side of the building, gun drawn and ready, and ran smack dab into her. They tumbled to the ground and rolled over several times before Puddinhead came out on top.

Dana was actually a little relieved to be caught. After all the running, whizzing, twirling, spinning, zigging and zagging, almost getting mowed down by Kimmy's car, not to mention shot at, she felt like she had been the star of an elaborately choreographed bullet ballet. And she was plumb tuckered.

Puddinhead straightened up and aimed his gun right between her eyes.

"I give up," Dana said. "Calf-rope and uncle. I'll go peacefully. Just don't shoot me in the head."

He holstered his gun and pulled out his cuffs. Dana sneezed again, spraying his face.

"Sorry, I'm allergic to men," she said. She would have wiped her nose, but he was pinning her arms to the ground with his knees. Instead, she snuffled.

The snuffling had the reverse desired effect and Dana reared back and let loose with a monster of a sneeze. She felt something shoot through her nasal cavity and explode out her right nostril. She had no idea what it was until she saw it embedded in his forehead. It was her temporary crown. Her second molar crown had come unglued again and she had sneezed it through her nose. It bullseyed Puddinhead in the middle of his forehead.

He looked surprised for a split-second, then he rolled his eyes back and keeled over.

She panicked and—

Holy Mother of Crapola, I killed him.

—bucked his limp body to the side, clambered to her feet and hopped into his police cruiser, which was still running with its lights flashing. She burned rubber, swerving onto the street and followed the direction that Kimmy's Mustang had disappeared.

Her breath came in short bursts and echoed in her ears. She was hyperventilating.

I'm a wanted woman now. Wanted for murder. Not any old murder either, but the murder of a police officer.

Dana made a couple of turns, the gas pedal pressed all the way to the floorboard, tires squealing, when she saw Kimmy's Mustang sitting at a red light.

She was filled with a cold rage that froze the blood in her veins.

If it wasn't for her, I wouldn't be in this mess.

Holding on to that one thought, she pulled the police cruiser up behind the Mustang. She picked up the handheld microphone, flipped the toggle switch, and shouted over the cruiser's speaker, "Kimmy, pull over!" Her voice reverberated through the roof. She liked how authoritative she sounded when her voice was amplified.

Kimmy floored the Mustang, shooting through the red light. Dana pursued her, yelling into the mike, "Kimmy, pull your car over! We need to talk!"

Kimmy looked over her shoulder and flipped Dana the bird. Dana mashed the accelerator all the way to the floor, yelling, "I saw you back there! I saw you porking somebody in The Best Little Hairhouse!"

Kimmy made a right turn without signaling. Dana followed, taking the turn on two wheels. A group of trick-or-treaters jumped back on the sidewalk as she whipped around the corner, screaming into the mike, "Kimmy Barnes is a two-timing slut!"

Dana caught up to the Mustang and tapped its back fender with her front fender. She shouted into the mike, "Pull over, you slut!"

Kimmy swerved into the next alley and raced to the end. Dana squealed her tires behind her. "Kimmy is a whore!" she announced. "She's a harlot. A hussy, a strumpet!"

Kimmy made a left turn. A kid on a bicycle darted into the alley, forcing Dana to slam on her brakes, narrowly missing the bike's back tire and spinning the police car into a donut of rubber and smoke. The kid fell over and quickly crab crawled to the sidewalk.

Dana yelled at the kid over the mike, "Didn't your mother ever tell you to look before you cross?"

She straightened the cruiser out and looked left. No sign of Kimmy. She turned right onto Main Street. The street was filled with costumed looky-loos wondering what all the noise and excitement was about. Seeing all the people staring at her gave Dana an idea. If she couldn't catch Kimmy, she'd do the next best thing. She would broadcast Kimmy's whoredom to the entire town.

Dana guided the cruiser, lights flashing, slowly down the street as if she were grand marshall in a parade. She spoke calmly and enunciated, "Kimmy Barnes is a slut! She screws anything that moves. Lock up your husbands! Lock up your wives! She is a tramp, a vamp and a floozy! Kimmy Barnes has crabs and diseases and her hoo-ha is bald. It's from the mange. If you see her bald hoo-ha, don't touch it. Step away from the bald hoo-ha. Kimmy Barnes is a walking contagion of sexually transmitted diseases. She is patient zero of STDs. Kimmy Barnes is a sex addict, a nymphomaniac, and she's not a nice person!"

Dana heard a police siren. She twisted in her seat and looked out the back window.

Crapola, it's a police car. They're going to lock me up and put me on the chain gang cutting down weeds beside the road.

She debated trying to outrun the police car, but that turned out to be a moot point when she saw two more police cars headed straight for her.

They have me cornered. I'm going to have to shoot my way out. Wait. I don't have a gun.

She slammed on the brakes and threw the car in park. She might go down, but she wouldn't go down without a fight. She spoke over the microphone, "Why don't you all go arrest Kimmy Barnes? She's the one who should be put away. Put her behind bars!"

The door was thrown open and a gun kissed her nose. Dana dropped the microphone. Puddinhead was holding her at gunpoint. He looked alive and no worse for wear unless you counted the temporary crown that was embedded in the middle of his forehead.

He grabbed Dana by the arm and roughly pulled her out of the cruiser. He threw her up against the hood, frisking her like he expected to find a concealed weapon in her tights.

The other cops were out of their cars and circled around Dana with their guns drawn.

Stupid hick cops are standing in a circle. All I have to do is duck and they'll shoot each other.

She laughed. She knew that maniacal laughter was making her seem more insane and out of control, so she choked back her hysterics and said, "I think you guys are overreacting. Any of you would've done the same thing if you'd caught your girlfriend cheating on you."

A burst of white light caused Dana to flinch. She blinked and caught a glimpse of CeCe White with her camera aimed right at her, snapping away.

Puddinhead pushed her nose into the car's hood, pulled her wrists behind her back and snapped on the cuffs. He grabbed her by the elbow and pulled her to the car's back door. He opened the door, put her hand on top of her head and pushed her into the back seat.

She waited until Puddinhead was settled behind the wheel before she asked, "Can I have my crown back now?"

"Nope," he said. "It's evidence."

* * *

I was in love/lust with Lisa Number Four for about half a day, if that long. I met her in the parking lot at the hospital. I had gone there to stick my Slave Labor flyers under all the car windshields.

I found her sitting in her car bawling her eyes out. This was one of those situations where I didn't know whether to offer comfort or ignore her and tend to my own business.

My nurturing instincts won out and I rapped on her car window. She looked up at me through a river of tears and our gazes locked for a brief moment before her eyes rolled back in her head. She made a weird hiccupping, shrill noise down deep in her throat like a dog's squeaky toy when you step on it. She shivered, sighed, then rolled her window down halfway.

Even with the puffy eyes and the tears and snot dripping onto her upper lip, she was stunning. Black hair, blue eyes, porcelain complexion. One of my very first crushes was on Snow White and that's exactly who she looked like. Without the bluebirds flying around her head, of course.

"Are you okay?" I asked.

She nodded, but fresh tears started dripping, so I said, "I was dropping off some flyers, but...I saw you crying and...do you need any help?"

"I was diagnosed with PGAD," she sputtered. "There's no cure. There's no hope." She wah-wah'ed loudly and then snorted, "It's hopeless."

I'd never heard of that disease, but any illness with an acronym had to be bad. I had no idea how long she was expected to live and asking a question like that might be construed as rude under the circumstances.

"How can I help?" I asked. I was hoping she would say that I couldn't help and she had it all under control, but instead she smiled with those bright red bow-shaped lips and answered, "You probably don't have time to babysit me." She swiped at her face with her jacket sleeve and looked pitiful. If she were a puppy, I'd take her home and rub her belly.

I knew a cry for help when I heard one, so I put on my Good Sam hat and offered, "Well, I can always do these flyers tomorrow. And you look like you could use a friend. You want to follow me in your car and we can go back to my house? I'm sure we can figure something out and deal with this."

I was thinking I'd give her some hot tea and maybe make a few phone calls to her relatives. Maybe I'd even call over at the Baptist church and see if somebody wanted to start a prayer circle or hold a bean supper or whatever those people do when somebody's dying. Lisa Four and I were barely inside my front door before she grabbed my hand and stuck it down the front of her pants. She shivered, eye-rolled and made that squeak-squeak noise again…this time it sounded like a hamster wheel spinning. It took me a while to realize that was the sound she made when she came.

She ripped my pants off, threw me down onto the stairs and rubbed herself against me like she was sanding the varnish off an old table with her crotch. This time she squeaked a little then let loose with a bullroar of an orgasm.

She did that five more times before we could even get upstairs to my bedroom.

For the next twenty-seven hours we rolled around the room like two cats trapped in a paper sack. I had ten, maybe twelve orgasms until I was completely gazzed out. Lisa Four had, I don't know, I lost count when I blacked out, but I know she had somewhere in the vicinity of three hundred orgasms.

We had sex every way possible and some ways not so possible. By the next morning, my chin and lips were chapped and bleeding. My thighs were rubbed raw. My hoo-ha was swollen and throbbing and I think my clitoris had defected and gone AWOL.

I was done. I knew without a doubt she was going to kill me if I didn't make her stop. I pushed her away and gasped, "What's PGAD?"

"Persistent Genital Arousal Disorder."

That explained it.

"I don't think I ever want to have sex again," I said.

"Me either," she said, humping my pillow. Her eyes rolled back in her head and her eyelids twitched. "Eek eek eek eek," she squeaked, followed by a long "Aaaahhhhhh."

She collapsed on top of the pillow. Ten seconds later her hips were thrusting again.

I jumped out of bed and ran to the bathroom. I closed the door and turned the thumb lock. I cowered in the tub in a fetal position and listened to the squeaking from my bedroom. After a few moments, Asscat scratched on the bathroom door and meowed plaintively for me to let him in.

"No," I hissed at the closed door. "Every man for himself."

A couple of hours later, Lisa Four left. I slathered Udder Balm all over my privates and face and slept for forty-eight straight hours.

To this very day, whenever I hear a squeaky noise, I panic, my mouth goes dry and my clitoris retracts.

CHAPTER TWELVE

Dana found out that the worst part about being arrested wasn't the handcuffs biting into her wrists. It wasn't the embarrassment of being pushed into the back of a police car by her arch-nemesis, Puddinhead, and being paraded into the city jail. It wasn't even the mug shots. It was the mocks and jeers of the policemen.

As she was being fingerprinted, two policemen who obviously thought they were a modern day Laurel and Hardy kept up the comic patter.

"Hey, look what Wilson caught. It's Wonder Woman!"

"Hey, Wonder Woman, where's your invisible plane?"

"It must be parked right outside, we just can't see it!"

"Hey, Wonder Woman, know what I wonder?"

"What?"

"I wonder where your pal Catwoman is!"

Dana ignored their taunts as she wiped the ink off her fingers on a coarse paper towel.

"What'sa matter? Catwoman got your tongue?"

Dana kept her lips buttoned and shunned the two like they were Amish outcasts. As Puddinhead was leading her to her jail cell, Laurel and Hardy called after him. "So, Wilson, who you bringing in next?"

"Batgirl?"

They guffawed.

* * *

In Dana's humble opinion, the city jail cell was actually kind of nice. She'd paid to stay in motels that were much worse and this room was free. The cot was clean and halfway comfortable, and there were even two pillows that smelled faintly of Lysol. They had cross-stitched pillowcases. One pillowcase had an embroidered bouquet of flowers on it and the other had the cross-stitched slogan "Jesus is watching you."

That was the part about Jesus and Santa Claus that had always bothered her.

Do they watch me on the toilet? While I'm in the shower? Masturbating? While I'm doing the dirty deed? Santa looked like the type that would, that dirty old letch.

She rummaged under the mattress and found a couple of old *People* magazines to while away the time. She read the magazines cover to cover, even though they were written in Spanish and her Spanish was limited to Ricky Martin's "Livin' La Vida Loca." She was surprised how much of it she understood. Popular culture must transcend language barriers.

After she was all caught up on Brangelina and their latest adoption, she uncovered an old *Glamour* magazine from under the cot. She didn't usually read fashion magazines (the skinny models made her feel like crap), but she wasn't usually in jail either. She flipped through the pages. Surprisingly, she found that she was right in style. She looked at the cover. It was dated November of 1983.

Note to self: Stop wearing boxers as outerwear.

She closed her eyes, flipped some pages and pointed. It must have been fate because the pages fell open to a quiz titled

"How to Know if Your Relationship is on the Rocks." One of those perfume sampler things fell out from between the pages. She rubbed it under her arms, then decided to take the quiz. What could it hurt? But when she looked closer, she found that somebody had already taken the quiz and circled the answers. Looking at their answers made her realize she wasn't the only victim of a cheating spouse.

Dana threw the magazine against the wall. She didn't need advice from a bunch of skinny magazine women. She could write her own quiz. After so many failed attempts, she was an expert on rocky relationships.

Dana laid back on the cot with her hands behind her head and imagined the type of article she would write for *Glamour*. It would be titled "Ten Telltale Signs That Your Girlfriend is a Cheating Whoredog."

1. Does she come home wearing different clothes than she left the house in?

2. Does she text while she's talking to you?

3. Does she answer her phone, leave the room and talk to somebody for hours at a time and then tell you it's her mother even though you know her mother is dead?

4. Does she disappear for hours or days at a time and not tell you where she's been?

5. Does she come home from "work" smelling like pussy?

6. Does she never have sex with you anymore?

7. Has she started calling you pet names (like Monkey Girl or Biscuit Butt) even though she's never done that before?

8. Does the passenger seat in her car keep changing from its usual position?

9. Has she developed a sudden interest in the mail and try to look at it before you do?

10. You follow her late at night and find her talking to somebody in the back of the beauty shop and a cop stops you and she runs away and you get shot at and arrested?

Dana sighed and put the magazine back under the cot for the next woman who found herself in jail because of a broken heart and shattered dreams. She flopped back down onto the cot and wished there was room service.

"Dana?"

She blinked her eyes a couple of times to try and wake up. She didn't realize that she'd fallen asleep, but she must have, because she was having a nightmare that her mother was looking at her through the bars of the cell.

"Mom?" Dana muttered.

"I oughta known you'd end up in jail," Leona said through the bars.

Dana sat up and rubbed her eyes. "That really you?"

"They say you accosted a police officer," Leona said.

"I sneezed on him," Dana corrected. "It's not like I hauled off and hit him."

A fat cop (Hardy) squeezed by Leona and unlocked the cell door. He swung the door open and said, "Your mother here paid your bail. You're free to go till your court date."

Dana eyed her mother warily and didn't move.

"C'mon," Leona said. "Let's go have breakfast. I'm buying." She turned and swished away. Hardy leered after Leona's ass. Dana shook off her stupor and followed her mother down the hallway.

She heard the cell door clang shut behind her like in all those old prison movies. Dana studied her mother's back as they walked down the hall. It wasn't fair that Leona got the svelte gene and didn't pass it on, leaving Dana to fight the battle of the bulge alone. Leona didn't even look like how a mother was supposed to look. She looked like a country and western singer all dressed up to go onstage at the Grand Ol' Opry—red cowboy boots with silver wingtips and roses stitched into the sides. The boots matched her red jumpsuit, which had a belt that hugged her hips. Rhinestones marched up and down every seam. She had bangles and bracelets on both wrists, several necklaces and enough cubic zirconia in her ears to blind a person. All flash and trash, Trudy would say. When Dana was little she thought Leona looked like starshine. But what was bright and shiny to a little kid looked faded and jaded to an adult.

The policemen who were gathered around the coffee pot stopped talking and watched Dana and Leona as they walked by.

Leona held her chin high and defiant, daring the men to stare. Dana shuffled along behind her mother with her chin tucked into her chest like she was walking into a dust storm.

As soon as the door shut behind her, Dana heard the policemen break into loud laughter. She wrapped her bathrobe-cape tightly around her butt.

* * *

Dana marveled that her mother was still driving the same white and red Thunderbird convertible that she remembered as a kid. It was an old car even back then. The Thunderbird had not only survived, but it had passed through the stages of being cool, uncool and old and now was regal in its vintage status.

Leona drove with one hand, the other holding her cigarette. The interior of the car filled with smoke. Dana rolled down her window and let the cool air slap her face.

"Still smoking, I see," Dana said, feeling rather uppity about quitting but wanting a cigarette all the same.

"Smoking helps keep me slim," Leona said. "You should give it a try."

Dana flinched. "No, thanks."

Leona ran her eyes up and down Dana and frowned. "Nice costume," she said.

"I like yours too," Dana said back.

Leona stared straight ahead for a long while. After several turns, she lit another cigarette off the butt of the last one. She crushed the old one out in the overflowing ashtray, pointed her nose in Dana's direction and laughed softly.

"What's so funny?" Dana snipped.

Leona shook her head and her words curled around a stream of smoke. "Nothing. Not a thing." She flipped the Thunderbird into the parking lot at BJ's Diner. She parked, filling up two spaces, and didn't seem concerned about it.

Judging by the size of the crowd, BJ's Diner was the place to be at six a.m. There was about ten years' worth of grease on the walls and counters and the place smelled like the bottom of an old cowboy boot. Near the front door sat an old man who looked like Yoda except Yoda had smaller ears. He was sitting before that old type of cash register with the round buttons that are hard to push down. There was a yellowed sign taped to the front of the register that said, "If our food and service don't live up to your standards, please lower your standards."

Scotch-taped to the wall behind the old man was another sign. This one read, "Guys…No shirt, no service. Gals…No shirt, no charge."

Dana pretended she didn't see all the stares aimed at her Wonder Woman costume.

Haven't you ever seen somebody dressed up for Halloween?

Leona scooted into an empty booth by the window and left Dana the seat that had a big duct-taped X where the brown Naugahyde had been slashed. Dana took a menu out of the holder and studied the dull pictures of pancakes and eggs like she was going to be tested on it later. Anything to not look at her mother.

Leona lit another cigarette and blew a stream of smoke at Dana's menu. Brenda, the waitress, sidled up to the table with an order pad and pen poised. She squinted through the gray cloud. "You all want coffee?"

Dana nodded. Leona looked up at Brenda's tall beehive hairdo and mumbled, "Bring me some tomato juice and some 'what's-this-here' sauce."

Brenda used her pen to point at a bottle of Worcestershire sauce that was sitting on the table next to the ketchup and the Tabasco. She asked, "You all know what you want?" She used the back of her pen to scratch at the thigh of her shiny support hose.

"The two by two by two, please," Dana said.

"Juice," Leona said without taking the cigarette out of her mouth.

"Be right out." Brenda moved to the next table.

"You could hide something in that tall hair of hers," Leona said, not bothering to lower her voice. "There could be a whole nest of rats in there. Or a bag of spiders." Brenda shot her a look that drilled twin holes in the back of her head.

Dana looked at her mother's cigarette and wished she had one. She avoided Leona's eyes and whispered, "She's worn her hair that way for thirty years."

"That don't make it right."

Brenda moved on to the back room and Dana breathed a sigh of relief.

Leona stared at Dana until she looked at her. "You're all grown up," she said.

"That happens over time."

"I don't know where you got those boobs. Sure wasn't from me."

Dana glanced at her mother's plunging neckline. She was right. "Why are you here?"

Leona shrugged and squished her cigarette out in the ashtray. Brenda appeared at the table, setting a glass of tomato juice in front of Leona and a coffee by Dana's elbow. Dana smiled at Brenda, but she only walked away. Leona added three shakes of Worcestershire sauce to her juice and gulped a third of it down in one long swallow. She pulled a silver flask out of her big purse and added vodka until the juice turned pink and was level with the rim. She stirred it with a butter knife and then drank deep. She smacked her lips a couple of times and asked, "What's the matter, aren't you happy to see me?"

Dana ignored Leona's tomato mustache and shrugged. "I don't know what you want from me is all." She made a big show of adding a package of fake sugar and some dry creamer to her coffee.

"A thank you would be nice. Seeing as how I bailed you out of jail."

"Thanks," Dana mumbled. She mashed the dried clumps of creamer in her coffee with her spoon.

"That didn't sound too sincere."

Dana looked at her mother. "What do you want me to say? You want me to ignore the fact that you're an alcoholic? You want me to tell you that my life is all peachy keen and swell? You want me to absolve you of all guilt for abandoning your children?"

Leona took her time lighting another cigarette even though there was still one burning in the ashtray. She picked a stray piece of tobacco off her tongue and wiped it on a napkin. "I'm not an alcoholic. I'm a drunk."

"What's the difference?"

"Alcoholics go to meetings."

"That joke wasn't funny the first time I heard it." Dana added five spoons of real sugar to her coffee. She sipped it and grimaced.

"I hear you're a lesbian now," Leona said.

"No," Dana corrected. "I'm not a lesbian *now*. I've been one for a long time."

"You have a girlfriend or whatever you call them?"

Dana let her eyes wander. She looked out the window and her gaze settled on the Thunderbird. "Sort of," she answered.

"What's that mean, sort of?"

Dana shrugged. "I have a girlfriend, but she's cheating on me."

"Kick her ass out. My third husband was a philanthropist too. That's what I did to him, kicked his ass out."

"You mean he was a philanderer."

"That's what I said."

"It's not that simple, Leona."

"You want me to get rid of her? I know a guy who'll do it for a hundred bucks and a six-pack."

Dana looked at Leona. "You talking about killing her?" she whispered harshly.

Leona shrugged with one shoulder and blew a stream of smoke at Dana's left ear. "She'll be gone is all I know. I never asked him where they go off to."

Dana rolled her eyes. "I can kill my own girlfriend, thank you very much."

Brenda put Dana's order in front of her, asking, "You going to kill your girlfriend?"

"No." Dana picked up her fork and knife and cut her eggs.

"Somebody will," Brenda said. "She's going to piss off one wife too many and somebody'll kill her. Might as well be you."

Dana clanged her knife down on the tabletop, saying a bit too loudly, "I said I'm not going to kill her, Brenda."

"I understand." Brenda winked at Dana and made that gesture like she was locking her lips and throwing away the key.

"Another round," Leona said, holding up her almost-empty glass. Brenda pretended not to hear and marched away. Dana giggled at the snub.

Leona watched Dana put away her breakfast in silence. Dana picked up a triangle of toast and slathered jelly on it. The act of eating made her feel better. Not so cranky. Now that her blood sugar was higher, she decided to take a magnanimous approach. "You married?"

Leona pushed back her cuticles with a toothpick. "I was. Then I wasn't. Then I was. Now I'm not. I've been living in Nashville for the most part. Writing songs."

"Any money in that?"

"Ever heard of the country song 'Time Sure Flies When You're Having Rum'?"

"Sure. It was top ten for like a year."

Leona leaned across the table far enough that Dana could smell the alcohol on her breath and said, "I wrote that song." She tapped her red fingernails on the Formica tabletop. "That song was stolen from me."

Dana mopped up egg yolk with another toast triangle and considered what Leona said. "Hmmm…" She took a big bite.

"I wrote it, all right," Leona said like Dana had said otherwise. She set her empty glass down like an emphatic period at the end of a sentence and pointed her pinky at Dana. "I was at the Bluebird Café and I got up on that li'l stage and sang the song I'd just written down on a cocktail napkin. A big, really big, music producer who shall remain nameless was there. After I sang and went back to my table, the music producer was gone and so was my napkin."

"I invented the Roomba," Dana offered.

Leona squinted at her over her cigarette smoke.

"I did," Dana said. "I had an idea one day to make a robot vacuum cleaner and I wrote it down on a paper towel. The paper towel got thrown in the trash and a couple of months later the Roomba came out on the market." She took a bite, chewed and swallowed. "I also invented the spork, except I called it a foon, but somebody stole that from me too. Just goes to show you— you should always wear your tin foil hat."

Leona didn't blink. "You think I'm a liar."

Dana shook her head. "No, not a liar. Crazy maybe. Insanity does run in the family, you know. Everybody in our family is crazy. Why should you be the exception?"

"Not true. My daddy was as sane as the day is long. He died from melatonin. It said so right on his death certificate."

"You mean melancholia."

"That's what I said."

"He was too crazy," Dana said. "He killed himself, didn't he?"

"True. But he was sane when he did it."

Dana reached for the last piece of toast, the one she had coated with strawberry jelly, but Leona slapped it out of her hand. "You'll thank me later." Leona patted her thighs and clucked her tongue a couple of times.

"I'm not fat," Dana said without conviction.

"I'm not an alcoholic," Leona retorted. She reached across the table, picked up the toast and wadded the whole thing into her mouth like Helen Keller but with fewer manners. "Saving you from yourself," she mumbled with her mouth full.

"How long you planning on staying in town?" Dana asked, not bothering to hide her disgust.

"Didn't you know? I moved in with you."

Crapola. Just when I thought my life couldn't get any worse.

"One big happy family," Dana said under her breath.

"Yep. The whole famn damily is back together." Leona slapped fifty cents on the table for a tip and headed for the cash register.

* * *

Leona guided the Thunderbird up in front of the house. When Dana saw Kimmy's Mustang in the driveway she let out a sigh that sounded like a slow leak in an air mattress.

"That her car?" Leona asked.

"Yep."

Leona looked both ways up and down the street then turned to face Dana. She barely moved her lips as she said, "All you have to do is say the word and poof, she's gone."

"I don't want you to *poof* her. Understand?"

"Whatever you say." She looked unconvinced.

"No poofing. Promise me."

Leona held her hand over her heart and said solemnly, "No poofing."

Dana opened the car door.

"Unless—"

"No poofing!"

"Okay." Leona sighed. "I'll be back in a little. I'm going to Walmart to pick up one of those rototiller chickens for supper."

"You mean rotisserie."

"That's what I said."

Dana got out and shut the door. She watched the Thunderbird peel off down the street, ribbons of black smoke curling out its tailpipe.

* * *

Dana found Kimmy in the kitchen, sitting at the table with her entire hand stuffed inside an olive jar. Kimmy was nuts over green olives. She liked to drink the juice out of the jar after the olives were gone. She filled up ice cube trays with olive juice and used the ice cubes to spice up her drinks.

Kimmy was wearing red go-go boots, thong underwear and a white T-shirt two sizes too big. She wasn't wearing a bra and her boobs were droopy and sad.

Looks like it's time for that 3,000-mile tire rotation.

Dana sat down at the table and watched as Kimmy struggled to get her hand out of the olive jar without opening her fist. If she opened her fist, she lost the handful of olives. If she kept the olives in her fist, she couldn't get it out of the jar. It was a Kimmy conundrum.

"Use a pickle fork," Dana suggested.

"These aren't pickles, Miss Smarty Wonder Woman Pants."

"It'll work on olives too."

Kimmy gave up, loosened her fist and took her hand out of the jar. She flapped her hand in the air, flicking juice everywhere. Then she lifted the jar to her mouth and drank the juice. When the juice was gone, she shook the jar a little and several olives plopped into her mouth. She set the jar down and chewed happily. "There's more than one way to let the cat out of the bag."

Dana retorted, "A bird in the hand catches the worm."

Kimmy licked her juicy fingers like a preening cat. "What were you doing last night?

"What were *you* doing?"

"I was at work," Kimmy said in a "duh" tone.

"Work, uh huh. *Working* out your nether regions."

Kimmy scrunched her nose. "My what? You know I don't speak Spanish."

"I want to know what you were doing at the beauty shop last night."

"I was doing inventory for Wanda."

"I bet. I guess that's why you left so fast when you saw me. I guess that's why you tried to outrun me in the police car."

"That was you chasing me?"

She plays stupid really good. Not much of a stretch, though.

"You were all alone in the shop?"

"Yep."

"I saw you through the window. Talking to somebody."

"That was you who tried to break in?"

"Don't play stupid, Kimmy. It insults us both."

"I'm not playing stupid, Dana, I really am stupid. Wait. I didn't mean that like how it sounded." She speared an olive with her fingernail and popped it in her mouth. She seemed pleased with her newfound ingenuity as she speared another. "Easy as shooting fish in a haystack."

"I saw you talking to somebody."

"Oh yeah? So, what was I saying then?"

"I don't know, but I saw your mouth moving."

"Maybe I was chewing gum."

"Maybe you were talking to your lover."

"Maybe I was singing along with the radio."

This line of questioning was getting Dana nowhere fast. "Forget it."

"Okay, truce. Olive?" Kimmy held out an olive speared on her artificial fingernail like it was an olive branch.

Dana waved it away. "Kimmy, we need to talk. Seriously talk."

"Is this about your weight again?"

"No. And I really wish everybody would shut up about my weight." Dana forced a smile, more for herself than for Kimmy. "We need to talk about us. I have a few questions and I would appreciate truthful answers."

"I have a question too," Kimmy said, chomping on another olive. "How do you think they get the little pimento into the little hole? Do they pay little people to put them in there? Wouldn't that be an awful job to have all day long, stuffing pimentos into olive holes?"

"Machines do it."

She crinkles her forehead in thought. "Really?"

"We're getting off track. Back to us. I haven't seen you in a week. You never come home except to change clothes and wax your pussy. Where have you been and who with?"

"Okay," she said with an exaggerated sigh. "I'll tell you the truth."

"Please do."

"I'm trying to better myself," she said.

Great. She's trading up. I'll be the first to admit that I'm not that great of a catch, but I do own my own business and I can lose twenty pounds if I really want to.

Kimmy said, "I'm taking a night class over at the college."

Dana was stunned. "Wha'?"

"I'm studying accounting. Five or four more classes and I could be an accountant. I wouldn't have to be a beautician anymore and I'd probably make a lot more money."

"You're bettering yourself through the college's continuing education classes?"

She nodded. "I could be the accountant for your business. Aren't you proud of me?"

"Sure," Dana said. She felt horrible. Horribly guilty for thinking such bad thoughts about Kimmy when all she was doing was trying to improve her lot in life. "That's great."

Dana slumped down in her chair until her chin was eye-level with the table.

"Well, you sure have a funny way of showing it," Kimmy said. She tossed an olive in the air and caught it in her mouth.

Dana said half-heartedly, "Well, I'm glad you're being pro-active about taking care of yourself."

"I'm doing it for us."

Dana peeked over the edge of the table. "Does that mean you love me?"

"Why do you always ask that?"

"Because I want to know the answer. A truthful answer."

Kimmy pursed her lips and thought hard. Dana figured if Kimmy had to think that hard about it, she already had her answer.

"I think," Kimmy said, "love is never having to say 'I love you.'"

If our relationship were a movie that would be the perfect tagline.

"Next question." Dana sat back up and looked her directly in the eye, daring her to lie. "Are you seeing somebody else?"

Kimmy met her gaze head-on and answered, "I could say no and you wouldn't believe me and you'd get mad. I could say yes and you'd believe me and you'd get mad. Either way you're going to get mad, so why don't you save yourself some time and go ahead, get mad and get it out of your system."

She had a point. Dana tried another question, "Where do you see us going with our relationship? Do you think we should stay together? Do you think we're even good together?"

Kimmy put an elbow on the table and cupped her chin. "Truthfully, Dana, I don't know. All I know is that I go to work, I come home and you're always sniffing around me like I did something wrong. I can't go to the bathroom without you knocking on the door and asking what I'm doing. You're very needy, you know. If you ask me, you're the one who has the commitment issues, not me."

"I am committed!"

"Sometimes people commit to the wrong people for the right reasons. You should set aside some time for self-examination. Maybe you could get a grip on your neediness."

"You think I'm needy? Because I want to be the only lover you have? That's not needy, that's normal."

"You're not exactly in danger of anybody calling you normal," she stated.

"So you think I'm crazy?"

She let out a long, exasperated sigh. "Let me put it this way. You rotate towels and dishes and your underwear. You always do things in threes. You still live with your grandmother and talk to your cat. You say you're a writer, but you never write. Everybody down at the beauty shop is talking about how you joined up with AA and that you must be a closet drinker because nobody's ever seen you have a problem with it. So you're either pretending to be an alcoholic or you think you really are one. Either way, it's crazy."

"Well, if you say it like that..." Dana's head was spinning out of control. She began to defend the accusations by saying, "I rotate stuff because that only makes good sense. If I didn't rotate my stack of underwear from top to bottom then I would always end up wearing the same seven pair of underwear and they'd get all raggedy-ass and—"

Kimmy had heard it all before. She interrupted Dana's harangue. "You know, sometimes I worry for my safety. I'm afraid to go to sleep because you might make sure I don't wake up. You know how scary it is to sleep next to somebody who's crazy?"

"I'm not going to poof you if that's what you think."

"Poof?"

"It's an expression. It means kill."

"Do you want to kill me? Because I woke up one night and you were staring at me in the dark.'"

"You had stopped breathing. I was checking to see if you were alive."

"I was holding my breath because you were staring me."

"You know, Kimmy, I may do a few small crazy-like things, but I don't think you're really scared of me. I think you're scared of commitment."

"There you go with the K word again."

"C."

"See what?"

Dana sighed. "You're so scared of the *K* word that you can't even turn on your car's blinker."

Kimmy shook some more olives into her hand. "I might change my mind. How am I supposed to always know that I want to turn left a whole half a block ahead of time?"

"Most people know where they're going."

She looked Dana in the eye and said slowly, punching each word. "Do you?" She tilted her head back and looked down her nose at Dana. "Do you know where you're going? Do you even know who you are? Look at yourself. Are you Wonder Woman? Are you Dana Dooley, the writer? Are you Dana Dooley, the alcoholic? How do you expect me to love somebody that doesn't even know who they are?" She screwed the lid back on the olive jar.

How is that somebody so damn dumb can be so insightful?

The lid slipped off the jar and toppled on the table, spinning round like a top. Kimmy grabbed the lid and tried to screw it back on the olive jar. It fell off again.

"Righty tighty," Dana said.

"Huh?" Kimmy asked.

Dana picked up the lid and handed it to her, saying, "Lefty loosey, righty tighty."

Kimmy puts the lid back on the jar and turned it to her left. "Your other right."

Kimmy reversed direction and the lid spun on.

"Kimmy, you know what?" Dana said. "Let's break up. You can stay here until you find a place if that's what you're worried about. I'll even help you find a nice apartment. I'll even promise you your first accounting job after you finish your CPA thingie-ma-jig."

Kimmy thought that over for a full two seconds. "No, thank you. I'll stick it out with you. You need me to take care of you."

Dana should've seen that one coming. Every time in the past she'd ever made noises about breaking up, Kimmy would come flying into her arms.

"But you said it yourself. You can't love me. You don't know who I am."

"No. What I said was that *you* don't know who you are." Kimmy reached across the table and took Dana's hand in her hands. "It's not rocket surgery, Dana. You can figure it out. I believe in you."

Dana pulled her hand away and crossed her arms over her chest. "I want to break up. I want you to move out. I want you to take your dog and leave." There she said it. She couldn't be more clear than that.

"Is there somebody else?" Kimmy asked.

How does she do this? Now she's the one accusing me of playing around? How'd that happen?

"No, there's nobody else."

Kimmy stood, threw one leg over Dana's lap like she was getting on a horse and licked her ear. "Can she do this to you?"

"There isn't anybody else."

Kimmy placed her palms over Dana's boobs and flicked her nipples with her thumbs. "Can she do this?"

"I said there isn't anybody else." Dana felt her nipples harden and silently cursed them for being traitors. "But if there were somebody else, then yes, I suppose she too could pinch my nipples."

Kimmy looked at Dana, trying to catch the lie somewhere on her face. They locked eyes for a long moment. Dana was reminded of that old adage that said the eyes were the window to the soul. If that were true, then there was a sign hanging in Kimmy's window that said "gone fishin'."

Kimmy pressed her lips against Dana's. Dana liked green olives but not enough to taste them secondhand. She tried to squirm out from under Kimmy.

"And this?" Kimmy asked, darting her tongue in and out of Dana's ear. "Can she do this?"

A moan escaped Dana's lips and she squirmed again, but this time she may have squirmed a little against her, instead of away from her. Kimmy moved her hand to Dana's crotch, urgently caressing her through the unitard. She moaned in Dana's ear, "I love how you feel."

It had been way too long since Dana had had sex. She felt her body caving in and her mind going on strike. Kimmy's rubbing became more insistent and Dana's breath caught in her throat.

"I want you to come for me," Kimmy breathed into Dana's ear, sending shivers down to just the right spot. "I want you to come hard."

"Good God," said a voice behind Dana.

Kimmy stopped and looked over Dana's shoulder. Her eyes grew wide and she asked, "Who are you?"

Dana twisted in her chair and saw Leona. Her lit cigarette was dangling out of her mouth and she had a plastic Walmart bag slung over her shoulder like it was a purse. She smelled like lemon pepper chicken.

"Don't stop on account of me," Leona said. She pulled her flask out of her pocket and took a snort. She placed the bag on the table and sat down across from Dana and Kimmy. She inhaled on her cigarette and said, "I'm not a prude. I saw a lesbian porno once. But it looked like two straight women rubbing soap bubbles all over each other and giggling. This looks more real."

Something inside Dana clicked. "I need some fresh air."

She pushed Kimmy out of her lap and stood. "I need to leave."

She walked out of the kitchen. "I need a new life."

She walked out of the house. The screen door slammed shut behind her.

Kimmy's voice taunted Dana as she headed down the street, "What about *my* needs?"

* * *

Dana had only walked about two blocks when the Thunderbird pulled up alongside her. The window rolled down and a cloud of cigarette smoke boiled out.

Dana stopped and faced Leona.

Leona didn't brake. The Thunderbird kept moving. She stopped the car about twenty feet away. Dana watched as Leona shifted the car into reverse. The tires rolled and crunched over gravel until Leona's face in the window was right in front of Dana.

Dana spoke first. "I need a cigarette."

Leona leaned out the window and shook a pack of Marlboro Reds. Dana took a cigarette out of the pack and stuck it in her mouth. She sucked on it. And exhaled slowly.

Leona reached out with a cigarette lighter, but Dana waved it away. "I don't smoke anymore."

Leona coughed.

Dana blew twin streams of non-smoke out her nostrils. "I hate you, you know that?"

"I figured."

"I've spent most of my life hating you."

"You're not so special. Lots of people hate me."

"Why are you here then?"

"Believe it or not...I love you."

"You got a funny way of showing it."

"It ain't all that funny."

Dana sucked on the cigarette and fake-ashed. She took a moment to formulate her thoughts, then said, "Most of what's wrong with me is your fault, you know. What you see standing before you is your creation."

"How could that be? I wasn't even around for the most part."

"I'm a lesbian because I never had a proper father figure and because I'm always trying to find a mother in my choice of mates."

"Bullshit. You're a lesbian because you got that gene from your daddy's side of the family. His own sister was a dyke. At least you didn't get her little beard problem."

"Hush up!" Dana exploded. She punched the air between them with her finger, saying, "That's one of the problems. Nobody ever listens to what I have to say. They're too busy telling me what they want me to think and say."

Leona hushed up.

Dana holstered her pointing finger and in a calmer tone said, "Let me do the talking, please. For once, let me speak my mind without being interrupted."

Leona nodded and inhaled on her cigarette.

"Okay, I was born a lesbian, I'll grant you that much. It makes life harder, but it's not that big of a deal. Most of the time I like it."

Leona nodded.

"But all the other stuff is your fault."

"What other—"

"I said hush it!"

Leona did.

Dana continued, "I grew up thinking my own mother didn't love me. I filled the hole you left with peanut butter and ice cream and cake and beef jerky. I was a fat kid who turned into a fat teenager who became a fat woman and all that fat is nothing but unhappiness weighing me down. My unhappiness is so heavy that some days it's too hard to even pick up my feet. All that fat and sadness has me squished down so low you could sweep me up in a dustpan and throw me in the garbage…and nobody would even notice."

Dana blinked away tears and continued in a trembling voice, "I can't eat one little thing without thinking about how many calories it has or what kind of carbs it has and everything sits inside me like a hunk of lead and even with all that in my belly, I'm still hungry, still wanting."

Leona exhaled a stream of smoke out her mouth and sucked it right back up her nose.

"I can't hold down a relationship because I'm always afraid they're going to leave me. They're going to leave me like you did. And I'll end up fat and alone."

Leona exhaled words with the smoke. "Sounds like you got a bad case of the poor me's."

Dana tossed the cigarette to the ground and squished it with an angry twist of her shoe. "You know what I have to say about that? Eff you!"

"You can't even cuss right. How'd I ever end up with a daughter who can't even cuss right?"

"Fuck you!" Dana kicked gravel toward the rear of the car.

"That's good. Now if you could say that to people once in a while you'd feel a whole lot better about yourself."

"Yeah, thanks for the great fucking advice." She turned and stalked down the street.

Leona called after her. "And you're not fat. You're beautiful."

CHAPTER THIRTEEN

Dana headed for Trudy's but then realized Trudy was probably at work by now. So she turned the other direction and headed on foot toward The Best Little Hairhouse, where she had left her car before she was unjustly arrested. Hopefully it was still there and they hadn't impounded it.

She turned a corner and was almost run over by a little boy riding his bike. His bottom half was dressed as a cowboy with jeans, boots, plastic spurs and twin six-shooters on his hips. His top half was dressed Indian-style with a fringed shirt and a war bonnet on his head. The cowboy/Indian slammed on his brakes and looked her up and down. Embarrassed by the boy's open scrutiny, Dana pulled her bathrobe-cape around herself.

"Who're you supposed to be?" the boy asked.

"Good question," Dana mumbled and kept walking.

A couple of blocks later, she saw Lloyd the Mailman's mail truck. She figured she could save him a trip up her sidewalk if she stopped and got her mail from him. Lloyd the Mailman was a really old guy with arthritic knees that looked like tree burls under his shorts and he'd probably appreciate the courtesy. She walked up to the front of the truck and looked inside. He wasn't there. She looked up and down the street, but Lloyd the Mailman wasn't anywhere to be seen.

She was about to walk away when the mail truck bounced up and down. She froze. She stared at the truck. It rocked. Then stopped. Then swayed. And stopped.

She took a tentative step toward the truck. "Lloyd?"

The truck vibrated, then bounced up and down.

"Lloyd, is that you in there?"

When there was no answer, Dana's imagination kicked into high gear and she conjured up all kinds of scenarios: Lloyd the Mailman was hog-tied in back of the truck, beaten and bleeding. He'd been robbed and left for dead. Somebody had stolen all the disability checks he was carrying.

It was the first of the month.

Or he could've been the victim of a gang rape.

That would explain the bouncing up and down.

Maybe it was because she had on her Wonder Woman costume, or maybe it was because she needed a way to channel all her untapped sexual energy, or maybe the caffeine was just now hitting her bloodstream, but whatever it was, she flew to the rescue. She ran to the back of the truck, threw open the rolling door and yelled, "I command you to stop this monkey business right now!"

"Shut the door!"

Dana did a double take. It was Ellen. Ellen was dressed in Lloyd's polyester postal uniform. The pants were pooled around her ankles. She was squatting and her bare butt was aimed in Dana's direction. If she wasn't so startled she would've taken the time to admire the view.

"What're you doing?" Dana asked. Because even though she was a writer who possessed a more vivid imagination than most people, she couldn't imagine a scenario that would fit this strange display.

"What's it look like?" Ellen yelled over her shoulder. "Shut the door."

Dana quickly jumped inside the back of the truck and rolled the door closed, plunging everything into darkness. Dana stood absolutely stock-still lest she Dooley over something in the pitch black. After a moment, she heard a water faucet turn on.

Dana barraged Ellen with questions, "Where's Lloyd the Mailman? What've you done to him? Where's that water coming from? Did you kill him? Did you dress in his clothes? Are you trying to steal the disability checks? You'll get caught, you know. You can't kill a federal employee and steal government checks without getting caught."

The faucet turned off.

"You're talking nonsense. Have you been drinking?" Ellen asked. "You can open the door now."

Dana rolled the door back up and the sudden daylight made her blink. Ellen was fully dressed in a mailman costume and holding a Gatorade bottle in her hands.

Dana inched away from her, saying, "You killed Lloyd and stole his costume, didn't you?"

Ellen laughed. "By that logic, I could accuse you of killing Lynda Carter."

"Huh? Oh, yeah," Dana said, grasping Ellen's meaning. "But the difference is that she's figmental and Lloyd's real. Or was real."

Ellen grinned. "Lloyd retired. I'm the new letter carrier. I've taken over his route."

"Oh." Dana relaxed, remembering that Ellen had told her she'd gotten a job transfer and she moved paper from one place to another for a living.

Ellen handed Dana the Gatorade bottle. "Don't drink that," she warned. "It's pee." She buckled her belt.

"You were peeing in a Gatorade bottle?"

"Letter carriers have to pee too, you know," she said, hopping out of the back of the truck. "What am I supposed to do, knock on a door and ask if I can use their bathroom? Gatorade bottles have a wide mouth."

"Wow. I never realized."

"We all pee in bottles. It's a trade secret." Ellen took the bottle away from Dana, jumped out of the back and walked around to the passenger side of the vehicle. Dana followed and watched as Ellen tossed the bottle into a box heaped with other full Gatorade bottles. "I keep forgetting to throw them away," Ellen explained.

"That's a lot of pee. You know," Dana said brightly, "you could sell that to people who have to take drug tests for their jobs."

"Is there a category for that on eBay?"

"I don't know, but I can check it out for you."

Ellen looked Dana up and down. "Are you on your way home from a costume party?"

"No, I'm walking over to get my car from where I left it last night."

"You've been drinking?"

"Of course not."

Ellen raised an eyebrow in a "really?" expression.

That was when Dana remembered she was a faux alcoholic. What with rescuing Fat Matt and almost catching Kimmy and a stint in jail and her mother walking in on her having sex, she had forgotten that she was supposed to have a drinking problem. Some alcoholic she was. She was going to have to try a lot harder if she was going to be convincing. She amended her statement. "But I sure do want to, you know, get inebriated and stuff. I can't stop thinking about wanting to get falling down intoxicated. Yessirree, I'd kill for a glass of alcohol right about now. You know, some 900-proof stuff." She rubbed her belly in circles and made a yummy noise.

Ellen nodded sympathetically. "You can want. Everybody *wants* to drink. Promise me you'll get through today without a drink. Can you do that? One day?"

"I'll try."

"Good." Ellen reached over and took Dana's hand in her own.

Dana flinched and her eyes grew wide. "Did you feel that?"

"Feel what?"

"That jolt. It was like you tasered me," Dana said.

Ellen's smile faded.

Dana panicked. "Did I say something wrong?"

Ellen leaned in close, her lips millimeters away from Dana's, and replied, "I want to kiss you, that's all."

"Okay by me," Dana whispered. When Ellen's lips touched hers, Dana forgot all about her lip gloss or that she had to pee like mad or that they were kissing in broad daylight for anybody to see.

Ellen pulled back. "Sorry," she said. "I promised myself I wasn't going to do that again."

"I'm glad you didn't keep that promise."

Ellen turned and walked to the back of the mail truck and hopped inside. Dana followed.

Ellen scooted around several trays of mail and some packages. "You kick out that girlfriend of yours yet?"

Dana shook her head. "I tried. I almost caught her, but it didn't work out too well."

"What happened?"

Dana shrugged, not really wanting to tell her she had just gotten out of jail. "It's a long story and involves an alien crop circle, a loose crown, my mother and olives."

"I'm still trying to catch my girlfriend cheating too," she said. "My story involves clogging and donuts."

That was when an idea hit Dana like a bolt of lightning, frizzling from one side of her brain to the other and shooting out her mouth. "I know what we can do!" Dana continued in a rush of words. "I saw this Hitchcock movie once when I had the flu and the sound wasn't working on my TV so I was lipreading and I had a fever so it was kind of hard to follow and it turned out the sound was turned down because my cat sat on the remote, but that's another story."

"Wait…What?"

Dana was so excited, she jumped out of the back of the truck and paced the road. After a few seconds, she stopped pacing and fired a question. "Have you told anybody about me and you?"

Ellen shook her head.

"Good. I haven't either. I mean, we were seen at the AA meeting, but I saw forty other people there too, and it's a small town, so of course we know each other—"

"What're you talking about?" Ellen interrupted.

"Just listen. We both have cheating girlfriends, right?"

"Right."

"And they're hiding it from us, right?"

"Right."

"*But*," Dana emphasized, "your girlfriend isn't hiding from *me* and my girlfriend isn't hiding from *you*."

"Soooo?" Ellen said, trying to fit all the pieces together.

Dana climbed back into the back of the mail truck and rolled down the door. Blackness enveloped them. Dana lowered her voice to a whisper. "It'll work like this: I follow your girlfriend and you follow mine. Like in the Hitchcock movie I saw where they kill each other's wife and get off scot-free because there's no link between themselves and the wife they killed. Get it? We pull the old switch-a-roo."

"But, Dana, I don't want you to *kill* my girlfriend—that seems a little harsh."

"Sshhh," Dana said, even though they were all alone in the back of the truck. "I didn't say kill. We'll follow each other's girlfriend, maybe take a few photos of them being dirty birdies, and that'll give us the proof we need to get rid of them."

Ellen was silent for so long that Dana wondered if she was still over there in the dark. "That might work," Ellen finally said.

"It will work," Dana said. "It worked in the movie like a charm and Hollywood doesn't make this stuff up, you know."

She sounded dubious, "It's worth a try."

"It'll work. It has to."

"Can I kiss you now?"

Dana homed in on those words like a bat with sonar. She aimed her lips for Ellen's and bullseye! Dana kissed her until she was afraid she'd spontaneously combust and all that would be left of her would be a giant wet spot.

* * *

Lisa Number Fives's real name wasn't Lisa. It was Aude Lisa. She was French, being born and raised in

Paris. She was black too. I had to admit most of my attraction to her was the novelty of having a girlfriend with ebony skin who spoke French. It was about as far away from Oklahoma as you could get.

Aude was pronounced Odie, like the dog in the Garfield cartoons. Trudy used to make fun of her behind her back, calling her "Odie-wan-kenobi" and "Odious Matter." I took to calling her Lisa because it was easier and was less likely to be made fun of.

Lisa Number Five moved to Dooley Springs from Paris her last year of high school because her father got a job teaching at the college. When she came to America, she couldn't speak any English whatsoever. She locked herself in her bedroom for a whole month and learned to speak English by watching *The Addams Family* reruns on TV. After that she thought all American children were named after days of the week and she snapped her fingers a lot.

I fell in love with the French language more than I fell in love with her. Until then my entire knowledge of French was from Pepe Le Pew. One time in bed she whispered French nothings in my ear and I had my first multiple orgasm ever. The next morning, I asked her to translate what she'd said. It went something like this: "Your pores are tres big. You should splash cold water on your face and exfoliate more."

Our main problem was the language barrier thing. She took everything literally. One time we were walking around *le parc* and she was deep into some a story about a guy named Gomez and a disembodied hand and I said, "I don't understand. Back up."

She looked at me kind of funny, then backed up two steps.

Of course, I couldn't resist that temptation so I said it again, "I don't get it. Back up."

She backed up two more steps.

Well, now I was thinking this was great fun so I kept saying it. I had her backed all the way up into the middle of the street before a car honked at her and slammed on its brakes. She ran for the sidewalk, saying, "*Merde!* You try to kill moi!"

I laughed. She didn't. She never did understand American humor.

Lisa Number Five and I broke up the day I came home from work and found her *voulez-vous coucher moi'ing* with a woman named Jan Dingle who was only five feet tall and looked like Pugsley. Dingle was really her name. I don't think I ever got over that. I was cheated on with a Dingle. That hurt.

When I caught them in bed sixty-nining each other I grabbed some of Lisa Number Five's crap and heaved it out the window. Dingle woman scurried out of the room with her hands over her pussy, while Lisa Number Five went ballistic. She screamed in her French accent, "I never like you! You person bad!"

I grabbed another armload of her crap and tossed it out the open window. I scoured my brain for all the French words I knew and shouted as I threw more of her belongings, one at a time. "There goes your *baguette*! Oh, looky, your *frère Jacque* and your *à la mode* are flying out the window!"

"You are person *fou*, you are person crazy!" she shouted.

I grabbed the top drawer out of the dresser and shook the contents out the open window. "Oh, no! There goes your c'est la vie and your *au contraire* and your que *sera, sera*!" I picked up a pair of her shoes and threw them into the yard below, making sure to aim at Dingle as she scampered for the street. "*Bon jour, déjà vu*!"

A shoe boinked Dingle in the back of the head and she fell to her knees. I laughed and hung halfway out the window, razzing her, "*Adieu*, Dingle *beaucoup! Bon voyage, pomme frites*!"

Dingle rose unsteadily to her feet and ran serpentine for the safety of her car.

Lisa Number Five advanced on me and spit into my face, "You are creepy, you are kooky, mysterious and spooky, altogether ooky!"

She snapped her fingers twice and left.

She always did have to have the last *bon mot*.

* * *

Dana's lips were still tingling from Ellen's kiss when she found her car exactly where she'd left it—in the alley behind Wanda's shop. She turned the key in the ignition and went over the facts Ellen had told her about her girlfriend. The girlfriend worked the graveyard shift over at Hole In One Donuts. Every Monday, Wednesday and Friday afternoon, she had a dance class over at the Tsa La Gi Senior Village Activity Center. They were rehearsing for a local production of *Riverdance*.

In turn, Dana gave Ellen all Kimmy's info: She worked days at The Best Little Hairhouse but hadn't been home lately much because she'd been taking a continuing ed course at the college at night.

Dana put Betty in reverse and backed out of the alley, swinging in a wide arc onto the main road. She put the car in first gear. She was planning to head over to Hole In One first. That way she could check on Ellen's girlfriend's work history and maybe score some of those pigs in a blanket they made.

She pressed her foot to the accelerator and Betty shot backwards. She stomped on the brake and screeched to a halt right before she took out a garbage can. She mashed down on the clutch, slipped the stick shift out of first and re-stuck it back into gear. She slowly let off the clutch and pushed on the gas pedal at the same time.

Betty went backwards. Dana braked right before she backed into the truck coming up behind her. She tried to put Betty in first gear a couple more times, but each time the car headed backwards.

The truck behind her honked and Dana stuck her arm out the window, waving it around. The driver honked as he swerved around Dana, shaking his fist.

Dana gave up on getting Betty going forward. This had happened before. Betty was temperamental. She wouldn't go forward for weeks at a time, then suddenly she would. Dana patted her dashboard and cooed, "It's okay, Betty. We all have our hormonal issues."

Dana turned in her seat so she could see out the back window and drove in reverse all the way to the donut shop.

The Hole In One was on Choctaw Street in the middle of town. When Dana was a little kid it was on the edge of town. That was how much Dooley Springs had grown over the past thirty years. Fly-by-night businesses, check cashing places and pawn shops had sprung up like mushrooms on either side of the Hole In One only to disappear just as quickly. (Once there was even a sushi place that had tried to make a go of it. The locals refused to eat raw fish and called it The Bait Shack. It closed down after only two months.) But the Hole In One remained a permanent fixture.

And according to Dana's acute sense of smell, it was still heaven on earth. She gained ten pounds by opening the door and getting a whiff of all that sugar and grease.

She hadn't been inside the shop in ages, but it was just like she remembered. The tables were topped with green Formica with little red apples, matching apple orchard print curtains and the plank floor had a wear pattern from the front door over to the big glass case where all the pastries sat looking scrump-dilly-ishus. There was a collection of famous musicians' pictures, autographed and hanging on the walls. All the Oklahoma-spawned country music greats smiled down on the tables while the customers ingested artery-clogging treats. There was Hank Williams, Garth Brooks, Reba McEntire, Roy Clark and, of course, Carrie Underwood.

Rush hour must have been over because the tables were empty and the trash barrels were stuffed with paper cups and napkins. Dana followed her nose up to the counter and her stomach loudly announced her presence.

"Hungry?" the woman behind the counter asked, setting aside the newspaper she'd been reading. Her white apron had "Maude" embroidered across the chest. Maude was in her sixties if she was a day and had the body type of somebody who stood on her feet for a living—skinny legs and no butt to speak of. She made up for it with her big belly. She looked like a marshmallow balanced on top of two toothpicks. She had a pained expression on her face that made Dana think either her shoes were too tight or that the hairnet on her head was restricting the blood flow.

"My stomach sure thinks so," Dana replied. "Can I have a dozen of your little sausage and cheese rolls to go?"

"No," Maude replied.

"No?"

"Sold out on those hours ago, honey. All's we got left is the spicy ones."

"Okay. I'll take a dozen of those then."

Maude picked up a pair of tongs and began to drop sausage rolls one by one into a white paper bag. Her lips moved silently as she counted. Dana needed to pry some information about Ellen's girlfriend out of this woman, but she knew it wouldn't be easy because Maude's face was scrunched up like a lemon that'd been sucked dry. It was an unforgiving face, one that didn't meddle and didn't gossip.

Dana leaned an elbow on the glass case, tossed her bathrobe-cape cavalierly over her shoulders, trying to look casual, and asked in an overly friendly tone, "You must work all night making the donuts, huh?"

"No."

"No? You come in early then?"

"That's right."

"How early?"

Maude let out an exasperated gust of air, dumped all the sausage rolls out of the bag and back into the pan. "You made me lose count," she said.

"Sorry," Dana mumbled.

She watched Maude start over, counting sausages and dropping them into the sack. Dana let her get all the way up to six before she asked, "So nobody works nights here?"

"That's right." Her lips moved, counting eight and nine.

Dana knew somebody was lying and she bet dollars to donuts it was Ellen's girlfriend. Working nights—that was a convenient excuse to not be at home and go cheating around town.

She pumped Maude for more information, "You going to see that new show, *Riverdance*?"

Maude's tongs stopped in mid-air. "Is that the one where they're Irish cloggers?"

"I think so, yeah."

"Is it coming to town?"

"No, I heard that the local dance studio's putting it on. They have a clogging class or something that's going to put it on out at the senior center."

"I think you're wrong. I'm a clogger, see?" She pointed with her tongs over to a photo on the wall. It was a black and white 8 x 10. In the picture, Maude was a good forty years younger, missing her donut belly, but still wearing the same sour expression. She was standing beside a trophy half her height.

"Wow. What's the trophy for?"

Maude puffed out her chest. "National clogging championship. I teach clogging over at the dance studio. And I think I'd know if we was doing a show."

"Oh. I must've been mistaken."

Maude sighed heavily, gave Dana a "shut-your-mouth" look, dumped all the sausages back into the pan and began counting again.

"Sorry," Dana mumbled. Maude counted all the way up to eight sausages this time before Dana asked, "So nobody's here at nights, you say. Nobody at all? A cleaning woman maybe?"

Maude eyed her suspiciously. "We close at two p.m. every day and we don't leave no cash in the till, so don't go getting no funny ideas."

Dana quickly backtracked once she realized Maude thought she was casing the joint. "No, you see…A friend of mine told me she worked nights here. I'm trying to find her."

"I done said nobody works here but me and my husband."

"You never hired a woman to work…maybe temporarily?"

"What's this friend's name?" Maude asked like she was sure Dana was lying.

"Well, I don't rightly know, you see—"

Maude's eyes popped and her jaw went slack. She slowly looked from Dana's face to the paper she'd been reading. Dana's eyes followed Maude's and—

Holy cow!

—there was a picture of her right on the front page. It showed her handcuffed with Puddinhead pushing her up against the police car. The bold headline read: "'Wonder Woman' Arrested." The smaller type under the headline continued. "After a local officer stopped 'Wonder Woman' during a potential breaking and entering, she assaulted the officer and hijacked his car."

Dana snatched the paper off the counter, but she was too late. Maude recognized her picture, which wasn't too hard unless there was another Wonder Woman roaming around town. Maude quickly ducked under the counter where Dana couldn't see or reach her.

"Harold! Get out here!" Maude yelled.

"Hold on a minute, Maude," Dana pleaded.

"Harold!"

"Who's Harold?"

"We're being robbed!"

"I'm not robbing anybody!"

Harold hurried out of the back room, his feet pedaling way behind his big belly. He was red-faced and holding a half-eaten bear claw in his hand. "What's happening? We're being robbed? Who's robbing?" he asked.

"I am! I mean, I'm not. I mean, you're not!" Dana yelled.

"Why are you shouting?!" he shouted.

"I'm not shouting!" she shouted. Dana slapped the newspaper down on the counter, trying to emphasize her point and it popped loudly, sending Maude scurrying back under the counter. Harold clutched his chest like he'd been shot through the heart.

"Give her the money before she kills us dead!" Maude yelled from somewhere down below. "She's a dangerous and wanted criminal!"

Harold stuffed the other half of the bear claw in his mouth, hit a key on the cash register, grabbed all the bills and shoved them into the white sack with the eight sausages. He nervously threw the bag and it hit Dana dead-center in the chest. She caught the bag before it hit the floor.

"You don't understand…" Dana squeaked.

Harold held his hands up in the air *a la* stick-up mode and said, "Leave. You got the money, just leave. Don't kill us. We're hard-workin', church-goin', peace-lovin' people here, please—don't shoot us."

"I wasn't going to—"

He grabbed a nearby broom and pointed it across the counter, poking Dana in the belly with the bristly end. "Shoo! Bad girl, bad! Shoo, shoo!"

Dana backed toward the door, trying to explain, "I only came in here for some sausage rolls. I wasn't trying—"

"Shoo!" he shouted and heaved the broom at her.

Dana ducked out the front door and closed it as the broom thudded against the glass. She looked back through the door and saw Harold—

Crapola! He's calling the police.

—with a phone in his hand.

Dana ran to Betty, jumped inside and it took her three tries to get the engine to turn over. She peeled out in reverse and backed down Main Street. She pushed the accelerator to the floorboard and sped away—going twenty miles per hour, Betty's top speed in reverse gear.

She realized she had the sausage bag stuffed with money in her hand. Never one to waste food, she rooted around in the bag, found a sausage roll and took a bite to calm her nerves.

After five minutes of driving backwards, ignoring all the honks and stares, Dana realized that making a getaway by car wasn't as fun as the TV made it out to be. Especially in reverse. Her neck was already developing a crick, so she didn't know how she was going to drive much longer.

She had no plan, no idea where she was going. She bit a hunk off another sausage roll and put her brain to work. She was a wanted fugitive. She had robbed a donut shop.

Who was going to believe I didn't when I have a sack full of money and sausage breath? And she was on bail for assaulting a police officer. Her future didn't look so bright.

She wheeled around a curve and a truck loomed up on the road behind her, which was actually in front of her. She shut her eyes and slammed on Betty's brakes.

When she opened her eyes she saw that the rear-end of the car was only an inch or so away from the truck's bumper. And the truck was none other than Maw Maw's ice cream wagon. It was pulled off onto the shoulder, but half the truck was blocking the lane.

Dana knew exactly what that meant…Maw Maw was up to her artistic shenanigans again.

Dana cut off the engine and got out, slamming the door behind her. She walked around the truck and saw what she knew she would: another one of Maw Maw's "Christian Roadkill Artistic Projects." Or as Dana called them…CRAP. This one was a work in progress. Maw Maw had set up an old coffee table alongside the road and there were ten or so frozen critters—opossums, armadillos, dogs, cats—arranged around it. Dana could tell in one glance that it was a rendition of the Last Supper. The only one missing was Jesus.

"Maw Maw! You're blocking the road!"

Dana squinted at the tableau. She took a step closer. Oh no, it couldn't be. But it was. A stuffed Snickerdoodle was sitting to the left of Paul. "You killed Snickerdoodle?"

Maw Maw threw open the service window and poked her neck out. "I didn't kill him, he died of a pickled liver." She looked Dana up and down, then ordered, "Gimme a hand in here." Her head disappeared back inside like a turtle hiding in its shell.

Dana sighed but resigned herself to do as asked. She might have Johnny Law chasing her, but that was a whole heap less scary than Maw Maw's wrath.

She dragged her feet up to the truck, stepped inside through the side door and found Maw Maw bent over the deep freeze. Dana shut the door and said, "Still working with the frozen dead, I see."

Maw Maw was up to her shoulders in cold mist and her voice echoed from the bowels of the freezer. "Only until I get my embalming recipe perfected. I'm on the verge of finding a recipe that not only preserves the remains, but also repels insects. Until then my art is going to be temporary, I'm afraid."

Dana nervously cleared her throat and took the plunge. "I'm

going on a surprise vacation. Don't know exactly when I'll be back."

Maw Maw didn't even so much as lift her head. "No, you're not, little lady. You're staying put."

"I need to get out of town for a bit."

"Is this because of your mother being back?"

"Yes." That was the first lie Dana had ever told her grandmother and to her surprise, it was easy to do. But it left a bad taste in her mouth like she'd put a cup of salt in a recipe that called for a cup of sugar.

"Don't fib to me. Why are you running?"

Dana came clean. "The law's after me. They think I robbed the Hole In One."

Maw Maw's head popped up. "Did you?"

"Of course not."

"Then there's nothing to worry about." She poked her head back down into the freezer.

"It looks like I did, though. I kinda sorta have a bag full of their money and eight, I mean six, of their sausage rolls."

Maw Maw lifted her head and said simply, "Then go give it back and explain what really happened."

"I don't think it's that simple. Harold threw a broom at me."

"I've known Harold and Maude since God was a child. They're decent folks. I was at their wedding. I schooled both their kids and all their grandchildren." She wiped her hands on the front of her dress like that decided that. She bent back over the fridge and rooted around inside. "You saw your mother, I take it?"

"Yes." Maw didn't lift her head or say anything more so Dana continued, "I'm not going to forgive her if that's what you're getting at."

She jerked her head out of the freezer and looked at Dana. "That's your prerogative." She pulled a cigar out of her dress pocket, along with a pack of matches. Dana knew the cigar meant she was in for a lecture. Cigars were Maw Maw's way of giving weight to her words. Maw Maw had a cigar in her mouth the day she gave Dana the sex talk, the day she told Dana her Paw Paw had died, and the day she didn't get a clock for Christmas.

Dana knew it was odd, but when she was nine years old, more than anything in this whole wide world, she wanted a clock for Christmas. Not a watch. A clock—like the kind most people have hanging on their kitchen walls. When Christmas morning came Dana unwrapped an Easy-Bake Oven and scads of new clothes most girls would kill to have, and she didn't find a clock—not even one single timepiece of any kind. Dana flung herself headfirst into a full-blown, throw-down hissy fit. Maw Maw picked her up and tossed her into the middle of the backyard, went back in the house and locked all the windows and doors. It didn't take Dana long to realize that having a fit without an audience wasn't worth the trouble. When she worked up the nerve to knock on the door, Maw Maw let her back in, lit a cigar and gave her what-for in the gratitude department.

Maw Maw stuck the cigar in her mouth and chewed from one side to the other, looking out the window for a long moment.

"Your mother…Leona…"

"I don't want to talk about her if you don't mind."

"I'm not asking you to talk. I'm asking you to listen."

Dana sighed, but other than that, she kept quiet.

While Maw Maw talked, her eyes roamed around the interior of the truck, lighting on everything except Dana. "Leona was born angry. Angriest baby you ever did see. She was never happy. Always sassing back, getting into trouble with teachers and the like. It was like life wasn't big enough for her and she always wanted more and when she couldn't have it she got mad. Most of that was my fault. I didn't ever spank her, never raised my hand to her, and maybe I should have."

She paused to light the cigar before continuing, "She got it into her head that life was supposed to be exciting. And when it wasn't exciting enough to suit her, she would make it that way. That got her into all kinds of trouble. By the time she was a young woman, she was drinking and carrying on. Right out of high school, she moved in with that man, the one with the beard and the guitar, had two babies, but even that didn't settle her down or make her happy. At that point she was so fed up with her lot in life that she couldn't have found happy if it'd bit her in the butt."

Dana stared at the cigar's red embers.

"After that man left her, she tried to make ends meet. But she couldn't raise two little ones on a waitress's salary. She finally broke down and wrote me a letter asking for money. A loan, she said, for diapers and food. That's why I drove to Nashville and loaded up you and your little brother and brought you back home with me. Oh, Leona squawled and carried on, but she knew I was right in doing that. Even if she couldn't see it at the time."

"You went and got us?"

Maw Maw squinted at her through the curly-cues of cigar smoke.

Dana continued. "All I remember is her shoving me and Matt out of the Thunderbird in front of the house. I remember her dropping us off, not you bringing us back."

Maw Maw said, "You must be remembering that time when she tried to kidnap you."

Dana couldn't keep the surprise out of her voice, "Kidnap? When?"

"She came back to town with the idea of kidnapping her babies back. Said she couldn't live without you all. She had a pocketful of money for writing some country song that got sold and she thought she could make a go of it for a living. She had you both in her car and almost got out of town too, but li'l Matt started crying and screaming so hard for his Maw Maw, it broke her heart and she brought you all back to me. Dropped you all off in front of the house and drove away bawling her eyes out."

Dana shook her head, confused. "I don't remember any of that."

"Memories are funny things, aren't they? They're like your own private little picture show. You can edit and splice and put 'em together any way you want."

Dana sat down on top of the deep freeze and tried to make some kind of order out of all the thoughts swirling around in her head. Her mother didn't abandon her like she thought. She even came back to get her—that was a big pill to swallow all at once.

"Your mother is no saint and that's a fact, but she does love you in her own way. And if you'd give her the time of day, you might find that out."

Dana nodded.

"Good," she said, swatting Dana's leg. "Now get your butt off my freezer."

Dana hopped down and Maw Maw opened the lid, rummaged around a minute, then pulled out two big furry blocks of ice. She thrust them in Dana's direction and asked, "Which one do you think looks more like Jesus? The tabby cat or the collie dog?"

"Collie dog. Obviously. Look at his face."

She placed the cat back in the freezer and handed Dana the frozen dog, saying, "That's exactly what I thought."

Dana gripped the frozen Jesus by the tail and held him out at arm's length. She peeked inside the freezer and was amazed by how full it was. "You've been busy."

Maw Maw shut the freezer lid. "Had a good harvest. Summertime's always the best season 'cause all the animals come out and try to cross the roads."

Maw Maw was a picky harvester. She didn't collect and freeze any old roadkill. It had to meet her high standards. Her criteria were four-part: 1. It had to be completely dead. 2. It had to be whole, not in parts. 3. It had to free of all blood. 4. And it had to have a certain *je ne sais quoi*.

Maw Maw took the dog from Dana and cradled him in her arms. "Look at the *je ne sais quoi* on this one," she said.

Dana stared into the glassy, cold eyes of the dog and just to humor her said, "This one is your best Jesus yet."

Maw Maw looked lovingly into the dog's face. "Your Paw Paw used to look at me the same way."

Dana didn't know if that was a good or a bad thing, so she nodded.

Maw Maw straddled the dog on her hip and rummaged around in some big cardboard boxes, flinging costumes and cheap jewelry every which way. She pulled out a purple apron and draped it over Jesus's shoulders.

"I hate to interrupt you when you're in the middle of a creative orgy, Maw Maw, but I thought you were going to quit doing your art displays. You said you couldn't afford to keep paying for all the fines."

"I thought of a better way to handle the situation."

"What better way?"

"I'm not going to pay those fines."

"You want to go to jail? That's a heavy price for some little ol' roadside display."

She shot Dana a stern look. "They're not displays. They are drive-by art that connects to the soul with a mighty moral punch."

That was an exact quote from some Christian magazine out of Arkansas that interviewed Maw Maw about three years ago. They compared her to John the Baptist as a modern "voice crying in the wilderness." They didn't bother to mention that John the Baptist was bat-shit crazy from eating all those locusts and only wearing animal skin dresses like Barney Rubble.

"Now grab that possum," Maw Maw said, pointing into the belly of the freezer. "He'll make a good Judas."

Fifteen minutes later Maw Maw had all the varmints arranged like the photograph of The Last Supper painting that she had ripped out of a magazine.

"You got it wrong," Dana said, studying the magazine photo. "The woman to the left of Jesus should be facing out more."

"That isn't a woman, Dana," Maw Maw corrected. "That there is the Apostle John."

Dana scrutinized the photo from an arm's length away, then again at only inches from her nose. "It sure looks like a woman to me."

"Men looked like women back in the olden days," Maw Maw said. "They all had long hair and wore dresses."

"No, it's definitely a woman. Look, no Adam's apple and check out her soft hands." Dana stuck the picture under Maw Maw's nose so she could inspect it.

Maw Maw refused to look and waved the paper away. "They all looked feminine back when. Especially Jesus. That there's the Apostle John all right. I oughta know, I taught Sunday School for thirty years."

Dana gave up. Maw Maw could argue with God and win.

CHAPTER FOURTEEN

Dana drove the ice cream truck back into town because Maw Maw had insisted on switching cars with her so Dana could remain undetected by the police. Maw Maw said if the cops hauled her off to jail for aiding and abetting it would be a great adventure. In Dana's humble opinion it wasn't a good trade. It's not like she could be inconspicuous in an ice cream truck that blared the tune to "Jesus Loves Me, This I Know."

Dana told herself that she would sneak in and out of town quickly. She wanted to pack some clothes, (she wanted to get out of her cockamamie Wonder Woman costume) and maybe say goodbye to Trudy before she ventured out and lived a life in the underbelly of society as a renegade outlaw fugitive. But if she were being totally honest with herself, she wanted to see Ellen one last time. She envisioned a tearful goodbye. Ellen would burst into tears, lamenting the love she'd never have. Then Dana would relent against her better judgment and invite Ellen to go on the lam with her. It would be like Bonnie and Clyde except it would be Bonnie and Bonnie.

"But life won't be all roses. You have to understand that. I'll always be a wanted woman," Dana would say. "We'll have to live on the road, always on the move, the law chasing us from one nameless town to another, eating bologna and raw weiners out of an ice chest."

"I love you and that's all the matters," Ellen would say. Then, just like in her favorite book, they would drive off in the ice cream truck toward the orange sunset and the *Go, Dog. Go!* party tree.

Dana's romantic fantasy was interrupted by another round of "Jesus Loves Me, This I Know." The song jangled every last nerve she had in her body. She scanned the dashboard and punched and twirled every button she could find, but the stupid song still tinkled from the overhead speaker. She had been in the ice cream truck five minutes and she felt like ripping out her hair.

She swerved left into her neighborhood and drove up and down the streets slowly, hoping to catch a glimpse of Ellen or her mail truck.

Bingo! Dana found her about five blocks away from the funeral parlor.

She parked the ice cream truck behind Ellen's mail truck. She turned off the engine and was rewarded with instant relief when the song stopped too. She walked all the way around the mail truck but didn't see Ellen anywhere.

She was about to climb back in the ice cream truck when she saw the mail truck shaking—

Ellen sure has a small bladder.

—and bouncing up and down.

She started back for the rolling door but stopped when she heard something mighty peculiar. It sounded like whales mating. She knew that sound because she liked to watch *Animal Planet* when she had insomnia.

She figured that Ellen was either really sick or was a really bad singer. She rolled up the back door of the mail truck and once again came face to face with Ellen's bare butt. But this time Ellen wasn't squatting over a Gatorade bottle. This time she had her butt in the air and her nose buried between a woman's thighs.

The woman who belonged to the thighs, leaned up and looked over Ellen's shoulder.

And the woman was—*drumroll*—none other than—*drumroll*—Kimmy! *Rimshot!*

Dana screamed inside her head and clasped her hands over her ears like that Culkin kid in the *Home Alone* movies. It was incomprehensible, yet the evidence was irrefutable. Dana was staring right at the butt of her girlfriend while she was going down on her girlfriend. Her girlfriend's girlfriend was her girlfriend.

Ellen lowered her butt and looked over her shoulder. "Dana?"

Dana looked from Ellen to Kimmy. "Kimmy?" she asked.

"Dana?" Kimmy asked.

"Ellen?" Dana asked.

"Kimmy?" Ellen asked.

"What the hell are you doing, Ellen?" Dana asked.

"You two know each other?" Kimmy asked.

"Who's Kimmy?" Ellen asked.

"Her. The woman you're going down on," Dana said.

"That's Jeannie," Ellen said.

"Who's Jeannie?" Dana asked.

Ellen pointed at Kimmy. "She's Jeannie."

"That's not Jeannie. That's Kimmy," Dana said.

Ellen and Dana looked at Kimmy and asked simultaneously, "Who *are* you?"

Kimmy stood up and wiggled back into her panties, pulled her skirt back down, saying to Dana, "Never you mind who I am, who are you?"

Dana shouted. "You know who I am! I'm Dana!" She pointed at Ellen and asked Kimmy, "Who's that?"

Ellen said, "You know who I am! I'm Ellen."

Dana rolled her eyes and put her hands on her hips. "I know who you are and you know who you are and I know who I am and so do you and we know who each other is, but what I want to know is who are you to her?"

"Run that by me again," Ellen said, standing and pulling her pants up.

Kimmy jumped out of the back of the mail truck.

"Kimmy, where are you going?" Dana asked.

"Her name's not Kimmy. It's Jeannie," Ellen said.

"No, it's Kimmy," Dana said.

"She's my girlfriend, I ought to know her own name," Ellen said.

"She's my girlfriend and I say her name is Kimmy," Dana said.

"We have the same girlfriend?" Ellen asked.

"Apparently, you're the one Kimmy's been screwing behind my back all this time."

Ellen said, "So, you're the one Jeannie's been screwing behind my back."

"I should've known," Dana said. "I should've known you were too good to be true. You've been lying to me all along."

"Oh, no, you don't. I'm not the liar. You can't blame this on me. If anybody lied, it's you!" Ellen shouted.

"I never lied to you!" Dana shuffled her feet. *Except for that one part about being an alcoholic, but that's not what we're talking about right now.* "You're the one telling me how much you like me and want to be with me, then having sex with somebody else."

"She's my girlfriend. I can have sex with her anytime I want."

"In the back of a mail truck during work hours? That's where my tax money's going? Isn't that like a federal offense or something?"

"It's my lunch hour! And, like you haven't been having sex with her too," Ellen said disgustedly. "And don't talk to me about breaking the law. Lesbianism is illegal in Oklahoma so you're guilty too."

"Both you *and* Kimmy Jeannie are cheating on me! That does it! I'm breaking up with you both!" Dana made a memorable exit, hopping out of the back end of the mail truck, slipping in the gravel and landing smack-dab on her rear end. "Crapola!"

Ellen leaned out of the back of the mail truck and looked down at Dana. "Are you okay?"

"No, I most certainly am *not* okay. Your girlfriend stole my ice cream truck."

"*My* girlfriend? I thought she was *your* girlfriend."

Dana stood up and brushed the gravel and dust off her rear end. "Not anymore, she's not. You can have her."

"But I don't want her."

"Tough titty said the kitty." Dana did an about-face and walked away as fast as she could without actually running. She looked like a speed walker, a very angry speed walker. She had no idea where she was going, but that didn't matter. All that mattered was that she get far away from Ellen.

* * *

Three minutes later Dana was still walking, though not as speedily as before. She was headed for Trudy's because that's what best friends are for and besides, she had nowhere else to go. She was about two blocks from the funeral parlor when she heard the unmistakable tinkling of "Jesus Loves Me, This I Know."

Dana quickly jumped off the sidewalk and hunkered behind a hedge. She peeked over the hedge edge in time to see the ice cream truck varoom down the street with the music blaring over the tinny-sounding speaker. A whole passel of kids were frantically chasing after the truck, waving dollar bills. They were red-faced, wheezing and yelling, "Stop! I want ice cream! Hey! Get back here, where're you going?! I'm going to tell my mom on you!"

Kimmy stuck her head out the window and shooed the children with her hand, yelling, "Stop following me! Go away!" When the fastest kids caught up to her, she accelerated and careened around the next corner on two wheels.

The pack of kids outsmarted her by running through a yard, heading down the alley and cutting her off one street over.

"Leave me alone!" Dana heard Kimmy shout from two blocks away. "I don't have any friggin' ice cream!"

Dana laughed. She doubled over, held her belly and laughed. She laughed until she had tears streaking down her face.

* * *

"Let me get this straight," Trudy said, "Ellen is your girlfriend's girlfriend? You're dating Kimmy and Ellen is dating Kimmy and you and Ellen are dating?"

Dana was too busy crying to answer. It was like the dam had broken and she was drowning in her own tears. She was lying on top of Trudy's make over table, face-down, head buried in the crook of her elbow, sobbing and hiccupping.

"Which one are you crying about?" Trudy asked. "Are you heartbroken over Kimmy or Ellen?"

"Ellen!" Dana sputtered through tears and snot.

Trudy wrapped her arms around Dana's shoulders and nuzzled her nose into her hair. "Aw honey. I know it hurts. But, you know, someday we'll be laughing about this."

"I don't think so," Dana said. "I was so in love with her. Big Love, with a capital L."

"You've been through worse times than this, Double D. Remember Lisa?"

"Which one?" She sniffled.

"Any of them. All of them. You thought you were in big love with all of them."

"I wasn't in love with Lisa Four."

"Riiight," Trudy said. "I know you, remember? Every time you kiss a girl, you think it's love."

"Doesn't matter. It's over now."

"You're not really going to run away, are you?" Trudy asked.

Dana sat up and asked brightly, "Hey, you want to go with me? We could go to a big city and you could start up your dead celebrity look-alike business."

Trudy looked away and shook her head. "I'm not ready. I still have to...I have lots to do."

Dana nodded her head and said, "Okay, but you're going to be sorry. I'll be out there somewhere having a grand ol' time and you'll be here still playing wet nurse to a dream."

Trudy looked stern. "This isn't one of your TV movies, DD. This is real life. And in real life when people run away from the law, they get caught and when they get caught sometimes they get dead."

"I won't get dead," Dana promised. "And you know what?"

"What?"

Dana hopped off the table. "I'm sick and tired of being stomped on. This time I'm going to do the stomping." To prove her point, she stomped her foot.

Trudy was dubious.

Dana faced Trudy and squared her shoulders. She smiled. "I feel free. Like I'm a bird who somebody let out of the cage." She raised her arms and stretched her wings.

Trudy was dubiouser.

"You know, I think I'll do something…I'm going to take Leona's advice and do something I wouldn't have done before. Call it a final fuck-you and fare-thee-well to cheating girlfriends."

Trudy took two steps back. "You're kinda scaring me, Double D."

Dana snapped her fingers and asked, "Does your daddy still have all those magnetic letters for the sign out front?"

"Sure. But what're—" Trudy stopped. Her face lit up with a grin. "You're not going to…?"

"I sure as tootin' am," Dana said, rubbing her palms together. "Now, go fetch me those letters."

* * *

The Last Chance Baptist Church was the biggest and richest and proudest church in Dooley Springs. It was three stories of red brick and had a pointy spire taller than any other building in the county. The membership had just completed erecting its brand new sign overlooking the four lane bypass. Magnetic letters made up messages that changed on a weekly basis. This week's message read, "I kissed a girl and I liked it. Then I went to hell."

Four more Baptist churches were lined up down the bypass and each one had their very own magnetic letter sign. The churches' dueling scripture and cheesy messages kept the non-religious of Dooley Springs thoroughly entertained. Sometimes denizens drove the bypass on a Sunday to read the new messages. It was cheap entertainment.

Trudy pulled the hearse into the Last Chance Baptist Church parking lot (they had decided they had to use the hearse because it would hold the long ladder and cops never pulled over a hearse) through the portico and parked it around back so nobody could see them from the road. Trudy had coaxed the keys away from her daddy saying she was going to take it for a wash and wax. She figured as long as she ran it through the Not-a-Spot car wash before she brought it back, he wouldn't be any the wiser.

"Keep the engine running," Dana said. "And keep a lookout while I do the work."

"Okay, sure," Trudy replied. "But what do I do if I see somebody coming? You might not see it if I scratch my butt."

"Honk twice, then get the heck out and save yourself. I'm already a wanted fugitive. You have more to lose, so don't hesitate, go."

"Okay," Trudy said.

Dana pulled the ladder out of the back and propped it up against the tall sign. She scrambled up the ladder and picked off the magnetic letters, tossing them to the ground.

Trudy sat behind the wheel of the hearse, playing with the radio and keeping a lookout for cops or Baptists.

Dana climbed down the ladder and fished around in the big cardboard box of letters looking for the ones to spell out the message she had in mind.

"Dangit!" Dana yelled.

Trudy powered down the window. "What?"

"I don't have enough letters."

"Why? What're you going to put up there?"

"Well…" Dana said, "something along the lines of 'Kimmy is a cheating whoredog slut who is going to hell and I hate her and she can't even cut hair good and she has a bald hoo-ha.' You know, something generic like that."

"May I make a suggestion?" Trudy said.

"Sure."

"Cut down your message a little. Make it something simple like 'Kimmy is a slut.' You know, that really says it all right there."

"Okay, but I want to do all the Baptist signs along the bypass. I want the whole town to see them. And I don't have enough M's to do 'Kimmy is a slut' that many times."

Trudy scrunched up one side of her face and thought for a moment. "I know!" she said. "Do one of those progressive sign things."

"Huh?"

"Like those advertising signs on the way through west Oklahoma. One word per sign. This sign would say 'Kimmy,' and the next one down the road will read 'is' and the next one 'a' and the next will be 'slut'. Like that."

Dana rubbed her palms together, envisioning it. "I love it! Then as people drive down the highway, they'll read the message one sign at a time."

"Exactly." Trudy powered her window back up.

Dana quickly rummaged around in the box, grabbed the letters M, I, Y, K and M, stuck the K between her teeth, the others in her bathrobe-cape pockets, and headed back up the ladder.

* * *

"If I'd known revenge was this much fun, I'd have tried it years ago," Dana said. She fake-puffed on a cigarette and handed it to Trudy.

"I can't believe you wouldn't let me see them!" Trudy clenched the cigarette between her teeth as she drove the hearse down the bypass. "What did you write? Tell me!"

"No!" Dana giggled. "I want you to read it just like how all the cars driving by will see it. That way you can give me a purely objective opinion."

"Okay, here comes the first sign," Trudy said.

Dana took back the cigarette as Trudy drove the hearse by the first sign and read the message out loud, "'KIMMY.'"

Trudy nodded. No surprise there.

"Here comes the next one," Dana said.

Trudy neared the sign for the Free Will Baptist Church and read its message out loud, "'IS.'"

Trudy snickered in anticipation. "'KIMMY IS' what?"

Dana stifled a giggle. "'KIMMY IS...'" She beat a drumroll with her fingertips on the dashboard.

Trudy read the next sign, "'A SLUT AND...'"

Dana echoed, "'KIMMY IS A SLUT AND...'" Drumroll again.

"And what?"

"Keep driving," Dana urged. "Here it comes."

Trudy craned her neck around the wheel to read the last sign. "'EATS POO-POO.'" She burst into gales of laughter. "'Kimmy is a slut and eats poo-poo'? You actually wrote 'poo-poo'!" After laughing herself out, she asked, "Why didn't you write 'shit'?"

"I was all out of S's, and I had a surplus of O's."

CHAPTER FIFTEEN

Dana slept like the dead.

She woke up early the next morning and it took her a full two minutes to realize she was inside a coffin. She had fallen asleep there the night before because she couldn't go home and it was a perfect hiding place. Trudy and Dana had stayed up late giggling and talking like they used to in high school before husbands and girlfriends got in the way of their friendship.

Dana availed herself of the facilities and took a quick sponge bath in the ladies room. She used the cheap soap in the hand dispenser to wash her face and neck and hands and arms. The rough paper towels left her skin feeling red and raw. After that, there was no way she was going to use the soap and towels on any of her tender parts.

She had told Trudy that she wouldn't leave until she came into work, but Dana decided that maybe she should sneak home and grab a quick shower before going on the lam. And maybe she should pack a lunch. And change clothes too. Wonder Woman was too conspicuous. There was probably an APB out for her by now with a detailed description of her costume. She could always come back by and tell Trudy goodbye right before she left town.

Dana put her bathrobe-cape back on, this time putting her arms in the sleeves and wearing it like a bathrobe. She tied the belt around her middle and hoped that hid most of her costume.

She crept out the back door and disappeared, superhero stealth-style.

* * *

"Jesus loves me, this I know…"

Dana froze in the middle of her packing and strained her ears.

Clump.

She looked at her bedside clock and watched the second-hand tick off a full minute. There was no more clumping or music so she resumed packing.

It was already six a.m. and she hadn't even taken a shower or changed out of the Wonder Woman costume yet. She was going to have to hurry. The problem was she couldn't decide what to wear. Jeans or sweats? Should she pack both? How many pairs of underwear should she pack? Finally, she dumped her whole underwear drawer into a paper sack. That way she wouldn't have to worry so much about finding a laundromat.

I bet I'll lose weight. I've never heard of a fat fugitive. No time for eating, let alone overeating. That's a definite bonus.

She dumped all her bras into the sack. Dana didn't own a suitcase because she'd never gone anywhere before. She was sure going to make up for that now. Maybe she could take the time to buy a suitcase (or a new wardrobe!) after she got across state lines.

Was it important to get across state lines? Dana didn't really know. Was she safe if she crossed into Arkansas or could the Arkansas cops get her? She wished she'd paid more attention to those reality cop shows.

Clump.

There was that noise again. Dana thought maybe it was Asscat throwing another squirrel butthole on the porch. Or maybe it was the newspaper being thrown on the porch by the newspaper boy. But it couldn't be that. Dana had unsubscribed to the paper over a month ago when she had a tiff with the editor over the crossword puzzle. He ran the same puzzle two days in a row and when she did her civic duty and brought it to his attention, he told her it was a mistake. "A mistake!" she had bellowed over the phone. The only reason she had subscribed to the paper in the first place was for the crossword. Some days it was the only thing that got her out of bed. All Dana wanted was an apology and a promise that he'd be more careful from now on, but the editor had some bug up his butt about news stories being more important than puzzles and having a lot more important things on his plate to worry about than her puzzle needs and in the end, he refused to apologize sufficiently and she cancelled her subscription just to show him.

So, if the clumping noise wasn't the morning paper, then what the hell was it? Was it a clomping or a clumping noise?

Dana edged over to her bedroom window and peered around the curtain. The sun was peeking over the horizon and the only person up and moving was the old lady who lived in the house across the street.

When Dana was a kid she thought that house was haunted. Now that she was grown up, she *knew* that house was haunted. The rumor was that the little old lady who lived there, Willie Mae, had killed her husband in 1962, decapitated him with a hacksaw and sat his severed head out for the garbage. Dana sometimes saw his headless shadow roaming the house looking for his head.

Willie Mae was already up and about and winterizing her flower beds by throwing hay over everything. Willie Mae was the spitting image of those little troll dolls. She had fly-away blue-tinted hair, big gnarled feet and a bulbous nose. She straightened up from her hay tossing, put a hand on the small of her back and stretched. She peered over toward Dana's house. Dana squatted down real quick so she wouldn't be spotted. After a few seconds Dana poked her nose back over the windowsill and had another look-see.

Willie Mae was still looking toward Dana's front porch, but now she had her hand held up and was shading her eyes. She lifted the eyeglasses that were hanging from a dirty string around her neck and perched them on her nose.

Willie Mae stumbled backwards like whatever she'd seen had slapped her in the face. She turned and ran pell-mell for her front door.

Dana had never seen the old woman move so fast. She pressed her nose against the window and tried to see whatever had sent Willie Mae scurrying for her house. That was when she noticed the ice cream truck parked in the driveway. So Kimmy *had* come home. She squinted at the front porch and didn't see anything except—

What the heck is that?

—a foot. A foot with red toenails was hanging off the porch. The foot was connected to a shin and the shin was connected to a knee and the knee was connected to a she-didn't-know-what because she couldn't see that far, but Dana really hoped it was connected to a body because the thought of a leg all by itself on her front porch was enough to make her queasy. And that was saying something because Dana didn't quease up easily. Normally she had the stomach of a goat.

Dana ran out her bedroom door, leaped down the stairs two at a time with her bathrobe-cape flying behind her, hit the floor with both feet and bounded for the front door.

She stopped. She took a deep breath and counted to fifteen (a multiple of three) inside her head. She screwed her courage to the sticking point, opened the front door a crack and peeked outside.

Kimmy was lying on the front porch, naked, tits up.

Dana closed the door so quickly, she almost squished her own nose.

She shut her eyes and thought about what she just saw. Was Kimmy napping on the front porch?

Dana opened the door and peeked out. Kimmy was still there. Naked and motionless. She studied Kimmy, but she couldn't discern any movement. It sure looked like she wasn't breathing. She shut the door.

Holy crap. Kimmy is dead. That is Kimmy's dead, naked body on my front porch.

Dana opened the door, took three deep breaths and stepped out onto the porch. She stared at Kimmy's unbreathing body. Dana's brain told her feet to move, but her feet either weren't listening or they were glued to the porch boards.

She didn't have to check for a pulse to know Kimmy was dead. She could see that she wasn't breathing. An armadillo with tire tracks down its middle laying tits up in the middle of the highway couldn't have been any more dead.

Dana wished she'd had some coffee before Kimmy had gone and died and thrown herself on the porch. This was going to screw up her getaway.

She heard a far-off siren and this time her feet started running before her mind told them to. She followed her feet down the porch steps and through the front yard. She ran as fast as her feet would carry her with her long blue bathrobe-cape flowing behind her.

Dana only ran as far as her own backyard before she pulled a Dooley. Somehow, her left foot got hung up in her bathrobe-cape. The dangling belt wrapped itself around her ankle like a skeleton's hand reaching up from the grave and its bony fingers yanked her foot out from under her and she flew butt-first and head-second around the corner of the house. She had enough forward momentum going that she rolled the next thirty yards.

While performing these acrobatic somersaults, she saw the topsy-turvy world flash by her eyes. It was like looking at a scrapbook upside down while it spun on a lazy susan in the middle of a merry-go-round on a Ferris wheel. She saw the back of her house: a close-up of grass; a pile of petrified dog doody; a pink and orange sunrise; the back porch; and more dried-up doody.

As these snapshots whirred by and her body was otherwise engaged with rolling, her brain had time to think. It thought about Dead Kimmy. It thought about who had killed Dead Kimmy. Her brain knew it wasn't her. At this point she was the only suspect she could safely rule out. Sure, Dana hated Kimmy enough to kill her, but somebody had beat her to it. The murderer could be Ellen. Maybe Leona poofed her even though she had asked her not to. Or maybe Maw Maw did the honors. Dana realized if she thought about it hard enough she could find a motive for everybody in town—spurned lovers, unrequited lovers (not many of those), wives of lovers, husbands of lovers, lovers of lovers, you name it.

As Dana rolled, she asked herself a question: *Why did I run when I found her dead?* She answered the question: *Because she was on my porch and that made it look like I did it and I panicked.* Dana believed herself, but she didn't think the police would. *I didn't kill Kimmy, but it sure looks like I did.*

Half the town could testify that she had a motive. She had advertised her loathing for Dead Kimmy and not too subtly, either. Dana reviewed the list of things she did or said that could incriminate her. There were those highway signs. Puddinhead caught her about to chunk a hunk of concrete at Kimmy. She followed Kimmy in a police cruiser and yelled over the speaker at her. Brenda, the waitress at BJ's, had overheard her talking about killing Kimmy. She'd told Ellen she wished Kimmy would go away. She wrote about getting rid of Kimmy on her to-do list. And to top it all off, she'd become an alcoholic and everybody knew they did things they didn't remember afterward. She had Dooleyed this one up but good.

Dana rolled to a stop with her nose about three inches away from a fresh grave. She could bury Dead Kimmy's butthole out here with the squirrel buttholes. But there wasn't enough time for digging.

Dana untangled her limbs and sat up. She was sitting on top of the storm cellar doors. She took that as an omen and decided to do what any sane person would do when it looked like they'd murdered their girlfriend and said girlfriend was lying naked on their front porch: hide the body in the cellar.

They couldn't arrest her if there was no body. If there was no body, how would they know there was a murder? Dana had watched enough *CSI* to know that much.

* * *

Kimmy was dead weight. Dana tried to pick her up and sling her over her shoulder in a fireman's carry, but ended up dropping her on her head. It was a good thing she was dead because that would have hurt.

The police siren wailed closer and that sent Dana into hyperdrive. A hefty shot of adrenaline coursed through her veins and you know how those people who are good and scared can lift up the front end of a car to get the little kid out from under the tire? That was pure-dee bullcrap because Dana still couldn't pick her up. Instead, she grabbed Dead Kimmy's legs, turned her back to her, hitched Kimmy's knees around her waist and dragged her like she was a Clydesdale pulling a beer wagon.

If Kimmy weren't dead and feeling no pain, Dana might have felt bad about dragging Dead Kimmy's bare ass over the grass and gravel. And—in a passive-aggressive move—over a couple of piles of doggy doody. What was the harm? Dead Kimmy was dead and it made Dana feel better, so why not.

She put Kimmy's legs down long enough to fling open the storm cellar doors. She then reversed direction and backed down the cellar steps, pulling Dead Kimmy by her ankles. Dana's stomach lurched each time Dead Kimmy's head banged down the steps. It reminded her of the time she'd tried to bust open a coconut by throwing it on the sidewalk.

She pulled Dead Kimmy over to the middle of the cellar's dirt floor, ran back up the steps, grabbed one door handle and then the other and clanged them shut. And just in time too, because Dana heard tires screech to a stop on the street and a siren let out one last long *Whooooooop whoop whoop* before it cut out.

Dana headed back down the steps, but—

Crapola !

—the hem of her bathrobe-cape was caught in the doors and instead of going down the steps, she found herself hanging in midair. The robe was grabbing her under her arms and her toes couldn't touch the ground. Her feet were still in running mode, moving back and forth, and she looked like Fred Flintstone where his feet move in a big blur before they catch ground and take off. Dana swung back and forth a couple of times, using her legs as momentum like a kid on a swing. Finally, her arms slipped out of the robe and she was tossed to the floor in a heap right beside Dead Kimmy.

She didn't dare open the doors again to retrieve her bathrobe-cape since the police were there already. She had to hope and pray that they wouldn't see any fuzzy blue material poking out of the doors.

She wished Wonder Woman had an invisible cape like that Harry Potter character. No, wait, he had a cape of invisibility. What she needed was a cape that was invisible.

She crawled over to the far wall, rested her back against the cold concrete and hugged her knees to her chest. A good five minutes passed before she realized she was crying.

She swiped away the tears, disgusted with her weakness.

Wonder Woman doesn't cry.

She didn't even know why she was crying. Was she crying for Dead Kimmy or was she crying for herself? Maybe she was crying for Ellen and what would never be. Probably she was crying for all of those reasons.

Dana snorted the tears back up and tried to clear her mind enough to think. But the only clear thought that came to mind was that she was up that famous creek without a paddle. If Willie Mae saw Dana moving the body, the police were going to head back this way. If those doors opened up and they found her down here with a naked dead body... How would she explain that?

WWWWD? What would Wonder Woman do?

Wonder Woman would've called the police and told them she found a dead body. Too late for that now.

Dana looked at Dead Kimmy, but she just stared back with glassy eyes and was no help whatsoever. Dead Kimmy looked so vulnerable all naked and not breathing. She was lying on her back and her man-made boobs had low air pressure and were drooping off to her sides. Her nipples were pointing in different directions like Marty Feldman's eyes.

Dana rolled Dead Kimmy over onto her stomach so she didn't have to look at those weird eyes. Her real eyes, not her nipples.

No sooner had she sat back down than a thought hit her. She could pray. It couldn't hurt anything. The only trouble was she'd never said a prayer on her own before. Dana and Jesus had never been on what you might call speaking terms. The closest she'd ever come to being religious was when she was nine years old and went to summer Bible School. She made a picture of Jesus out of macaroni, pinto beans and Elmer's glue. Then she ate it. She hoped Jesus wasn't still mad about that.

Dana squished her eyes shut and prayed out loud, "Dear God..." She stopped. Did God have a first name? How did He know she was praying to Him and not some other god named God? That was when inspiration hit her upside the head. Why should she pray to only one god? Why not hedge her bets and pray to them all? She started her prayer over, "Dear God, Buddha, Allah, Athena, Jehovah, Zeus and that one god with eight arms: Please help me dispose of Dead Kimmy's body so nobody will find out and please don't let me get arrested for her murder."

She figured as long as she was asking for stuff, she might as well go whole hog. "And please let me be a rich and famous writer." She knew that might be asking too much since she was writing for the niche market of lesbian fiction. She amended her prayer, "And if the rich and famous part is too hard at least let me win one of those Goldie awards. Okay, thanks. Goodbye and amen."

Dana hung up the line and opened her eyes. As soon as she did, she realized she wasn't quite through with her prayer. She quickly shut her eyes again. "Are you all still there? You haven't hung up, have you? Listen, you can forget all that other stuff if you'll grant me one wish. Can you get Ellen to love me back?"

CHAPTER SIXTEEN

After what seemed like an eternity but was probably only about five minutes, Dana crawled across the dirt floor and sat on the bottom step. She took a deep breath and held it while she counted to thirty-three.

She heard voices. She quietly crawled up the stairs and listened with her ear pressed against the double doors.

"I don't see a thing, lady."

Dana would recognize that voice anywhere. It was Puddinhead. That was good and bad. It was bad because Puddinhead wanted to put Dana away forever and would think this was a great opportunity. It was good because Puddinhead was too stupid to figure out how to do such a thing.

Dana heard Willie Mae's voice crackle like two pieces of Velcro being pulled apart. "She was on the porch, I'm telling you. Dead. And as naked as the day she was born."

Puddinhead replied, "Where is this body now? Dead, naked bodies don't get up and walk off."

"I didn't say she walked off," Granny snapped. "Somebody carried her off. Probably one of those hemophiliacs who like to have sex with dead people."

"Necrophiliac," Dana muttered.

"So, you're proposing that a woman got naked, died on the front porch and then somebody stole the body for sexual purposes?" Puddinhead said.

"Can you think of another reason she was there and now she isn't?" Willie Mae asked.

"Maybe she was never there to begin with?"

"Don't sass me, young man."

"Or maybe she wasn't even dead. Just sunbathing."

"In October? On a porch? Are you calling me a liar, young man?"

"No, ma'am, I'm not accusing you of lying," Puddinhead said. "I'm saying you called last week about a gunshot next door and it turned out your neighbor was watching *Cops* with the volume at full blast. Then a couple of days later you called about a woman abusing her child and it was some cats going at it in the alley. Now you call and say there's a dead, naked woman across the street and some sexual deviant stole her body."

Dana put her hand over her mouth to stifle her giggles.

"Where are you going?" Willie Mae asked.

"I'm going to drive up and down the neighborhood looking for a sexual predator having sexual intercourse with a dead naked woman."

"I'm going to report you to your superiors! There's no respect anymore. There was a time when concerned citizens got some respect, when officers of the law actually cared about..." Willie Mae grumbled, her voice fading as she walked away.

Dana kept her ear pressed to the doors until she heard the faint sound of a car engine turn over and drive away. She counted to three hundred and then creaked open the cellar doors. She peeked out.

All was clear.

Dana's mission was to get Dead Kimmy out of the cellar and as far away as possible from her house. She grabbed her bathrobe-cape and threw it back over her shoulders, knotting the arms around her neck. She inched out of the cellar, lay belly down in the grass and army crawled across the backyard toward the driveway and the ice cream truck.

She peered around the corner of the house. Willie Mae was nowhere to be seen and her old car was gone. She probably had gone to file a report on Puddinhead.

Dana duck-walked over to the ice cream truck and jumped behind the wheel. Thank God, the keys were left in the ignition. She turned the engine over and flinched when "Jesus Loves Me" blared through the roof speaker.

She slumped down in the bucket seat, hoping a casual observer would mistake the top of her head for Maw Maw's head. Using only the side mirrors, she managed to back the truck across the yard and right up alongside the open storm cellar in only one try.

Dana left the engine running and went back down into the cellar. She whipped off her bathrobe-cape and wrestled Dead Kimmy into it. Dana was thankful that rigor mortis hadn't set in yet because it would be awful to have to break her arms to get her into the bathrobe-cape. She tied the belt around Dead Kimmy's waist and hefted her into a sitting position. Squatting behind her, she wrapped her arms around Dead Kimmy's chest and lifted. She got her about three feet off the floor before Dead Kimmy slipped out of her grasp and plunked down hard on her butt.

The next time Dana tried to lift her, she had her arms around Dead Kimmy's waist and her hands locked together. This time she got her all the way into a standing position, but it was like balancing a wet noodle on its end and Dead Kimmy crumpled to the ground.

Dana gave up before her back gave out. She grabbed Dead Kimmy by the wrists and dragged her to the bottom of the stairs. She pulled as hard as she could and managed to get Dead Kimmy's butt off the floor and about three stairs up. Dana leaned her back, buried her right shoulder into Dead Kimmy's belly, flopped her top half over her shoulder and lifted.

Dana staggered under Dead Kimmy's dead weight up the stairs and into the daylight. She dropped the body, ran around the ice cream truck and opened the passenger door.

She raced back to Dead Kimmy, dragged her up alongside the door and wadded her inside. Dead Kimmy ended up with her head in the floorboard, her butt in the seat and her feet on the dashboard. She was curled up tighter than a rolly-polly bug. It took Dana another five minutes of pushing and pulling before she got Dead Kimmy's feet below her head.

Dana turned to shut the door when she heard a noise like sweaty thighs ripping off a vinyl car seat. She looked at Dead Kimmy and saw that she had slid down in her seat and that the noise she heard actually *was* sweaty skin sliding down vinyl. Dana pushed Dead Kimmy's butt back up into the seat and, this time, held her in place with the seat belt.

Dana stood back about five paces from the passenger window. She walked in place, pretending to be walking down the street. She wanted to know what the casual observer would see if they glanced at the ice cream truck as it drove by.

Dana glanced at the truck. She looked away. She glanced again. She looked away. Just as she thought. It looked like a dead woman was slumped in the passenger seat.

Dana stopped walking in place and thought about the predicament. Maybe Dead Kimmy wouldn't look so dead if the truck was in motion when somebody looked at her. Of course, Dana couldn't drive the truck *and* look at Dead Kimmy through the passenger window at the same time, so she did the next best thing—she walked about twenty yards in front of the truck and jogged by. She glanced up at Dead Kimmy as she passed.

She still looked pretty dead.

Dana opened the passenger door and moved Dead Kimmy's legs out of the way so she could root around in the glovebox. She found an old pair of sunglasses with yellow-tinted lenses. She stuck the glasses on Dead Kimmy's face. They didn't make her look any more un-dead, but at this point anything was an improvement.

Dana walked about forty yards in front of the truck. She bent over, poised like an Olympic runner in the starting blocks.

She counted to three and sprang out of the blocks, racing as fast as she could by the truck.

She glanced up at Dead Kimmy. And looked away.

Dana stopped. She bent over with her hands on her knees. She was out of breath and probably would've thrown up if she'd eaten anything this morning, which she hadn't.

Dead Kimmy would have to do. If anybody asked, she'd say Dead Kimmy had drunk too much and passed out.

Dana climbed into the truck, drove out of the yard, down the driveway and onto the street. A couple of blocks over she turned onto Main Street and headed north. If she could get through town without being noticed, she might have a chance to dispose of the body. Fat chance with the Jesus music blaring over the speaker, but what else could she do?

Dana had no idea how Dead Kimmy came to be dead, but she did know that she had to get the body as far as possible away from her. And while she was at it, she could make Dead Kimmy's death look like an accident. Or even a suicide. That way Dana wouldn't be a suspect.

Dana looked over at Dead Kimmy as her floppy head rattled against the window.

Dead Kimmy has to die. Well, okay, she's already dead. Dead Kimmy has to die again.

A red stoplight interrupted Dana's thoughts and forced her to slam on the brakes. Dead Kimmy's body jerked forward against the seatbelt, then slammed back into the seat. Her head conked against the glass window.

"Whoops," Dana said. "Sorry 'bout that."

Dana forced a smile across her worried face while she sat through the light. It wasn't easy to look nonchalant while dressed as Wonder Woman and driving an ice cream truck bellowing Sunday School Muzak with a dead woman in the passenger seat.

Dana caught a few people throwing her sidelong glances. Or was it her imagination? She thought if she were seen talking to Dead Kimmy people might think Dead Kimmy was really Live Kimmy and their suspicions wouldn't be aroused. So she struck up a conversation. "I'm hungry. Are you?"

Dead Kimmy didn't answer.

"We could swing through McDonald's and get one of those McMuffin things. You wanna?"

Dead Kimmy didn't answer.

"Yeah, they're really fattening, but they're tasty, don't you think?"

Dead Kimmy ignored her.

"Well, okay, you don't have to get all upset. We won't eat a fatty McMuffin, then."

Dead Kimmy gave her the silent treatment.

Dana sighed. "I really need to go on a diet anyway. But every time I do, I end up getting so hungry that I eat more and gain weight. I'm the only person in the world who gains weight by going on a diet."

The light changed to green and Dana eased the truck through the intersection. By this time she was so caught up in her conversation with Dead Kimmy, it was only natural for her to assume both speaking roles for the sake of continuity. Dana attempted to do the ventriloquist thing and throw Dead Kimmy's voice without moving her lips. She made Dead Kimmy's voice higher pitched. "You don't need to go on a diet," Dana said as Dead Kimmy pretending to be Live Kimmy. "You are beautiful and sexy."

"Why, thank you, Kimmy," Dana said in a baritone voice. She tossed in a few exaggerated gestures. "But I can barely fit in my Wonder Woman costume anymore. I'd like to lose forty or thirty pounds. Or sixty would be even better."

"You're full of horsefeathers," said Dead Kimmy. "You are gorgeous and sexy and talented and I want to make love to you right now. Pull over."

Dana laughed as herself. "You sure know how to make a girl feel good. And, no, we can't make love right here in an ice cream truck on Main Street. We'd get arrested. And, besides, you're dead and that's gross."

"Well, if I were alive, I'd ravage you right here and now," said Dead Kimmy.

Dana braked at another stoplight and said, "Seriously though, I'm thinking of a new diet. I could only eat Pop-Tarts.

Nothing but Pop-Tarts. Or maybe I'll only eat foods that begin with a 'P.' Like popcorn. And peas."

"And peanut butter," Dead Kimmy said as Dana in a voice that sounded like Live Kimmy imitating Dana.

Wait a minute. I'm getting confused. She said that as me? I was saying things as myself and as her and now I'm saying things as her saying them as me? Who am I again?

Before Dana could answer herself, a lawn mower pulled up in the lane beside Dead Kimmy's window. Dana looked over and saw Hank standing up on his lawnmower and looking back at her. Dana smiled tightly. Hank grinned and tipped his hat. Then he looked right into Dead Kimmy's face, grinned and tipped his ball cap at her.

Dead Kimmy ignored him.

Hank frowned. He rapped on her window with his knuckles. Dead Kimmy didn't even flinch.

Hank looked back at Dana. He pointed at Dead Kimmy as if to say "What the hell's wrong with her?"

Dana smiled and playfully socked Kimmy in the arm, mouthing the words, "Hey, Kimmy, look, it's Hank. Wave at Hank." She reached over and grabbed Dead Kimmy's limp arm. She held on to her elbow below Hank's line of vision and raised Dead Kimmy's arm in the air. By turning her elbow back and forth, she made Dead Kimmy's hand do a twisting-in-the-lightbulb wave at Hank. Her hand was jiggly and floppy, but Hank didn't notice.

He grinned and flopped his hand back at her.

The light turned green and Dana floored the truck, leaving Hank sitting on his lawnmower, still waving.

* * *

Dana had made so many turns down gravel roads that she was lost. She pulled the truck to the side. While driving, she had been thinking up a course of action. She hadn't seen any marks—blood, bruises or cuts—on Dead Kimmy's body. Dead Kimmy's head was a little floppy, but she didn't think her neck was broken. That meant when Dana staged Dead Kimmy's fake death, she needed to make sure the body looked like that was how she really died. In other words, if Dana staged a hit and run, she better run over the body for real or the lack of bruises and broken bones would be a dead giveaway that it didn't really happen that way.

That was Dana's plan. Lay Dead Kimmy in the middle of the road and run over her with the ice cream truck. It was a sound plan, a foolproof plan.

Dana got out of the truck and opened Dead Kimmy's door. She unbuckled her seatbelt, and took her sunglasses off and put them on her own face. She turned around so her back was facing Dead Kimmy and draped her limp arms over her shoulders. She carried her like a sack of potatoes thrown over her shoulders. A really heavy sack.

Light as a feather. Light as a feather.

Kimmy was several inches taller than Dana, which meant Kimmy's bare feet dragged in the gravel behind her as she stumbled down the road. After about thirty yards, Dead Kimmy slipped out of her grip and crumpled to the gravel. Dana squatted down beside Dead Kimmy and counted by threes until she caught her breath.

Dana listened to the song playing on the ice cream truck's speaker. Why hadn't she turned off the engine? That song was going to be stuck in her head all day.

"Jesus loves me—"

Dana rolled Dead Kimmy out of her bathrobe-cape.

"This I know—"

She tied the bathrobe-cape back around her own neck.

"For the Bible—"

She grabbed Dead Kimmy by the ankles and scooted her around until she was perpendicular to the road.

"Tells me so."

Dana looked back at the truck, then down at Kimmy, then back at the truck like she was lining up her pool stick to sink the eight ball in the corner pocket. She moved the body a little more to her left. A few more inches and the truck's tires should hit her straight on and she wouldn't even have to aim with the steering wheel.

Dana looked back to the truck, double checking to see if—

Oh my God!

The truck was rolling straight for her! Dana had left the engine running and forgot to put on the parking brake!

The truck gained momentum as it rolled down the hill, headed straight for Dana and Dead Kimmy. Dana performed an acrobatic forward diving roll into the rain ditch. She jumped back up in time to witness the truck's right tire just as it was about to—

Ew, yucky. I can't look.

She put her hands over her eyes and cringed as she heard a grotesque, squishy noise that sounded like somebody stepping on wet bubble wrap.

Dana peeked through her fingers and saw the ice cream truck was picking up speed and barreling down the road. Dana fixed her eyes on the driver's side door and hauled ass. It took her a good fifty yards to catch up to the truck and another twenty to be able to grip the door handle. She was gasping for breath and felt like she was breathing fire as she threw open the door and heaved herself inside. She threw the truck into second gear, and a few moments later, she was driving down the road like nothing had happened.

Thumpity-thump, thumpity-thump, thumpity-thump.

"Oh no," Dana mumbled, "not a flat tire. Not now." She craned her neck to look in the right side view mirror, but she couldn't see a thing.

She pulled over to the side of the road and this time turned off the engine and put on the parking brake. She got out and walked around the front of the truck, checking the two front tires. They looked okay. She headed for the back and—

Holy Moly!

That noise wasn't a flat tire. It was Dead Kimmy. Her dead arm had got caught in the rear bumper and the truck had dragged her all the way down the hill. How the hell had she missed that?

Dana didn't have much time to deliberate on what to do next because she saw a cloud of dust about a mile back up the road. There was a car coming. And from the looks of it, it was headed her way at a pretty good clip.

Dana quickly opened the back doors of the truck, untangled Dead Kimmy from the bumper and threw her body inside. She jumped inside the truck and closed the doors behind her. She dragged Dead Kimmy over to the freezer and lifted her body inside with the other dead animals. She had to curl Dead Kimmy's head down between her knees to get her to fit. That would keep her from stinking the place up while Dana decided what to do. She should've thought of that earlier.

She jumped into the driver's seat just as CeCe White's purple Gremlin slowly passed by. Dana smiled and waved. What CeCe was doing out here, Dana had no idea. And she didn't want to find out either.

Two minutes later, Dana pulled out onto the highway and was formulating Plan B.

* * *

Dana drove up and down a maze of country roads until her nerves were somewhat calm and Plan B was concocted. She stopped the truck alongside a cow pasture and opened up the deep freeze. Getting Dead Kimmy into the freezer was a lot easier than getting her out. She was like one of Maw Maw's frozen roadkills except bigger. Dana had to knock a lot of ice off Dead Kimmy's extremities (extremi-titties) to pry her out of the freezer.

She laid Dead Kimmy out on the floor to inspect the damage. There was a tire track across her boobs (fake boobs must make good bubble wrap because she didn't appear to be crushed at all), gravel embedded in her butt, freezer burn on her nose, nipples and toes, but surprisingly enough, that was all.

A clap of thunder and a burst of lightning made Dana jump. She looked out the front windshield and saw a barrage of big, fat raindrops. Another clap of thunder sent Dana flying into the driver's seat. She was going to have to hurry with Plan B before she got rained out.

Dana turned the truck into the next left, bumping over a cattle guard and aiming for a lone tree in the middle of the pasture. She flipped a U-ey and backed up to the tree.

It took her about two minutes to find a long rope in back of the truck and about three more minutes to tie it around Dead Kimmy's neck in a respectable noose. Thank God for those Girl Scout badges she'd had to earn.

Dana threw open the back doors and hopped out into pasture, splattering mud and cow poop all over her Wonder Woman boots. She rolled Dead Kimmy out of the back of the truck, and let her plop into the mud. She dragged her by wrists through the pouring rain and situated her under a limb of the big oak tree. It took Dana four tries to throw the end of the rope over the limb.

Where's a golden lasso when you need one?

Dana pulled on the end of the rope and, using her body weight, jerked Dead Kimmy into a sitting position. The more Dana pulled, the more Dead Kimmy flopped around like a Raggedy Ann who was missing all her stuffing. Dana pulled as hard as she could but only managed to get Dead Kimmy's butt about six inches off the ground.

Dana wiped her wet hair out of her eyes, gritted her teeth, held her breath and leaned all her weight into the rope and then pulled again. That got Dead Kimmy about a foot higher in the air. Now she looked more like a puppet with some broken strings.

Dana peered through the rain and saw a herd of curious cows had come up to inspect the commotion. The cows formed a loose circle around Dana and Dead Kimmy, eyeing them suspiciously.

I wonder if I could get one of the cows to pull for me?

Dana held on to the rope with one hand and stretched out her other to the friendliest-looking cow. "C'mere, cow. C'mere cow-cow."

The cow looked at her like she'd gone mad. Dana clucked her tongue. "Sooey. Soo, cow, sooey."

The cow rolled her eyes.

"Okay, then, don't help me. Just for that, I'm having a hamburger for dinner."

Then an idea hit her. It was so simple. She could use the truck to pull Kimmy. She tied the rope to the bumper of the truck. The bravest of the cows plodded over and sniffed Dead Kimmy. Dana jumped back into the truck and put it in gear. She figured if she drove about ten feet or so, that would be enough to lift Dead Kimmy into the air and hang her. Then all she had to do was turn the truck around and make a pass under the limb, then park, climb up on the roof and tie the rope into a knot around the limb.

Dana pressed on the accelerator. The truck's wheels spun. And spun. And spun.

Crapola! I'm stuck!

Dana floored it. The engine vroomed, the tires spun madly, then the back of the truck fishtailed, whipping about in the soft earth. Mud splattered high in the air and rained down on the front windshield.

A second later, the back tires caught hold and the truck lurched forward. The steering wheel whipped out of her hands and when she tried to wrestle it back into control, the truck ended up doing a donut in the middle of the pasture, spinning round and round and round…

Dana grabbed the wheel, braced her right foot on the dash and pulled the wheel the other way. The truck leaned on two wheels, threatened to topple, then thudded back onto all four wheels. During all the whoopty-do, Dana must've kicked something on the dashboard because now the music was playing triple time—

"JesuslovesmethisIknowfortheBibletellsmeso…"

—and sounded like Alvin the Chipmunks on helium.

Dana quickly put the truck into neutral and rolled down her window. She stuck her head outside and tried to see behind her through the sheet of rain. She could make out the tree, but not Dead Kimmy.

Oh my God, I don't even see the limb she was hanging from.

Dana jumped out, ran to the back of the truck and skidded to a halt when she saw Dead Kimmy stretched out beside the tree limb, covered in mud. The limb had broken and she'd dragged both it and Dead Kimmy through the mud.

Dead Kimmy looks like a chocolate éclair.

Dana's stomach growled.

A cow appeared out of the rain and walked slowly toward Dead Kimmy. Another cow appeared. And then another. Until the whole herd had Dead Kimmy surrounded. They stared at Dead Kimmy with a wild, feral look in their eyes.

Dana was no expert on cows or cow diets, but she figured if she thought Dead Kimmy looked like a dessert, then they might too.

She hurried back to the truck, jumped inside and peeled out. She drove for the gate as fast as the wheels would go, dragging Dead Kimmy behind her, bouncing over ruts and cow trails, plowing through a bale of hay, slip-sliding in the mud, and when she got to the gate—it wasn't there.

Where's the effing gate?

Dana wiped the condensation off the front windshield and squinted through the driving rain. She jerked the wheel to the left and circled the perimeter of the pasture, looking for the gate.

She looked in the side mirror and saw—

Holy cow!

—the herd of cows were chasing her. Or rather, they were chasing Dead Kimmy as she bounced through the muck behind the truck.

Dana sped up, zig-zagging around the pasture, but every time she zigged, the cows zagged. She couldn't shake them off her tail. She whipped Dead Kimmy around the muddy pasture three times before she found the gate.

Dana blasted the truck out the gate, over the cow guard and onto the dirt road. She stopped the truck and jumped out, running to the back.

The cow guard had stopped the cows from leaving the pasture, but they were lined up along the barbwire fence staring, daring her to come back inside.

Dana walked back to where Dead Kimmy was lying in the road with the noose around her neck. She looked like she'd been tarred and feathered with mud and hay and maybe even cow poop. Her neck looked fine except for an Indian burn on her skin. The branch must've broken before she could hang too long.

All that swerving had loosened the speaker on the roof of the truck and it was dangling over the side, hanging by two wires, bleating out musical notes like a homesick goat. In a fit of fury, Dana grabbed the speaker and hurled it at the leader of the cow pack. The herd scattered and the speaker sank into the mud.

Silence. Merciful silence.

Dana bundled Dead Kimmy back into the freezer and drove off.

* * *

So far, Dana had tried Plan A: Make Dead Kimmy's Death Look Like an Accident and Plan B: Make Dead Kimmy's Death Look Like a Suicide. Both plans had failed miserably. Plan C was less convoluted. Its objective was to hide the body.

Dana drove the truck out to the Boy Scout Hole. This was nothing more than a wide space in Four Mile Creek that snaked through the county and eventually met up with the Illinois River. It was always cold water and always sparkling clear. And at this time of year nobody would be there.

She backed the truck up to the edge of the creek and turned off the engine. She hauled Dead Kimmy out of the freezer and dumped her onto the gravel bank.

Dana thought she heard another car's tires crunching down the gravel road, but when she peeked around the side of the truck, she didn't see anything. She waited and listened a while longer, then after not hearing anything else, she waded out into the cold creek, dragging Dead Kimmy behind her. Once the water was up to her waist, she stopped. Dead Kimmy was floating in the water face up. The rainstorm had the creek moving pretty fast and before Dana could deliberate about weighing Dead

Kimmy's body down with rocks or even removing the rope around her neck, a current swept her away.

Dana watched the fast-moving creek bang Dead Kimmy over boulders and carry her around a bend. "Bye, Dead Kimmy," Dana said.

Exhausted, she stuffed herself back into the driver's seat. It was raining again. She turned on the windshield wipers, but they didn't even make a dent in the downpour. In fact, it was coming down so hard, she couldn't see two feet in front of her.

She heard a noise like somebody was crying. When she saw herself in the rearview mirror she realized that she was the one crying. And it wasn't really raining, those were her tears that she couldn't see through.

Dana felt a sudden pain in her chest. Her left boob twitched and a series of pins and needles shot through her ribs.

I'm having a heart attack!

She heard a buzzing sound like a vibrator buried under a pillow.

Oh. My bad. It's my phone.

She dug out the phone, looked at the caller ID and answered. "I'm so glad you called."

CHAPTER SEVENTEEN

Dana had left her stealth superpowers in her other cape. So she did the next best thing and drove through town only using the alleys. She turned into the bank's parking lot and squeezed the ice cream truck in between a big Dodge truck and a Smart car.

Dana figured the best way to not look like she was murderess was to act like she was innocent. So, she leisurely strolled into the city park and whistled all the way up to the monkey bars.

She casually looked around but didn't see anybody. She nonchalantly leaned up against the monkey bars and scrutinized her fingernails.

"Psstt."

Dana looked up.

"Pssstt. Over here." The voice was coming from a big mulberry bush. For one panicked moment, Dana thought the bush was talking to her. Historically, it had happened before. Except the bush had been burning at the time.

Trudy stuck her nose through the brambles of the bush and whispered, "Get over here, DD."

"What're you doing in there? Are you peeing?"

"No," Trudy hissed. "I'm hiding."

"Are you hiding from me?"

Trudy put her fingers in the shush gesture over her lips. "C'mere."

Dana crawled toward her on all fours and worked her way through the bush to Trudy's cozy little hiding place.

Trudy whispered, "Do you have to be so noisy?"

"You said 'c'mere,' you didn't say 'c'mere *and* be quiet,'" Dana whispered back.

"I wasn't kidding when I called, Dana. The whole town and the whole police force is out looking for you. There's a five-state manhunt going on. They think you killed all those Lisas you dated."

"The police think I have a penchant for killing Lisas?"

Trudy nodded. "Witnesses are popping up everywhere. They say you had a series of Lisas living with you, one after another, then they disappeared one day without explanation."

"I'm not a Lisa killer!"

"Sshhh," Trudy warned. "The cops are digging up all those graves in your backyard. And they can't find Kimmy anywhere. They think you killed her too."

"I didn't!"

"That damn CeCe White has pictures of you with Kimmy. Running over her with the ice cream truck and hanging her from a tree and drowning her. Now the police are saying they want to question you, but it's more like the whole town's on a witch hunt. "

"Damn, that CeCe White! I didn't know she saw me doing all that."

"You did it?"

"Oh, don't be so alarmed. I didn't kill Kimmy. I found her already dead and was trying to dispose of her body."

"DD, you have to get out of town. Out of the state. Hell, out of the country. I found Ellen like you asked and talked to her.

She's waiting for you. She says she has something important to tell you."

"Is she going to go with me or is she waiting to tell me goodbye?"

"I don't know," Trudy said. "I don't even know if *she* knows yet."

Dana looked Trudy up and down. "What the heck are you wearing?"

"A dress," Trudy mumbled.

"A dress? You look like a buccaneer."

"It's a wench's dress. I'm a Moor."

"And where's your wig?"

"I'm not wearing a wig. What's wrong with that?"

"I've never seen you without a wig on. Not since grade school."

"What about it?" Trudy said defensively.

"Heeeyyyy," Dana said. "You're going out with Bob Wyer, aren't you?"

"So what if I am?"

A twig cracked and they froze. They stared at each other wide-eyed and listened. After a minute, Dana said, "You know what's weird?"

"No, what?"

"I've known you for almost thirty years and this is the first time I've ever been inside your bush."

"That's not funny, DD."

"It's a little bit funny."

"No, it's not."

"A tiny bit funny?"

"Okay, a tiny bit. This is some serious shit you're in, Dana."

"Okay, wait, let me put on my serious shit face." Dana knitted her eyebrows, pooched out her bottom lip and frowned.

"Now you look like you're pooping."

Dana relaxed her face. "Where's Ellen waiting for me?"

"She's at the Last Chance."

"Why'd she pick a church?"

"She said she has a key because she delivers their mail. She told me to tell you she's left the back door unlocked. You're supposed to sneak inside and meet her there."

Dana nodded.

Trudy put her car keys in Dana's hand, saying, "Take my car so you won't get caught." She gave Dana a little shove. "You have to hurry."

"Trudy?"

"Yeah?"

"If I never see you again…I want you to know…that I…"

"I love you too, DD."

"I was going to say…have fun with Bob Wyer. I think he's the one for you."

Trudy pulled Dana into a big hug. Neither one of them wanted to be the first to let go.

* * *

Dana parked Trudy's car behind the Last Chance Baptist Church alongside Ellen's mail truck. She pushed open the church's back door and stepped inside. She closed the door behind her and blinked in the darkness. She felt her way down a long hallway and tripped up a couple of steps until she found herself in a large spacious area. Judging by the shadows and dark shapes, Dana figured she was on the dais at the front of the church.

"Did you lock the door?" a voice asked.

"God? Is that you?"

"It's Ellen."

"I know. I was kidding." Dana walked toward the voice. "Where are you? I can't see in here."

"Good."

"You sound like you're mad."

"Why shouldn't I be mad?" Ellen said. "You were sleeping with my girlfriend and pretending to be in love with me."

Dana turned toward Ellen's voice. "I most certainly was not! You were the one sleeping with my girlfriend!"

"She was my girlfriend!"

"No, she was my girlfriend!"

"Mine!"

"Mine!"

"Stop repeating everything I say!"

"Stop repeating everything I say!"

"I'm not repeating!"

"Neither am I!"

Silence.

"What does it matter whose girlfriend she was or wasn't? You wanted to be rid of her," Dana said.

"So did you."

"Well, we got what we wanted, didn't we?"

"Not exactly."

"What do you mean, not exactly?"

Ellen's voice said softly, "I wanted you."

"Well, isn't that sweet?" another voice said.

The overhead lights flicked on and Dana and Ellen flinched at the brightness. Jenny McCoy stumbled up the center aisle between the pews. She was holding a purple decanter in her hand.

"Jenny?" Dana said.

"Well, if it isn't the two lesbian lovebirds," Jenny slurred.

Dana noticed that Jenny's hairdo looked like she'd missed her last hair appointment. "Are you drunk?"

"Noooo," Jenny said. She took a step forward and fell against a pew. She grabbed the back of the pew and held herself upright. "Don't be ridicule…ous."

"Why are you in church and drunk?" Dana asked.

Jenny pointed one long accusatory finger at Dana. "I could ask you the same thing!"

"Ummm…I'm not drunk," Dana said. She squinted one eye at Jenny. "Have you been partaking in the blood of our Lord?"

"Ssshhhh," Jenny said, fanning her hand in the air. She almost toppled over before grabbing hold of the pew. She pointed the decanter toward the ceiling, whispering, "He can hear you." She giggled.

Ellen walked toward Jenny with her palms out, saying, "Do you need some help? I could make us all a pot of nice, hot, black coffee."

"I know you," Jenny blurted. "You're the mailman woman."

"That's right," Ellen said.

A siren wailed in the distance. Dana and Ellen looked at each other. "You didn't call the cops, did you?" Dana said.

Ellen shook her head. "Of course not."

"I did," Jenny said. "I heard you breaking in and called in the calvary."

"Cavalry, not calvary," Dana said.

"You think you're so smart," Jenny hissed. "You always thought you were better than the rest of us because you're Wonder Woman and went to college."

"This is a Halloween costume," Dana said.

Undeterred, Jenny continued. "Just 'cause your name's Dooley and you're so almighty pretty and you have big boobs."

"What?" Dana gasped.

"You're too good to be around us. Ever since high school, you think you're so...so...superior."

"Who thinks that?" Dana asked.

But Jenny was too busy passing out to answer. Before Ellen could catch her, Jenny nose-dived into the carpet. The decanter landed in the middle of the aisle.

"Ouch. That's gonna hurt," Ellen said.

Dana and Ellen watched the last of the wine leak onto the carpet like a pool of purple blood.

"She was jealous of me? Imagine that," Dana said, looking at Jenny's unmoving body.

The police siren was joined by another. And another. And another.

"Crapola," Dana said. "It does sound like the whole cavalry."

Ellen ran to Dana and took her hand. "You need to go. Fast," she said, guiding Dana toward the back exit.

But once they reached the hallway, Dana pulled Ellen up a narrow set of stairs. "Where we going?" Ellen asked.

"Brazil. Will you go with me?"

"I meant right now. Where do these stairs lead?"

"The bell tower probably. Will you go to Brazil with me?"

"Are you serious?"

"It could be like the end of a romance novel. We could raise fainting goats and live off goat cheese. You could grow vegetables in a garden in back of our bungalow."

"Fainting goats?"

"Sure, they're funny. You scare them and they faint. Rich people buy them for laughs. We'll get us a whole herd, breed them and sell them," Dana said.

"I don't know the first thing about goats."

They reached the top of the stairs. "I don't know anything about goats either," Dana said. "But we can learn." She opened a door and they walked out into the bright sunshine. "And I'll teach myself to crochet and make you cute sweaters. The kind with little leather patches on the elbows."

The sirens grew closer. Ellen looked up at the giant bell hanging right over their heads. She moved to the half-wall and leaned on it.

Dana stared at Ellen's back. "You don't want to go?"

"I'm still stuck on the fainting goats thing."

"It doesn't have to be goats. It can be sheep." Dana joined Ellen at the wall. Ellen wrapped an arm around her and they gazed out at the entire town of Dooley Springs laid out before them.

"Sheep faint too?"

"I don't know. If we scared them bad enough, they'd probably faint."

"How do you scare a sheep?"

"Boo, sheep! Boo!"

Ellen laughed. "That *was* scary."

"And with sheep, we could get our own wool that way."

"For you to crochet me little sweaters."

"Uh huh."

"So, if we're going to Brazil, why'd you bring me up here?"

Dana grew serious. "I'm tired of running. I've spent my whole life running."

"From what?"

Dana looked away and whispered, "Myself, I think."

They watched as three, four, five police cars screeched into the parking lot below them with their sirens still wailing. A long line of cars pulled in after them. It looked like the entire town had followed the police to the church. The parking lot quickly filled up.

Dana turned to Ellen. "Listen, Ellen. I have a confession. I'm not who you think I am."

"You're not Wonder Woman? Well, then, that's a deal breaker."

Dana took Ellen's hand. "No, I'm not really an alcoholic. I was only pretending to be."

After a long moment, Ellen whispered, "But why?"

"Because I wanted to be around you. I thought if we had something in common..."

"So you pretended to...have a disease?"

"Well, it's not like I told you I had elephantiasis or something. It arose organically," Dana explained.

"Telling everybody at the AA meeting that your dad was fried in a chimney as Santa Claus was organic?"

"I really Dooleyed this one up. I'm so sorry. You have every right to be mad."

"Actually I'm glad," Ellen said.

"You are?"

"Yeah, call me crazy, but I'm actually glad you're not an alcoholic. One of us is enough."

"You forgive me then?" Dana asked hopefully.

"Is there anything else you lied about? You're not really a man are you?"

Dana laughed. "No."

"Then I forgive you. But don't lie to me again."

"I won't," Dana said.

Ellen pulled Dana into her arms and kissed her.

The policemen jumped out of their cars. Leaving their doors open, they crouched down with weapons drawn and aimed right at the bell tower.

One policeman shouted into a megaphone, "Dana Dooley! Put your hands in the air!"

Dana laid her head on Ellen's shoulder. She looked out over the town and said, "Look, I can see my house from here."

CHAPTER EIGHTEEN

An hour later, half the county was milling around the parking lot of the Last Chance Baptist Church. The news teams from Tulsa, Channels 7 and 5, had their news vans, cameramen and reporters interviewing people who claimed to know Dana personally. Channel 12 out of Oklahoma City even had its helicopter buzzing over the church getting long shots of all the action.

Most of the people were looky-loos, mingling peacefully, except for a contingent of Baptists that was shouting and throwing rocks at the bell tower like they were trying to stone Dana. The police had roped off the front doors and were busy trying to hold back the crush of people.

Up in the bell tower, Dana and Ellen were huddled on the floor against the wall.

"This is the end, I guess," Dana whispered. "I have to give myself up."

"But you didn't do anything. You didn't kill her."

"I know that. But they all think I did. Everyone down there hates me."

"It's not you they're hating. It's more like they're hating on who they think you are."

"People have always hated me."

"That can't be true."

"It is true. They hate me because I'm fat. They look at me and see their worst fear."

"I don't know where you're getting this fat thing from. You are so *not* fat. And it's starting to piss me off that you think you are."

"C'mon, Ellen, look at me. I look like Wonder Woman on steroids."

"You do not! I think you're gorgeous and sexy!"

"You're just saying that to get in my unitard."

"So if I think you're gorgeous, what's that say about me? That you think I'm stupid?"

"No…"

"Let me ask you a question. Do you think I stink?"

"Stink?"

"You know, stink. Smell bad."

Dana leaned in and sniffed Ellen. "No."

"Well, all through school kids called me Smellin' Ellen. Does that mean I really stink?"

Dana laughed. "Really? They did?"

Ellen nodded. "I'll make you a deal. You don't call me Smellin' Ellen and I won't call you fat."

"Okay."

"You feel better now?"

Dana shrugged. "I can't change my self-image just like that."

"No, but you can try."

"Okay, I'll try."

"Try to see yourself through my eyes. My eyes see a gorgeous, sexy woman."

Dana blushed. "Thank you."

"Now can I get in your unitard?"

Dana laughed. "Right now?"

"Well, as soon as we get out of this mess."

"It's a deal."

"Okay, then." Ellen stood and brushed off the back of her pants. She kissed Dana. When she pulled away, she said, "I think I'm in love with you."

"Ditto."

Ellen opened the door, then turned back to Dana. "I'm going to go Google fainting goats. Stay right here." She ran down the stairs.

* * *

Tracy Savage, the blond, blue-eyed, ninety-eight-pound reporter for Channel 7 was in her element. This could be her big break. She had the news story of the century unfolding before her very eyes and she was on the scene reporting it blow by blow. Those know-it-alls from the Chicago station who rejected her audition tape were going to be eating their words when they saw her coverage of the biggest standoff in recent Oklahoma history.

Tracy smiled for the camera and intoned with perfect inflection into the microphone, "This is Tracy Savage reporting to you live from the Last Chance Baptist Church in Dooley Springs. I have with me Brenda Risenhoover, a waitress at BJ's diner." Tracy turned to Brenda, making sure to keep her face quartered toward the camera. "Brenda, you say you overheard the suspect and her mother planning a grisly murder. Can you tell the Channel 7 viewers exactly what you heard?"

Brenda popped her gum and said, "She was dressed as Wonder Woman. And she said that she was going to poof her girlfriend. She said it just like that too." She popped a bubble. "'Poof!'"

"You heard it here first, folks! Remember, this is Tracy Savage with Channel 7…where it isn't news until you've heard it from me."

Brenda grabbed the mike and added, "And all she left for a tip was fifty cents. Cheapskate."

* * *

Two teenage boys with matching mohawks stood beside Ellen's mail truck. One boy kept lookout while the other reached inside and pulled out the cardboard box full of yellow Gatorade bottles.

"Hey, lookit what I found," said one boy. "We could sell this and make some easy bucks."

The other boy grinned. "Let's hit up the Baptists first. They look thirsty."

The boys carried the box toward the crowd.

* * *

"This is Enrico Gonzales with the Channel 5 Eye On Oklahoma News Team. I'm standing outside the Last Chance Baptist Church where there is a hostage situation playing out right now." Enrico Gonzales rumpled his dark hair and loosened his tie for the camera. He wanted to appear hardworking and earnest like his viewing audience. He continued. "Dana Dooley, a local woman, is wanted for the murder of her girlfriend and allegedly the murders of up to twenty others. At this moment, Dooley is holed up in the bell tower. It appears she has taken a local letter carrier hostage. At this point, it is not known whether she has any weapons."

The microphone was jerked out of Enrico's hand and Bob McCoy angrily shouted into the mike, repeating himself like a real-life version of Foghorn Leghorn. "This is what happens, I tell you, I tell you, this is what happens when women are allowed to wallow in sin with other women!"

Enrico reached for his microphone, but McCoy placed his palm in the middle of Enrico's chest and pushed him away.

"I am the preacher, the preacher, of the Last Chance and I am God's heavenly servant on earth! I tell you, I tell you, Dana Dooley has been a blight and a sore on the hind-end of Dooley Springs for years! This is what happens, what happens!"

A crowd of red-faced, frothing-at-the-mouth Baptists circled behind their preacher, egging him on. Bob shook his fist up at the bell tower, yelling, "Get down here, Dana Dooley! Meet your fate! Murderers and homosexuals should be stoned, should be stoned!"

A few of the most zealous Baptists threw handfuls of gravel toward the church's front doors.

Enrico grabbed for his microphone and this time managed to wrestle it away from Bob McCoy.

Out of breath and panting, Bob McCoy wiped his sweaty brow with the back of his hand. Satisfied that he made a good appearance on TV, he raised a yellow Gatorade bottle to his lips. He stopped right before he drank and shouted, "Onward, Christian soldiers!" He raised his Gatorade bottle in the air for a toast.

The crowd raised their own Gatorade bottles in the air and repeated in unison, "Onward, Christian soldiers!"

They all drank.

* * *

Tracy Savage moved in close to Wanda and counted off to her cameraman, "Ready and action!" She spoke into her microphone. "Tracey Savage back with you, reporting live from Dooley Springs at the hostage situation. I have here with me Wanda Jackson, owner of the The Best Little Hairhouse. Dana Dooley, the suspect, worked for you, is that correct?"

"Yes, she cleaned my beauty shop every Friday." Her dentures *clicked*.

"And you once had a conversation with Miss Dooley, did you not? A conversation that seems rather incriminating?"

Click, click. "I don't know if I should say anything, but yes, Dana one time told me that she wanted to kill her girlfriend and bury her in her backyard."

Tracy turned a cold smile to the camera. "This has been an exclusive report from Tracy Savage, Channel 7."

* * *

Unnoticed by the crowd and the police, Ellen had snuck out the back doors of the church and now had Maw Maw, Fat Matt, Leona and Trudy huddled off to one side like a football team. Ellen was giving orders like she was a quarterback who had ten yards to go on a fourth down.

They all put their hands in the middle of the circle, one on top of the other, and Ellen said, "Let's do it!"

The huddle broke and they each ran off to their positions.

Leona strode boldly to the policeman holding the bullhorn and said, "I'm Dana's mother. I bet I can talk her down outta there for you."

* * *

Five minutes later, Leona had center stage. The policemen were circled, holding back the crowd. All eyes were trained on Leona as she raised the bullhorn to her lips. She hesitated, lowered the bullhorn and pulled a flask from her hip pocket. She unscrewed the cap and raised it to her lips.

"You can do this, Ms. Dooley," said a policeman. "You can talk her down. If you don't, we have no choice but to enter the premises and bring her out at gunpoint."

Leona took another swig. "Give me a minute."

"You want her to die like this?" he asked. "Chances are that some bullets are going to fly and she'll be on the receiving end."

Leona handed the policeman her flask and raised the bullhorn. "Dana! This here is Leona speaking." She hesitated, then added for good measure, "Your mother, Leona."

The crowd murmured, hushing each other, then fell silent, listening to Leona's words. "Honey, I know things haven't always been…good for you."

Dana's head appeared over the edge of the bell tower wall.

Leona continued. "But you need to come on down from there before you get yourself shot."

"I'm not guilty! I didn't kill her!" Dana shouted.

"I know that, honey," Leona said through the bullhorn. "But if you don't come down, you can't explain that to these people."

"What do you care?" Dana said.

Leona looked to the policeman and said, "She didn't kill anybody, you know."

He said. "Try again. There must be something you can say to get her down. You're her mother."

Leona took a deep breath and spoke into the bullhorn again. "Listen, Dana. I'm the screw-up. Not you."

"You can say that again," Dana said.

"I love you," Leona said. "I know that's hard to believe, but I do."

"That's the vodka talking," Dana shouted.

Leona pushed her way through the throng of people and marched to the church steps.

"What're you doing?" called the policeman. "Where are you going?"

Leona stood on top of the church steps, faced the crowd and planted her feet shoulder-width apart. She raised the bullhorn and said, "Listen up, people! There's something you all should know!"

The crowd jostled each other for a better view of the action. They formed a tight semi-circle around Leona and waited silently for her next words. Leona patiently waited until the news reporters and cameras were trained on her before she said, "My name is Leona and I'm an alcoholic."

A few people in the crowd took their cue and shouted back, "Hi, Leona!"

She continued. "I drank my life away because I abandoned my two children." She shuffled her feet, then said, "I got no excuses. I did what I did."

Ellen pushed her way through the crowd and stood at the foot of the steps between the two reporters, looking up at Leona, confused. This admission wasn't part of the game plan.

Leona continued. "My daughter didn't deserve what I done. Neither did my son. I came back here to make things right, but I couldn't. I wanted to make it up for them, but I didn't know how."

Leona stood silent for a moment, then said, "So I did the only thing I could think of to make my daughter's life better."

She paused dramatically and added, "I killed that woman. Dana didn't do it. I did."

The crowd erupted into a frenzy. Camera flashes popped and the two news reporters turned to their cameras and began talking excitedly. Tracy Savage hurled herself through the crowd, motioning to her cameraman to follow. Enrico Gonzales slipped into the wake that Tracy Savage left behind.

Leona looked down at Ellen. Ellen gave her a thumbs up.

Tracy Savage thrust her microphone right under Leona's nose.

"That's right! I killed her!" Leona exclaimed over the hubbub.

Two policemen headed toward Leona. Leona handed the bullhorn over to Ellen and held her hands out to a policeman, saying, "Cuff me. I'm giving myself up."

The policeman spun Leona around and began to cuff her hands behind her.

"She didn't kill anybody! I did!"

All heads spun to see Ellen standing on the church steps. She had the bullhorn raised. Ellen spoke again, aiming her words toward Enrico Gonzales' outstretched microphone. "I killed that woman because she was cheating on me! I hated her and I killed her!"

"What the hell?" a policeman said.

Ellen dropped the bullhorn and held her wrists out to be cuffed. "Take me away, officers, lock me up. I killed her in a jealous lover's rage."

The policemen looked at each. One policeman asked, "What do we do?" His partner shrugged. "I've never had this happen before."

"You arrest *me* is what you do!" said another voice.

The crowd turned to see Fat Matt in his mayor's suit climbing the steps. Tracy Savage and Enrico Gonzales ran to Fat Matt and shoved their mikes in his face. Fat Matt picked up the bullhorn and shouted, "I killed that woman! I'm the guilty one! I'm the murderer. My sister and mother and this woman with the pokey hair were trying to protect me! I killed her because… because…because I'm a cold-blooded killer!"

"You didn't kill anybody!" another voice shouted. Maw Maw pushed her way through the crowd and grabbed the bullhorn out of Fat Matt's hands.

Tracy Savage and Enrico Gonzales turned, knocked into each other and fell on their butts. As they scrambled to their feet, Maw Maw bellowed into the bullhorn, "I'm the killer! I killed her dead! I'm a dangerous, old, crazy woman killer is what I am."

A policeman yanked the bullhorn out of Maw Maw's grasp. "Okay, enough of this nonsense. Now which one of you did it?"

Ellen jerked the bullhorn out of the policeman's hand and exclaimed, "I did!"

Fat Matt grabbed the bullhorn. "You did not," said Fat Matt. "I did!"

Leona pulled the bullhorn out of Fat Matt's grasp and said, "You're both lying. I killed her."

Tracy Savage and Enrico Gonzales shoved their microphones in front of Maw Maw's face. "I killed her more than all of you combined!" Maw Maw shouted. She turned to a policeman and said, "Take me in and lock me up before I kill again."

"You're all wrong," Trudy said, appearing at the bottom of the steps. "I killed her out of jealousy and spite."

"You did not!" shouted Leona, Fat Matt and Maw Maw at the same time.

Enrico Gonzales and Tracy Savage aimed their microphones at Trudy.

"I did too!" Trudy exclaimed. "You all are trying to steal my thunder!"

"This is ridiculous," said a policeman, throwing his arms in the air. "You all couldn't have killed her."

"Nobody killed her!" shouted a voice.

Everybody looked around to see where the voice came from. Finally, Maw Maw asked, "Who said that?"

"I did!" Dana shouted. Everybody looked up at the bell tower. Dana was leaning over the wall and pointing to somewhere behind the crowd. "Nobody killed her…because there she is!"

The crowd hushed. Over the silence was heard a *chug-a-chug-a-chug* like the little red engine that could. The crowd parted as Hank steered his lawnmower toward the church steps. He wasn't wearing a shirt and his fat belly jiggled over his belt. He had a lopsided grin on his face. Kimmy was perched on the back of the lawnmower like the queen in a homecoming parade. She was very much alive and wearing Hank's shirt. Her hair was twisted and knotted and she looked like she'd been on the receiving end of a really bad home perm. Her skin was splotchy and bruised, and large parts of her were smeared with dried mud. She had a rope around her neck and smelled faintly of fertilizer. She looked worse than Stephen King's Carrie after the prom.

Hank steered his lawnmower up to the church steps and cut off the engine. Kimmy got off the back, wobbled from side to side, regained her balance and looked blankly at all the expectant faces. "Did I miss something?" she asked.

* * *

A week later, Ellen and Dana sat on the sofa, as close to each other as they could get. Asscat was sprawled in Ellen's lap, purring loudly while Dana flipped through TV channels with the remote.

"Here it is," she said.

On the TV screen, Kimmy and Tracy Savage sat in a news studio under bright lights. Kimmy had a new, shorter hairstyle and so much makeup on it looked like her features had been chiseled out of pottery clay.

Dana turned up the volume and settled back into Ellen's arms to watch.

Tracy Savage smiled at the cameras, then addressed Kimmy. "So tell us what you remember...in your own words."

Kimmy smiled at the camera. "I came home late and was hungry. So I pulled something out of the fridge, I didn't know what it was, but it looked like sausage gravy. I heated it up in the microwave and poured it over some cold biscuits and ate it. It tasted a little funny, but I didn't think much of it at the time. Then I took off all my clothes and was headed to bed when I got dizzy. I guess I got so dizzy, I got all mixed up and turned around and opened the front door instead of the bedroom door. Next thing I knew that old man was pulling me out of the Illinois River. He gave me his shirt to wear and drove me back to town on his lawnmower."

Ellen grabbed the remote and turned off the TV. She kissed Dana lightly on the lips.

Dana giggled.

"What's so funny?" Ellen asked.

"I'm happy is all."

"Me too."

Dana looked shyly at her. "Do you 'like my hat'?"

"I do," Ellen said. "I do like your hat."

They kissed.

EPILOGUE

One year later:

Jenny and Bob McCoy got divorced. Jenny now has her own business and travels the country selling food on a stick at all the county fairs. She has gained over two hundred pounds.

Trudy and Bob Wyer were married in Judge Tanner's cornfield. They moved to Kansas City where Trudy opened up her celebrity look-alike shop and has more business than she can handle. Trudy and Bob travel the country three months out of the year attending SCA festivals.

Leona attends AA meetings every Thursday night at the VFW. She hasn't had a drink in over five months. She wrote and sold a new country song, "Happiness is a Warm Gun." It topped the country charts at number eleven.

Maw Maw Dooley was written up in the *Los Angeles Weekly* as an up-and-coming installation artist. She had art showings in New York and Dallas. She is still working on her recipe for the perfect embalming fluid.

Fat Matt Dooley was reelected mayor of Dooley Springs. He disappeared two months after the election. Some people say they've seen him in the Cookson Hills roaming around with no clothes on. Other people say that's not Fat Matt, that's Bigfoot.

Tracy Savage accepted a new job offer. She's now a weather girl for the Fox Channel.

Wilson Drumright, aka "Puddinhead," moved in with his lover, Bruce the Fag, Trudy's ex-husband. They created the national phenomenon now sweeping the gay community of wearing your pants backwards.

Kimmy gained a short-lived notoriety and now sells artificial fingernails at a kiosk in a Tulsa mall.

Dana Dooley finally got her gold crown. And her book was published. It's not the great American novel she had hoped for, but it is short-listed for a Goldie award. The dedication reads: "For Ellen, my girlfriend's girlfriend."

And…Ellen and Dana are still enjoying their version of the party tree.